T0121842

One More CHANCE

Jim Crowgey

Order this book online at www.trafford.com
or email orders@trafford.com

Most Trafford titles are also available at major online book retailers.

Printed in the United States of America.

ISBN: 978-1-4669-8440-0 (sc)
ISBN: 978-1-4669-8442-4 (hc)
ISBN: 978-1-4669-8441-7 (e)

Library of Congress Control Number: 2013904153

Trafford rev. 03/12/2013

North America & international
toll-free: 1 888 232 4444 (USA & Canada)
phone: 250 383 6864 • fax: 812 355 4082

Dedication

This book is dedicated to the Backroad Bikers, retired GE engineering friends who have bicycled across southwest Virginia each Thursday for fifteen years. Our tight knit group includes Ralph Burr, Hal Cantrill, Thane Drummond, Walter Hill, Bruce Mitchell, Mike O'Meara, Gooch Rosebro, Jim Selvey, Tom Skelly, and Loren Walker.

Courtland County Bank
204 Main Street Virginia Route 301
New Court, Virginia

2011

JAN

SU	M	T	W	T	F	S
						1
2	3	4	5	6	7	8
9	10	11	12	13	14	15
16	17	18	19	20	21	22
23	24	25	26	27	28	29
30	31					

FEB

SU	M	T	W	T	F	S
		1	2	3	4	5
6	7	8	9	10	11	12
13	14	15	16	17	18	19
20	21	22	23	24	25	26
27	28					

MAR

SU	M	T	W	T	F	S
		1	2	3	4	5
6	7	8	9	10	11	12
13	14	15	16	17	18	19
20	21	22	23	24	25	26
27	28	29	30	31		

APR

SU	M	T	W	T	F	S
					1	2
3	4	5	6	7	8	9
10	11	12	13	14	15	16
17	18	19	20	21	22	23
24	25	26	27	28	29	30

MAY

SU	M	T	W	T	F	S
1	2	3	4	5	6	7
8	9	10	11	12	13	14
15	16	17	18	19	20	21
22	23	24	25	26	27	28
29	30	31				

JUNE

SU	M	T	W	T	F	S
			1	2	3	4
5	6	7	8	9	10	11
12	13	14	15	16	17	18
19	20	21	22	23	24	25
26	27	28	29	30		

JULY

SU	M	T	W	T	F	S
					1	2
3	4	5	6	7	8	9
10	11	12	13	14	15	16
17	18	19	20	21	22	23
24	25	26	27	28	29	30
31						

AUG

SU	M	T	W	T	F	S
	1	2	3	4	5	6
7	8	9	10	11	12	13
14	15	16	17	18	19	20
21	22	23	24	25	26	27
28	29	30	31			

SEPT

SU	M	T	W	T	F	S
				1	2	3
4	5	6	7	8	9	10
11	12	13	14	15	16	17
18	19	20	21	22	23	24
25	26	27	28	29	30	

OCT

SU	M	T	W	T	F	S
						1
2	3	4	5	6	7	8
9	10	11	12	13	14	15
16	17	18	19	20	21	22
23	24	25	26	27	28	29
30	31					

NOV

SU	M	T	W	T	F	S
		1	2	3	4	5
6	7	8	9	10	11	12
13	14	15	16	17	18	19
20	21	22	23	24	25	26
27	28	29	30			

DEC

SU	M	T	W	T	F	S
				1	2	3
4	5	6	7	8	9	10
11	12	13	14	15	16	17
18	19	20	21	22	23	24
25	26	27	28	29	30	31

Contents

Acknowledgments	xi
Chapter 1	1
Chapter 2	8
Chapter 3	17
Chapter 4	23
Chapter 5	30
Chapter 6	34
Chapter 7	39
Chapter 8	45
Chapter 9	50
Chapter 10	57
Chapter 11	62
Chapter 12	67
Chapter 13	73
Chapter 14	80
Chapter 15	85
Chapter 16	90
Chapter 17	98
Chapter 18	105
Chapter 19	111
Chapter 20	117
Chapter 21	123
Chapter 22	130
Chapter 23	136

Chapter 24 142
Chapter 25 149
Chapter 26 156
Chapter 27 161
Chapter 28 169
Chapter 29 175
Chapter 30 180
Chapter 31 185
Chapter 32 191
Chapter 33 197
Chapter 34 205
Chapter 35 214
Chapter 36 219
Chapter 37 223
Chapter 38 235
Chapter 39 242
Chapter 40 248
Chapter 41 258
Chapter 42 267
Chapter 43 272
Chapter 44 284
Chapter 45 289
Chapter 46 301
Chapter 47 306

Acknowledgments

With sincere thanks to:

Mary Beth Crowgey, my daughter, for again offering her literary talents as my editor and my mentor. The many hours she spent creatively critiquing the draft manuscript and suggesting improvements greatly improved the final published novel, and for this I am most grateful. I would also like to acknowledge her major role in designing the cover for this book.

Mike Smeltzer, my friend since high school days, for offering expert advice to assure that elements of the story involving legal matters are technically correct.

Chapter 1

Sheriff Cole Grayson watched the black van coming hell-bent for election up the highway toward him, firing up the engine on his white Crown Vic. He flipped on his siren and blue strobe lightbar as the vehicle whipped past, the cruiser's rear wheels slinging dirt onto the pavement. He accelerated until he was close behind, filling the rear view mirror of the driver ahead.

Cole saw that he was drafting a late model Ford with tinted windows, a dented back bumper, and an obscured license plate. The darkened glass prevented him from studying the person behind the wheel, but he had gotten a quick look earlier through the clear windshield of the approaching vehicle and knew his quarry.

A straight stretch of road gave Cole the opportunity to radio his dispatcher. "Tammy, I'm in pursuit of a black Ford van with dark-tinted glass that fits the description of one stolen off a used car lot in Martinsville. I'm glued on its bumper heading north on Route 301 toward West Virginia, now passing the turn off to Courtland Springs.

"It looks like a 2010 commercial model with Virginia plates, but I can only make out three of the numbers, 648. The tags are probably lifted off another vehicle. The driver is a young African-American male wearing a dark blue hooded sweatshirt."

"Is he a good enough driver to haul moonshine in Franklin County?'

"Pretty close. But he looks like a scared dude who's probably way too screwed up for your people to hire for the family business. Don't forget that this conversation is being recorded, Ms. Ewell."

"I copy that. I'll notify the Virginia and West Virginia State Police that a high speed pursuit is in progress and request road blocks ahead. Be careful!"

He continued to tail the van along the winding two-lane road up Painters Mountain, trying to stick close, hoping to get a better look at the driver through the tight turns. He had not learned a great deal more at the critical moment the two vehicles entered a blind curve and encountered four massive Black Angus steers standing in the road ahead, calmly regarding them, their two tons of prime beef blocking both lanes.

The sheriff watched as the van driver laid on his brakes, making a sharp turn off the pavement onto the right shoulder of the road, losing traction in the gravel and spinning around in a full circle before sliding through a patch of briars, nose-first into a drainage ditch.

Cole braked hard in a desperate attempt to slow before veering away from the cattle and following the van from the highway. But the Crown Vic was still carrying too much speed for him to maintain control when he hit the shoulder, and he skidded sideways through the dirt and weeds into the ditch, stopping only a short distance from his quarry.

The driver of the stolen vehicle made a futile attempt to restart his engine, then opened the door and bolted, vaulting the rail fence and starting across the cleared pasture, on a dead run toward a wooded ridge ahead.

Cole jumped out of the car holding his .40 Glock at his side, shouting, "Stop! You're under arrest!" He watched the man continue on, running with a sprinter's speed.

"Hold up or I'll shoot!" he yelled in exasperation, not bothering to raise his pistol.

He followed his man over the fence, ripping the seat out of his pants on a rusty nail, hauling it through the broom sedge in high gear, but quickly running out of gas and gasping for breath after only a short distance. The fugitive kept going until he reached the far side of the field, jumping the fence and disappearing into the trees.

Cole shouted out a last time in frustration, "I could have shot you, punk!" He lowered his voice, realizing the man was now likely to be out of earshot, adding for his own satisfaction, "You won't get a pass the next time."

The sheriff walked back toward the road, crossing the fence and jumping the ditch to reach his car, quickly getting on the radio. "Tammy, I'm over near Slate Bank on 301. The young guy I was chasing wrecked the van and has taken off on foot. I could have stopped him, but I wasn't about to cut down on some unarmed, scared looking kid."

"Can you give me the complete license tag number?"

"First things first. Tell Jake and Tank to get over here on the double and bring the dogs. We've only got a few hours before dark.

"The guy we're looking for runs like a track star, and he got away up into the side of the mountain. Put out the word that he's an athletic black male about six feet tall, around one-seventy. You already have the rest of his description.

"I'm getting ready to check out the stolen van right now, and I'll try to make out the plates for you. After I finish going over it, we'll need a wrecker to tow it back into town. The front end looks like it's torn up way too bad to run.

"And call Jack Gunther in Slate Bank. Tell him some of his beef cattle have gotten out onto the highway again, and that I'm going to be sending him the bill for getting the front end aligned on the cruiser."

Cole slipped on a pair of gloves, and walked over to the van. The front compartment offered few surprises, except for a half smoked joint in the ashtray, and a cheap pair of work gloves lying on the floor.

But upon opening the rear door he knew that he had hit the jackpot. Spread before him was equipment that could only be used for one purpose: making crystal meth.

The pungent smells of ammonia and ether assailed his nose, causing him to step back He could see a haphazard array of drug paraphernalia including pails, jugs, a measuring cup and funnels, rubber tubing, coffee filters, cheesecloth and towels, even a propane stove and ice chest. Keenly arousing his curiosity were two brand new Nike gym bags stashed to one side.

Cole returned to his truck and picked up the radio. "Tammy, back again. Cancel that call for a wrecker, and put in a call to the State Police in Salem. That stolen van is a mobile meth lab, and we need their hazmat technicians out here to investigate.

A short time later, Deputies Jake Johnson and Tank Krupski drove up in a Courtland County Sheriff's Department pick-up truck, unloading two excited German Shepherds, Greta and Beau. They had leashed the dogs and were conferring with Cole when a Virginia State Police cruiser pulled in behind, and three troopers joined them.

Cole recognized the senior officer as Lt. Tom Bowman, a man he trusted to have his back when needed. He was eager to hand the investigation of the stolen van over to the State Police, knowing that there was a complex protocol for dealing with methamphetamine production sites which required a Philadelphia lawyer to assure compliance.

He was far more interested in getting up into the side of Painters Mountain with Jake, Tank, and the two dogs to pick up the trail of the escapee. But Cole was curious to learn one thing before he left: what was in the gym bags.

Tom Bowman was obviously equally anxious to find out the same thing, slipping on a pair of gloves to gingerly retrieve both bags from the van. He unzipped the first one to reveal rubber-banded bundles of twenty, fifty, and hundred dollar bills. One of the State Police troopers let out a whistle, exclaiming. "We must be looking at more than a hundred grand!"

The second bag was filled with small packages wrapped in opaque plastic, making it impossible to see the contents. Tom dug a knife from his pocket and carefully slit one of the wrappers, exposing a handful of small ice-clear crystals.

"Just what we suspected," he muttered. "There's a lot of crystal meth here, and I'm guessing that if you were able to sell it on the street, you'd have enough money to fill another bag."

Cole asked Tom, "Now that we know what our fugitive was hauling, is it OK if my deputies and I leave you to handle this so we can go after him?"

Tom cut his eyes upward and responded with a sardonic grin, "Why not? Everybody ducks out and leaves the dirty work to Smokey."

"Get the dogs, and let's clear out of here before Lt. Bowman changes his mind," Cole directed his deputies. "I'll show you where we can pick up our escapee's trail on the other side of the field."

"Hold up one minute, Sheriff, before you hightail it out of here," Tom called out. "I was summoned to Arlington last week for a meeting of Virginia State Police and Federal DEA officials.

"All state law enforcement personnel are going to get a VSP communication about the growing problem with local production of this stuff. I don't care whether you call it crystal meth, crank, ice, speed, whiz, or any of another half-dozen names, it's creating a hell of a problem. Almost all of the heroin and cocaine, and a lot of the pot we interdict is smuggled in from Mexico, but meth is usually made in hometown USA.

"We believe that a lot of it is manufactured in rural areas like your jurisdiction, bucolic Courtland County. Kind of surprising that shit produced out in the boondocks ends up in the hands of drug users all over the place, but that's what's happening."

"I get the message," Cole replied. "We'll step up our efforts to get crystal meth off the streets in Virginia. Now my men and I need to get up in the hills and track down our man. Maybe he'll give us some leads on the local drug business."

"Good luck," Tom called out as Cole and his deputies turned to leave. "Don't let your conscience bother you about leaving me here holding the hazmat bag."

The sheriff led the way over the fence ahead of his men, Tank observing, "It's a good thing deer season hasn't opened, boss. With your underwear poking through those torn britches, some hunter might mistake you for a white-tailed deer and shoot you. You're quite a sight."

Cole didn't bother to turn around, countering, "If you don't like the view, son, you can look the other direction. I never told you or anyone else that I auditioned for the Chippendales."

Chapter 2

Buddy Grayson heard the hall bell clanging at three-thirty to signal the end of classes for the day at New Court Middle School, getting up from his desk to jostle with other students through the classroom door onto the concourse leading to freedom.

His sixth grade classmate and best friend, twelve year-old Mikey Dillon, caught up with him as he reached the door and both boys dashed over to bungee school books onto luggage racks, rolling their bicycles out of the school's iron pipe stand, quickly heading for the outskirts of town.

Buddy felt the cell phone in his pocket vibrate, pulling his banged up bike off the road to take the call, hearing the friendly voice of his dad's dispatcher, Tammy Ewell.

"Buddy, your father wanted me to let you know he's going to be late getting home this evening. He and two of his deputies are still up on Painters Mountain tracking a fugitive toward Waiteville. He doesn't want you or Mandy worrying about him—go on down to the Dairy Queen and get a cheeseburger when you get hungry."

Buddy slipped the cell phone back into his pocket and pulled back onto the pavement. "That was the dispatcher over at the courthouse telling me Dad's not going to be home for dinner. She said he's hunting down some criminal on Painters Mountain."

"Your father sure has an exciting job, running around up in the hills chasing crooks," Mikey commented. "All my old man does is run a one-hour dry cleaning store. His idea of excitement is finding a couple of quarters somebody left in their pants pocket."

"Yeah, but your father isn't likely to have some mean drunk point a gun at his head and threaten to shoot him while he's trying to break up a fight between the dude and his old lady, like Dad did last year.

"Dad got shot in the leg trying to help arrest a couple of fugitives back when he was working for the FBI in Washington, and I can still see him limping when he first gets up in the morning. Finding quarters in somebody's dirty clothes might be all the excitement you want when it comes to your family."

"You never told me your father got shot when he was an FBI agent."

"I don't like to talk about something as scary as having somebody try to kill your dad. I've had nightmares about that."

Mikey thought over the risks involved in law enforcement, silently agreeing with his friend about the advantages of running a dry cleaning business, then changed the subject. "Let's go over to your house and do some more work on our raft."

Buddy never missed a chance to give his friend a hard time and quickly seized the opportunity to strike again, knowing that Mikey had a secret crush on his pretty fifteen year-old sister.

"You sure seem to enjoy spending your free time after school working in my garage. Maybe when Mandy comes home from school you'd like to ask her if she'll come out and help you nail down the deck boards."

Mikey knew that his friend had seen right through him, replying red faced, "It would be OK with me if she wanted to. She probably knows a lot more about sawing and nailing boards than her dumb brother. You can't tell the difference between a hammer head and a handle."

"And you don't know your butt from a hole in the ground," Buddy countered, shifting his bike into a lower gear to accelerate away from his friend.

"Race you to the house. My sister's probably there right now, looking out the window for you."

*****

Mandy changed into her practice uniform of blue shorts, white New Court Rockets—Girls JV Volleyball t-shirt, white socks, and sneakers. She pulled her red hair back into a ponytail, glancing at the locker room mirror as she hurried to the gym.

The reflected image was a reminder that a growth spurt had propelled her to a height of five-nine, the same height as her mother, Jennifer. Or rather, the same height her mother had been less than three years earlier when an aortic aneurism had snuffed out her life in the blink of an eye.

The recollection of her mother's sudden death while driving home from work on an ordinary day, and all of the surreal events that followed, hit Mandy like a blow to the stomach. It was enough to take her breath away, and she silently slumped down on a bench, her eyes filling with tears.

Norma Patton had been standing by in the gym watching her junior varsity volleyball team assemble, waiting on the twelfth and last player to report. After several minutes, she impatiently headed back through the door into the locker room, spotting Mandy sitting alone, seemingly making no effort to join her teammates.

Norma did not try to conceal a coach's annoyance with a player reporting late to practice. "Are you planning to join us, or are you going to sit here all afternoon while the rest of the squad stands around waiting on you?"

Mandy quickly stood, quietly replying, "I'm sorry, coach," while carefully keeping her back turned.

Norma detected a break in her voice, and realized that the teenager had not been idly daydreaming. She crossed the locker room to face her youngest team member, spotting the damp cheeks. "What's wrong?" she asked softly.

The kindness in her voice pushed a button, and Mandy broke into tears. Norma put her arm around the young girl, sympathetically suggesting, "Let me ask Kelly and Kim to take over and get practice started. Then, if you would like, we can talk privately in the conference room."

The two walked side-by-side to the vacant office, closing the door behind them, silence enveloping the room as they sat facing each other. "Is there anything you'd like to talk over with me?" Norma inquired, drawing on her experience in counseling students. "If something's bothering you, and you'd like to air it out with a sympathetic friend, you'll find that I'm a good listener."

Mandy hesitated, and silence again cloaked their small quarters. Then she began to speak in a voice so soft that Norma had to lean forward to make out what the girl was saying, her first words capturing Norma's full attention.

"I'll never get over the way Mom died, without my even having the chance to tell her goodbye.

"We were living in Arlington. I was twelve years old and in the sixth grade. Buddy was in the third grade. Dad and Mom commuted to government jobs in Washington.

"I remember everything so clearly about that awful day. Mom gave me money to buy lunch, and she waited to talk to me before she went off to work.

"I was so wrapped up in my own little world, talking with a friend on my cell phone, that I didn't stop to speak with her before she left. She kissed me on the forehead and walked away, turning around with a smile as she went out the door. That was the last time we were together. I never told her I loved her."

Norma reached out to take Mandy's hand, sitting quietly with a lump in her throat, compassionately waiting for the girl to go on.

"I wish I could go back and change everything. I wish I could take Mom to a doctor and get all of her problems fixed so nothing bad would ever happen to her. I wish she was still here with Dad and Buddy and me.

"Mom died almost three years ago, and I still miss her as much now as I did then. Will it ever get any better?"

"Time softens the hurt of losing someone you love, but I'm sure hearing those words doesn't offer you much comfort now," Norma gently replied.

"I heard about your mother's death right after you moved here. News gets around fast in small towns. Everyone in New Court learned much more about your family when your dad was elected county sheriff.

"I was pleased that you signed up for the volleyball team this fall," Norma continued. "The other teachers and I have been watching you, and we could see that you weren't getting involved in school activities like many of the other girls. A lot of folks are concerned about you."

"It's been hard to go on living like nothing has changed," Mandy sobbed. "I don't cry around Dad or Buddy, but sometimes when I'm alone, I start to think about Mom, and I'll just bawl."

"There's nothing wrong with crying over the loss of someone you love, Mandy. But I don't think you should keep it all bottled up inside. I imagine that your father and brother are also struggling, and it might be good to let them know what you're still feeling.

"I hope that from now on you'll know that I care about you, and that you'll come to me when you feel the need to talk with a friend. My door's always open." Norma reached into a pocket and pulled out a tissue, silently offering it to her.

Mandy sat quietly, wiping the tears from her eyes before softly speaking, "Thanks, Ms. Patton."

"Would you like to have a few minutes to compose yourself, and then join the other girls, or would you rather just skip practice today, go home, and come back tomorrow?"

"I'm ready to go back to the gym with you, Ms. Patton. I'll be OK now."

Norma reached out to give Mandy a warm hug, keeping an arm around her slender shoulders as they left the conference room.

*****

It was after nine o'clock when Cole, Jake, Tank, and two tired and foot-sore German Shepherds got back to the Sheriff's Department at the Courtland County Courthouse.

Darlene Cumbo, the matronly second shift dispatcher, looked up to greet them as they entered. "I'm certainly glad to see Sheriff Taylor, Deputy Fife, and Gomer back in one piece. So that young man led y'all on a wild goose chase all the way to the West Virginia line, and then gave you the slip?"

"Yeah, Charlene Darling, we had a nice hike up the side of Painters Mountain toward Waiteville, but the dogs lost our man's track when we got to Painters Creek Road.

"I suspect that he caught a ride with a friend and made it into West Virginia in the trunk of a car, despite the State Police road block. But don't think that it was all a waste of time. Along the way we busted up a still and discovered a big of stand of ginseng that will bring us some serious money when we go back and dig it up."

Darlene turned her head to conceal a smile, not wanting to let the boss see that he had one-upped her. "Mandy called. She said that she and Buddy ate dinner at Bucky's Burgers, and are back at the house doing their homework. I think your kids worry a lot about you when you're out tracking a fugitive, ever since that shoot-out you got into last year."

"I don't think it goes back to that shoot-out. I think it comes from the morning Jennifer went off to work on an ordinary day, and they never spoke to her again. Anyway, I'll head on home now and spend some time with them."

Cole cleared off the top of his desk a short time later and prepared to leave for home, turning back to say goodnight to his staff. Darlene called out to him, "I gotta tell you, I really like the Calvin Kleins you're wearing, Boss. I didn't realize until just now that you went in for designer underwear."

He reached around to cover the ripped seat of his pants, replying, "I thought you knew designer duds are standard for the Sheriff's Department, Officer Cumbo. And by the way, all of the staff is going to stand for inspection here at the office tomorrow morning. I hope I won't have to write you up for improper uniform." He heard Darlene laugh as he departed the building and walked toward his dusty Chevy pick-up.

Cole recalled that he had wanted a bright red Silverado when he and Jennifer had gone shopping for the truck in Arlington back in 2005, but she had convinced him that white would not show dirt as badly, and he knew that as always, she was right.

He remembered Jennifer joking as they drove off of the dealer's lot, that every country music song in the last fifty years included some allusion to the love affair between men and pick-up trucks, wondering when and how male affection had switched from faithful horses to mindless machines. A few weeks later, she had given him several CDs to prove her point. He had listened to them right up to the time of her death, then put them away, never to be played again.

Only during recent times could he recall the happy days with Jennifer without being overwhelmed by feelings of insurmountable loss. Knowing that Mandy and Buddy were experiencing similar feelings, he had tried to conceal his emotions from them, hoping that neither had heard him break down in tears at night during the early months following her death.

Cole turned off the road into the parking lot of a convenience store to buy a half gallon of chocolate-pecan ice cream before continuing home. The kids had to settle for burgers and fries again tonight, he thought to himself. The least I can do is bring them a nice treat.

The front porch light was on, and Cole could see both Mandy and Buddy peering out of a window as he drove into the driveway, giving him a warm, reassuring feeling. Jennifer had often done the same when she got home first and knew he was on the way. With their children still providing the same loving presence, he knew that she would always be a part of his life.

Chapter 3

Saturday morning, Cole turned into the long gravel driveway leading toward a two-story frame farmhouse on a knoll overlooking Indian Creek Valley. The setting seemed more like home to him than his bungalow on the outskirts of New Court. It should, he reminisced. He'd been coming here since he started dating Jennifer Barker two weeks before Christmas in 1989.

Cole parked his truck in front of the house, and he, Mandy, and Buddy climbed the porch steps, letting themselves into the foyer through the glass paneled front door. Jane Barker got up from her chair beside the window, greeting each of them with a warm hug.

"It's so good to see you," she said happily. "Let's go right into the dining room. Breakfast is ready and waiting. I've been keeping the bacon and scrambled eggs warm on the stove, and I have a batch of my homemade cinnamon buns that you youngsters like so much just about ready to come out of the oven."

"Thanks, Grandmom," Mandy said appreciatively. "On Saturdays we usually go through the drive-through at Bucky's in town for a sausage biscuit. Your breakfast will be a real treat."

"Have you got a girlfriend yet?" Jane teased Buddy, trying to get a rise out of him as only a grandmother can. "I was in the sixth grade when your grandfather started trying to get me to notice him. He'd hang around in the afternoons wanting to walk me home from school. Once he kissed me on the playground, and I remember swatting him with a book, although I have to admit now that I liked it."

"Nope," Buddy replied through a mouthful of cinnamon bun. "I'm having too much fun to waste time on girls."

"Buddy's problem is that he can't find anyone who will have him," Mandy kidded. "But he really starts showing off anytime he sees Sarah Jackson. She's my best friend's youngest sister." She was prepared and waiting when her brother tossed the other half of his cinnamon bun at her, easily fielding it with one hand.

"What about you, Amanda?" Jane queried, turning her attention to her granddaughter.

"Nope, just like Buddy. I'm a loner, too."

"I don't think either of you is going to open up and tell Grandmom the truth, so we'll move on to something else. How about the three of you giving me a hand outside after breakfast? A section of fence in the north pasture has come down, and several calves got out yesterday.

"If you two youngsters would find where they've strayed, round them up, and drive them back through the gate, your father and I could replace a couple of rotten posts and get the fence back up at the same time."

"We'd be glad to help, Mama Jane," Cole replied, speaking for the three. "I'm probably the last man alive who actually enjoys working with a post-hole digger. Best exercise in the world for your shoulders, even better than lifting weights."

An hour later, Mandy and Buddy were hunting for the missing calves along a nearby wooded ravine, while Cole set to work with a hickory-handled post-hole digger that looked to be as old as Methuselah, lifting plugs of dirt from the ground with practiced ease.

He paused to catch his breath, glancing up toward the top of Indian Ridge to catch the sun's rays reflecting from a shiny object.

"Who do you think is on up on top of the mountain this morning?" he inquired. "Looks like someone's driving on the old gravel road along the ridge, and bear season doesn't open for over a month. Think that it might be one of your neighbors looking around?"

"It's likely to be one of the Goodes," his mother-in-law replied. "They own a strip of land right along the top of the mountain. The Dillons own most of the ridge on the north side, as well as farmland further down in the valley toward our place. The Goodes have been big land owners over on Barkers Creek since this area was settled, and the Dillons have been the largest property holders here in Indian Creek Valley for a long, long time. There's no love lost between those two families. It's a pity they can't get along, but as far back as I can remember, they've acted like the Hatfields and McCoys."

"That's pretty common knowledge here in Courtland County," Cole agreed. "I've wondered what created the bad blood. People I talk with don't seem to know for sure. It's as though the families' dealings with each other includes a Mafia code of silence."

Cole lifted a locust post to a vertical position and slipped the end into the hole he had just dug, holding it in place while Jane began shoveling dirt around the pole, firmly tamping it down. "The falling-out seems to go back to something that happened during the World War II era," she observed. "No one seems to know the details outside of the two families, and I'm starting to wonder how many of them still remember. Maybe this is a mystery for the sheriff to solve. Want to take on that job?"

Cole laughed, brushing his hands together to knock off the loose bark from the fence post. "Yeah, I'm running out of things to do and looking for more work right now, Mama Jane.

"I don't have nearly enough to keep me busy maintaining law and order between obstreperous drunks who threaten to shoot each other, trying to keep drug dealers from taking over the county, and helping investigate the deaths of two ladies on Carter Creek Road. Oh, and don't let me leave out trying to raise two adolescent kids as a single parent all the while.

"Nope, I think I'll take a pass on solving the mystery of the feud between the Goode and the Dillon clans, and leave that one to you."

"You're not going to unload that unpleasant job on me," Jane said with a laugh. "I'm pretty thick with Bayse Dillon, and I have a friendly relationship with Vernon Goode. Maybe both of us ought to let sleeping dogs lie."

At that moment, Mandy and Buddy started running toward them. "We came across all three of the calves that were out and herded them back into the pasture," Mandy informed them proudly. "But we found something else down in the ravine."

Buddy interrupted her to break the news. "The picked over carcasses of a couple of deer are on lying on the ground. Buzzards were feeding on them when we walked up. Guess what else we found?"

This time Mandy cut in. "We saw paw prints in the mud around the dead deer. Do you suppose that somebody's dogs were running loose and killed them?"

"More likely what you saw were coyote tracks," Jane answered. "I hear them at night, but I rarely see them, and have no idea where their dens are located."

"Coyotes!" Buddy exclaimed. "I didn't know you had anything like that around here. That sounds like Texas."

"I know what you mean," Jane agreed. "It's like frontier living out in these parts. And having a daddy who wears a sheriff's badge and carries a gun makes it even more exciting, doesn't it?"

"Yeah," Buddy replied, asking his father, "How long before I can have a .22 pistol and holster to wear around the place when I'm out here on Grandmom's farm?"

"I'd say at least four more years, maybe when you turn sixteen," Cole answered.

"Good," Mandy chimed in. "By then I'll be away in college. Grandmom, I'll start saving my money to buy you body armor and a steel helmet. Nobody will be safe for a mile around if Buddy gets a gun."

The two youngsters walked ahead, Cole and his mother-in-law following behind. "I'm going to go back on what I just said, and see if I can learn anything about what started that feud," Jane commented.

"Don't forget that curiosity killed the cat," Cole rejoined.

"I don't have a cat at the moment, so that doesn't worry me," Jane laughed. "I'll let you know if I find out anything."

"Good luck, he replied. "I'll be waiting to hear."

Chapter 4

Cole picked up the phone on Monday morning, recognizing the warm, upbeat voice of Connie Balfour, editor of the *Courtland Tribune*. "To what do I owe the honor of this call? You've got a family of skunks trying to move back under your building again, and you want me to come over and take care of them?"

"Do you really think I'd bother you to come over and deal with skunks?" Connie responded. "I don't need the sheriff or anyone else to handle small stuff like that," she continued with feigned annoyance. "For your information, Sheriff Grayson, if I were having trouble with skunks, I'd come back here with my Browning skeet gun tonight after dark and take care of business."

"I'm sure you would, knowing full well that there's an ordinance against discharging firearms inside the town limits, and that the smell from those skunks would run off neighbors for a half-mile around," Cole replied. "So now I'll quit guessing why you called, and politely ask what local law enforcement can do for you this morning."

"Meet me for a noon lunch at the Old Mill Restaurant in Slate Bank, and afterwards I'll flip you to see who picks up the check. I'm craving a good, lean buffalo burger with all the trimmings.

We haven't talked for quite a while, and I'd like to discuss something important with you."

"That's an invitation no gentleman could refuse, Ms. Balfour. What's the topic you want to kick around?"

"I'd rather wait until we meet to get into that."

"That's OK by me. I'll be there at high noon, and just for the record, I'll pick up the tab. I may be underpaid as the sheriff of this county, but I'm not in such bad financial shape that I need to flip a coin with a pretty lady to see who pays for a buffalo burger."

"Fantastic!" Connie laughed. "I believe I've finally found the perfect man—one who's generous, good-looking, wears a uniform, and knows how to treat a lady. See you at the restaurant."

During the drive across Painters Mountain later that morning, Cole thought about Connie, a sharp, attractive lady with a magnetic personality. He knew that the *Trib* had been a chronic money-pit for years before the publisher, who also operated a number of other small town rags, had hired her in a last ditch effort to save the business.

Connie had quit an assistant editor's position with the *Roanoke Times* to take on the challenge of running a newspaper out in the boondocks of Courtland County, hitting the ground running the first day on the job.

She had quickly replaced most of the *Trib's* burned-out staff, bringing in several young, energetic journalists, and she soon tripled the advertising base while simultaneously doubling the circulation.

The *Trib* had become an informative and entertaining paper due to her efforts. It focused on regional news, and it didn't pull any punches when it came to appraising the job performances of public servants.

The sheriff holding office at that time had sold out to county political bosses in order to get re-elected term after term, effectively retiring on the job. Connie was the one who had called him out with strong editorials accusing him of incompetence and conflicts of interest between public and personal business.

She had been instrumental in forming a committee to find a new candidate for the office, searching the state all the way into northern Virginia to secure a local boy with FBI experience. Connie had then spearheaded the grassroots campaign that resulted in his election in a close contest.

Cole knew that without her there was no way in hell he would be back in southwest Virginia living in his old home town of New Court, wearing the Courtland County Sheriff's badge.

He arrived at the small crossroads community, entered the Slate Bank General Store, and found his way to the restaurant in the back. He spotted Connie standing by a window, wearing a sweater, jeans, and Nike running shoes. Her casual outfit might have seemed unsuitable working attire for the editor of a newspaper, but it was in keeping with her independent personality, and certainly one which emphasized her striking figure.

Cole remembered that Connie had been a senior at New Court High when he was in the eleventh grade, which meant that she must now be pushing forty. However, no one would mistake the trim, athletic woman standing before the window as being over the hill. All it would take would be track shorts and a t-shirt to make her look ready to rejoin the girls' cross-country team at New Court High, where she still held one of the school records.

Cole quietly approached to stand directly behind her, and she reacted with startled surprise when she turned to find herself face-to-face with him. "Did the FBI train you how to sneak up on people?" she asked. "I didn't hear you come in."

"We sheriffs and marshals spend a lot of time working on stealth. Your life can depend on it when you become a lawman."

"You sound a little like Thomas Magnum," Connie replied. "But he was a private eye, not a lawman."

"Whatever, just as long as I remind you of Tom Selleck," Cole countered.

"More the voice than the looks," Connie laughed.

"Darn!" Cole responded.

A young waitress led them to a vacant table, took their orders, and disappeared toward the kitchen. Connie hesitated until she was out of earshot before speaking again.

"The local politicians have stepped up their payback campaign against the newspaper for its role in working to remove Sheriff Stoner from office and campaigning to help you get elected.

"Tom Bowling, who owns the Déjà Vu Consignment Shop downtown, called this morning to apologize, telling me he would not be renewing his advertising contract with the *Trib*. But that has nothing to do with my asking you to meet me for lunch today.

"Last month, I assigned my top reporter, Megan Porterfield, to work on a follow-up story regarding the suspicious deaths of two Roanoke College faculty members, Diane Kruger and Susan Helfey, back on May 11, 2008, on Carter Creek Road.

"She's uncovered some information that may shed new light on the case, and I'll share it with you if you'll promise to keep it confidential. Obviously, I want the *Trib* to break the story when the mystery is finally sorted out. Are you OK with that?"

"I promise that I won't disclose any information you share with me today outside of key personnel working with the Sheriff's Department and Virginia State Police task force."

Connie reached across the table to lay her hand on his, stating emphatically, "Megan doesn't think that the deaths of those two women resulted from an accidental house fire. She thinks both of them died as a result of premeditated murder, and the fire was staged afterward to disguise a hate crime."

Cole masked his surprise, asking, "What makes her think that?"

Connie unconsciously gave his hand a squeeze, replying, "Because this appears to be the third time in the last ten years that women from this region, cohabitating in what may have been lesbian relationships, have died under suspicious circumstances. She believes that all three of the crimes are the work of a serial killer with a pathological hatred of gays and lesbians.

"Megan discovered that two women living together in Giles County died in an automobile accident on May 12, 2002, after being run off of the road by a hit and run driver. Two other women in Monroe County, West Virginia, died in another suspicious house fire on May 8, 2005. No suspects have been identified in connection with any of these cases. Doesn't this start to sound like it might be the work of a serial killer?"

"Possibly," Cole agreed. "I'm probably telling you more than I should, but your reporter isn't the first person to think that the Kruger and Helfey deaths may be a double murder. However, your suspicion that this case might be connected to earlier unsolved killings is something new. I appreciate that lead."

"Is it a good enough to assure that the gentleman will pick up the lunch tab today?"

"Plenty good," Cole replied. "I'll even buy you a Klondike Bar for the trip home."

He casually draped his arm around her shoulders as the two walked from the store to the parking lot after lunch.

"Can we continue to share information about the Kruger-Helfey case that isn't confidential to the law enforcement task force?" Connie asked.

"I see nothing wrong with that," Cole replied. "You and your reporter have provided a promising new lead in an investigation that never seemed to go anywhere. It's not the first time in my career that I've had strong misgivings about the ruling of accidental deaths and the feeling someone got away with murder."

The two stood side by side as Connie fished through her purse for her car keys, Cole waiting to open the door for her. She glanced at him as she slipped behind the wheel, commenting, "Thanks for lunch. I really enjoyed visiting with you." She hesitated before starting her engine, as if waiting for his response.

Cole knew he had the chance to tell her something important, but he found himself only able to reply, "Me, too, Connie. We'll have to do this again before long."

Then she was gone, and he knew exactly what had caused him to fumble an opportunity to speak openly with her. He wondered whether he would ever be able to accept the crushing finality of Jennifer's death and the realization that she was gone from his life forever.

Chapter 5

"This afternoon we'll focus on passing the ball," Norma Patton informed the teenage girls standing before her in blue shorts and white New Court Rockets t-shirts.

"I call this the shuffle and deal drill. It will teach you how to shuffle, pass, and move to the ball. The first eight of you girls come over on this side and stand where I show you."

Norma was a good volleyball coach, still picking up new techniques two years after volunteering for the JV girls coaching job. She had played intramural volleyball at Radford University, rationalizing from the beginning of her assignment that any woman who taught high school chemistry and physics could easily master the fine points of the game.

Norma led the team through several practice drills before dividing the group into blue and white squads for a short scrimmage, the part of practice all of the girls eagerly awaited each day.

Melinda Moore was the best player on the Rockets JV team, a dominating six-one, one-fifty pound athlete with the physicality and competitiveness to spike winners against any defender. Melinda could soar above the net, striking the ball hard enough to make opposing players duck and cover.

Mandy was one of the tallest girls at five-nine, but too green in her first year on the team to be a starter. She had, however, inherited a competitive streak from her mother and dad, making her willing and eager to go to the net for blocks against anyone. That had created problems for her in the past, including an angry retaliation by hot tempered Kristen Callison.

A blue squad back row player bumped the ball to a teammate on the outside of the front row, and the second girl set the ball high for Melinda, who was standing near the center. Directly across the net, an intimidated white team player backed out of the line of fire, and Mandy moved in to fill the gap, going for a block

Melinda took two steps and jumped high in the air, meeting the ball at its apex, swinging her fully extended arm at full force to drive the ball downward over the net for the kill.

Mandy was still moving into position at the time the projectile arrived, and it caught her right between the eyes. She staggered backward, dazed, blood spurting from her nose.

Norma quickly whistled play to a halt and came out on the court to see how badly Mandy was hurt, finding that the ball had struck her high enough in the face to spare her from a broken nose.

Still, Norma decided it was a good time to wrap up practice for the day. "You girls hit the showers and get dressed. We'll pick up where we left off tomorrow afternoon. Mandy, I'll give you a ride home when you're ready to go."

As Norma was heading across town with her young passenger, she glanced across the front seat, commenting, "I'm glad you didn't end up with a broken nose like I did when I was in grade school.

"I was trying to hop my bike from the street up onto the sidewalk, and I ended up plowing into the curb and going over the handlebars. I never attempted to master that trick again."

Mandy laughed, "I've got to learn to block with my hands and not my head, particularly when Melinda's going for a kill. She's smacks the ball really hard, and when it hit me in the face, I saw stars."

"But you had guts enough to move in and try to block Melinda's spike after your teammate chickened out. I think you showed a lot of moxie. That's exactly what we need if we are going to be a championship contender."

Cole saw Norma pull into the driveway and stopped what he was doing to speak to her. He spotted two shiners starting to show on Mandy's face as soon as she stepped out of the car, asking anxiously, "Are you OK? What in the world happened?"

"I'm fine, Dad. I caught a ball in the face at practice, that's all. Miss Patton was nice enough to take care of me when it happened, and then give me a ride home."

Norma got out of the car to apologize. "I'm sorry about Mandy getting hurt today, Sheriff. Something like this doesn't happen very often in volleyball."

"Injuries are a part of most sports," he replied. "Thanks for giving Mandy a ride home. Feel free to call me Cole, Ms. Patton."

"I'll do that if you'll call me Norma. You would have been proud of your daughter today, taking on the biggest hitter on our team. Mandy just couldn't get into position in time to fill in for her teammate, and that's why she got hammered."

"Since it's dinner time, why don't you stick around and share some pizza with us," Cole invited, hoping Norma would join them. "Grocery store pizza isn't as quite as good as the stuff the pros make, but I still think it's right tasty."

"Thanks for the offer, Sheriff, I mean, Cole, but I need to get home and work on some lesson plans for tomorrow. Mandy, take care of yourself. I hope you'll be able to open both of your eyes when you wake up in the morning."

"She seems like a very nice lady," Cole commented as Norma drove away.

"She's my favorite teacher," Mandy replied. "Isn't she pretty?"

"I think you could safely say that," Cole replied with a gentle smile, slipping his arm around his daughter's shoulders as the two entered the house, detecting the delicious aroma of hot pepperoni.

Buddy glanced up from his seat in front of the television to chime in, "The oven timer just went off, and the pizza sure smells like it's ready."

He glanced up and caught sight of his sister, exclaiming, "What in the world happened to you today, Sis? Did you get into it with Kristen Callison again?"

Mandy rolled her eyes, replying, "Yeah, that's exactly what happened. Girls are always slugging it out in the gym or the locker room, just like the boys." Then she added sarcastically, "Buddy, you're a regular Sherlock Holmes."

The comeback was wasted on a kid brother who wasn't listening to a word she said, giving his undivided attention to the huge slice of pepperoni pizza on his plate.

Chapter 6

Jane Barker glanced down to be sure that her grocery list was on the seat beside her before putting Wesley's pride and joy, a '95 Ford F150 pickup, in gear and starting down the long driveway toward Indian Creek Road.

There was something about her late husband's farm truck that made Jane feel close to him whenever she climbed into the cab, and she often repeated her intention to hold on to the shiny sky-blue vehicle until the wheels fell off.

Nothing seemed out of the ordinary as she drove along the quiet country road, just an occasional squirrel frantically darting across the pavement, and a few black buzzards performing roadside clean up before flying away at the very last moment as she approached.

Most of the oncoming vehicles were easily recognizable, driven by long-time neighbors who gave her a friendly wave as they passed. However, one approaching vehicle was completely unfamiliar to her—a white crew-cab pick-up truck which slowed to turn onto a side road leading toward Indian Ridge. Jane squinted to make out the bold company logo on the door, WindEnerG, Inc.

She stared as she drove past, seeing the front seat passenger glance in her direction and then turn away. Vernon Goode did not react quickly enough to avoid her recognition, leaving Jane to mull over why he had just acted rudely, totally unlike the friendly way he had behaved toward her the last time she had run into him.

Then she considered one possible reason for his attempt to avoid eye contact—a desire not to be seen riding in a truck belonging to WindEnerG, Inc., heading surreptitiously toward his property on the top of Indian Ridge.

Jane pushed these thoughts from her mind as she pulled into the Kroger parking lot, focusing on her reason for the trip—stocking up on groceries to feed her hungry grandchildren on their next visit.

*****

Vernon Goode eased his aching back out of the truck to join the WindEnerG team, Jack Sanders, project manager, and two young engineers, and together they began their climb toward the crest of the ridge. Vernon noted with satisfaction that the Goode land was clearly posted with *No Trespassing* signs on trees lining the mountaintop road, discouraging the occasional hunter and hiker from lingering in the area.

All four were breathing hard by the time they made it to the top, the stunning view of Indian Creek Valley spread out below, with only the sound of the wind blowing through the tops of the towering bull pines.

"An absolutely perfect site for a wind farm," Jack observed. "Think about capturing this enormous natural energy with wind turbines and eliminating the harmful air pollution from coal-fired electric power plants. How could anyone not believe that harnessing this power is the right thing to do for the future of our country?"

Vernon gazed over the farmland below, wondering if all of the landowners in view would share Jack's enthusiasm, particularly the Dillon family. "How tall did you say those turbines will be?" he asked.

"They'll stand four-hundred forty feet tall. I know that seems big, but since this ridge is a good distance away from most of the homes, they won't be nearly as conspicuous as that may sound."

"You're aware that the Appalachian Trail crosses the valley further up the road, and those folks are mighty particular about what gets built where hikers can see it?" Vernon continued. "They'll fight it tooth and nail if it's in plain sight."

"We're planning to stay out of the AT view shed. WEG has spent a lot of time studying the permitting process a competitor completed in planning to build wind turbines on Poor Mountain in Roanoke County, and we have a high degree of confidence that we can get the required approvals from the Courtland County Board of Supervisors and any other regulatory body. All of the counties in southwest Virginia are searching for new jobs and additional tax revenue."

Vernon smiled sardonically, knowing one family which would undoubtedly be less enthusiastic than he and WEG about "going green" with a wind farm on the tip-top of Indian Ridge: Bayse Dillon and his clan, scattered in farm houses all across the valley below.

*****

Cole was preparing to kick back in his chair and close his eyes after lunch when the phone rang, and he found himself on the line with Tom Bowman of the Virginia State Police.

"Sheriff, we've identified the man you were pursuing a couple of weeks ago."

"You're talking about that young man in the stolen Ford van, the one that drives like a bootlegger and runs like a scalded dog?"

"That's the one. We were able to make a positive ID by checking fingerprints in the vehicle against the file for previously convicted drug offenders.

"His name is Maurice Jones, and it turns out that he was a track star in Henry County a few years back. He held the Virginia Double-A High School record for the quarter mile at that time.

"We still haven't been able to locate his whereabouts, and I suspect he's no longer in this area. I personally think it's likely that law enforcement people aren't the only ones looking for him right now. Some dealer must be mad as hell about him losing the big stash of money and drugs that we recovered, thanks to you."

"Can I get a copy of the State Police report on Jones? I want to have all the information about him that I can lay my hands on."

"I'll see that you get it," Tom replied. "A pity that the kid got mixed up with drugs. His athletic ability might have gotten him a college scholarship to play football or run track. He might even have gotten a look by Virginia Tech if he'd kept a clean record. Some kids miss great opportunities and really screw up their lives at an early age."

"Tell me about it," Cole replied. "I deal with them every day. So you're saying that this kid comes from a decent family?"

"Pretty much, although it was a typical low income, single parent household, with his mother drawing welfare and working part-time, minimum wage jobs. He was an average student, and an active member of a Baptist church."

"Maybe he's not totally incorrigible," Cole observed. "We'll try to keep that in mind when he's arrested. Thanks for the call."

Chapter 7

"You need to saw those boards on the sides a little shorter so they won't stick out and snag on the brush growing out along the creek bank," Buddy imperiously directed his friend.

"Who made you the captain of this ship?" Mikey asked in irritation, setting the rusty handsaw down to glare at his friend. "Remember, I was the one who got all the lumber to build this thing."

"Just give me the saw, and I'll do it," Buddy replied.

"Dad said that he'd haul our raft over to Carter Creek this afternoon and help us unload it near the swinging bridge. He warned me that we're not to float downstream past the Meyer property and get into that stretch of posted land."

Mikey finished driving a nail, replying, "That's as far as I want to go, anyway. Poling our raft back up-stream for a half mile will be a lot of work."

"We need the practice. The county raft race is coming up in May, and we may be able to win first prize for our age group if we learn how to maneuver this thing through shallow water."

"You think your sister will come out after lunch and help us load the raft on your dad's trailer?" Mikey nonchalantly asked, never looking toward his co-worker.

"You've really got a thing for high school girls, haven't you? Yeah, I plan to ask her to help us. We'll need at least four people to handle this battleship."

"I was just checking be sure we had enough people to lift it," Mikey shot back. "You're the one mooning over a girl and following her around everywhere she goes. Sarah Jackson ought to start calling you Lassie." He watched Buddy silently go back to work, knowing that, for once, he had gotten the upper hand.

Early that afternoon, Cole backed his truck up to the garage door, and he, the two boys, and Mandy set the raft onto the utility trailer, securing it with ratchet tie-downs before heading off for Carter Creek.

A short time later, the four unloaded the craft on the gravel bank just downstream from a rickety-planked swinging bridge hanging from rusty steel cables between tall trees on either side of the stream.

"You boys keep your life jackets on," Cole commanded, as he pushed the raft into the creek, and the two boys waded out to climb aboard. "There are some deep holes where the water is way over your head."

A few pushes on their long saplings, and the two adventurers were underway. "I'll be back before dinner time to pick you up," Cole called out. "Just be careful and stay out of trouble. There's no cell phone coverage out here, so you won't be able to call me. And don't forget what I told you about staying off of posted property."

Buddy and Mikey watched Cole and Mandy drive away before beginning the slow journey downstream, using their makeshift poles to steer into the mainstream and avoid rock ledges marked by riffles of whitewater.

The boys silently floated along, spotting a blue heron snatching a minnow before flying away with a pterodactyl's raucous squawk. Further along the way, several whitetail deer stood frozen, cautiously watching the boys slowly approach and then float past, bending their heads to drink again as the raft drifted away.

The boys lost track of time as the sun moved lower in the sky, neither expecting to so quickly complete the half-mile trip downstream through the Meyer property. Both were startled upon seeing the conspicuous cardboard signs nailed to trees on either side of the creek, proclaiming in bold black font: "No Hunting, Fishing, or Trespassing."

Mikey caught sight of a more ominous warning crudely lettered in red paint on a piece of plywood. "Look over on the left. There's a sign that says: 'Keep Out—Trespassers Will be Shot'." He looked at Buddy in alarm, whispering, "We need to clear out of here right now."

A boom shattered the stillness and echoed from the hillsides, and the boys saw a man holding a shotgun standing on the creek bank only a stone's throw away, angrily scowling at them. "You damn kids don't pay attention to signs, do you? Get the hell over here. I want to talk to you."

Buddy and Mikey froze, staring at the stranger, scared as they had never been before. He was big and unshaven, dressed in jeans and a camouflage jacket, long, greasy hair escaping his cap. They managed to pole the raft up against the bank where the man was waiting, their stomachs knotted.

The gunman sized up the two wide-eyed boys as he might a rabbit caught in his sights. "I'm going to let you little punks off this time, and give you a chance to pole that raft out of here and back upstream. But don't ever come here on my land again, or I promise you that you'll regret it. I won't go easy on you the next time. You understand me? Now get the hell out of here!"

"Yes, sir," Buddy replied, his voice shaking with fright. "Let's go, Mikey." The two boys leaned into their poles, pushing the raft away from the bank out into the middle of the creek, working hard to keep the bow facing into the current while slowly starting to move forward.

Neither glanced back when they reached the bend in the creek and heard the report of the shotgun a second time. Both were totally absorbed in the task at hand, digging their poles into the stream bed and pushing the raft against the flow with all of their might.

It seemed an eternity, defined by constant effort and aching muscles, before they approached the stretch of creek where they had put in, and were finally able to spot the old swinging bridge. They breathed a sigh of relief when they saw Cole and Mandy standing on the bank, waving.

Mikey turned to his friend, confessing, "I've never been that scared in my life. I nearly peed my pants when I heard his gun go off. It sure is good to see your dad over there."

Buddy let out a nervous laugh. "He scared the crap out of me, too. I was afraid he was really going to shoot us."

As they neared the bank, Buddy tossed the bow line to his dad, who pulled the raft into shallow water while the two boys waded ashore.

"You ought to hear what happened! Some mean looking guy with a shotgun jumped us and made us come over so he could chew us out. We both thought we might get shot."

"Where did you run into him? Did you go against my order not to drift pass the Meyer property and get onto the posted land downstream?" Cole asked.

"Yes, Dad. It all happened before we knew it. All at once, we saw a lot of posted signs along the creek bank, and then we heard a gunshot and saw this man motioning for us to come over and talk to him. He was one mean looking guy, about your size, wearing a camouflage hunting jacket and cap.

"He chewed us out, and let us go, but he fired his gun again to scare us while we were poling our raft back upstream away from his part of the creek. He's put up a sign warning that trespassers will be shot."

"I ought to kick both of your tails for doing exactly what I told you not to, but I suppose you've already been punished enough," Cole responded.

"I recognize the man you ran into from your description, and he's got a bad reputation. He's only owned that piece of property for a few years, but he and the crew who work for him have already had run-ins with the neighbors. He's obsessed with keeping everyone off of his land, and he's ready to butt heads with anyone who confronts him.

"He had every right to get on you for trespassing, but absolutely no right to fire that gun up in the air and scare you the way he did. I'm going to take one of my deputies and pay him a visit on Monday morning. That sign you saw, the one threatening to shoot trespassers, is going to come down."

"Why are people like him so mean?" Mandy asked. "Why do we have to put up with jerks like that around here?"

"I sometimes ask myself the same thing," Cole gently replied. "But there seems to be enough of their kind to give a sheriff job security for a long, long time, just keeping them in line and maintaining the peace."

"You're actually going back to talk to that man?" Mikey asked Cole. "He looks really tough. Aren't you afraid he might shoot you?"

"Don't you worry about a thing, son," Cole reassured him. "Law enforcement officers come up against troublemakers like him from time to time. I promise you he has a lot more to worry about in his dealing with me than I do in straightening him out."

What Cole did not mention to any of the three young people was the flow of adrenaline kicking in as he looked ahead to the coming confrontation.

Chapter 8

Gravel crunched under the wheels of the Crown Vic on Monday morning as Cole and Tank drove along an isolated private single-track road paralleling Carter Creek, ignoring "No Trespassing" and "Keep Out" signs posted on either side.

They continued through a dark hollow, densely overgrown with rhododendron and studded with rock outcroppings, until rounding a sharp turn to encounter a padlocked gate blocking the road. They had just stopped to consider their next move when a man wearing a camouflage coat and cap appeared from the underbrush, a shotgun slung under his arm.

Cole knew at once that this was the hot-tempered property owner who had terrified his son. He also knew from recent investigation that the man's name was Irv Sutton, and that he had previous convictions for disturbing the peace and assault.

Cole opened the car door, providing a clear view of the star on his chest. "Good morning. I'm Sheriff Grayson, and this is Deputy Krupski. We need to talk to you."

"I can see who you are, Sheriff," the man replied brusquely, no trace of civility in either tone or demeanor. "I haven't done anything to break the law, so I don't know what brings you out here this morning. Before we go any further, I'd like point out that your squad car is parked on a private road posted No Trespassing, and I haven't given you permission to come on my land."

Tank slipped his right hand down the stock of the short-barreled twelve gauge Remington pump shotgun resting beside his leg, index finger now resting lightly on the safety, prepared to take action if things got out of hand.

"Watch how you talk to the law," Cole cautioned in a flat, ominous voice, staring at Sutton unblinkingly. "If I have to go get a warrant from the judge to enter your property, I'm going to be a lot less friendly when I get back here.

"You're the man who scared the hell out of a couple of young boys floating down the creek on Saturday, aren't you, discharging a gun so they'd think you were going to shoot them? One of those boys happens to be my son, and whether he strayed onto your land by accident or not, you're damn well not going to terrify him or anyone else by pulling a stunt like that again."

Sutton held his ground. "Your boy and the other kid were on posted property. I own that section of the creek, and I'll not have anyone paddle in or set foot on the bank without my written permission."

"You heard what I just said," Cole tersely countered. "I also hear you've put up a sign beside the creek threatening to shoot trespassers, and I want that damn thing taken down right now.

"Courtland County is a peaceful place, and no one is going to move here and start acting up like some kind of goddamn terrorist. I'm letting you off with a warning this time, but don't make me have to come back out here to see you about this again."

Sutton glared at the sheriff, but held his tongue as Cole walked away and got back into the cruiser, turning the vehicle around in a tight U-turn before slowly driving away. Tank continued to look back, locked in an eye-to-eye stare-down with the seething landowner.

"I had your back, boss," he commented, lifting his finger off the safety and shifting the shotgun to rest the muzzle on the floor.

"I never would have gotten out of the car empty-handed to confront an armed man if you hadn't been here to cover me," Cole replied. "I owe you one."

"What do you plan to do about this Sutton guy? He acts as though he's had run-ins with police officers and sheriff department deputies before, and isn't a bit intimidated. The way I read him, he believes he can get away with doing whatever he pleases."

"If that what he thinks, he's in for a hell of a surprise living here in our jurisdiction. We'll keep watching to see if we can find out why he's so dead-set on keeping everyone off his land. He's bad news, and I'm positive that he's up to no good out here."

Cole's voice momentarily strengthened with emotion, adding, "For a minute, I was ready to cold-cock that tough talking, arrogant punk."

*****

Cole drove into the New Court High parking lot at 5:30, observing that there were still a number of cars parked beside the gym. He dialed in a radio station in Roanoke featuring country music, and sat back to patiently wait for Mandy. A short time later, she appeared at the door, walking toward his truck to climb in beside him and ride shotgun.

Cole was preparing to drive away when Mandy suddenly spoke up. "Dad, hold up a minute. Ms. Patton is standing over there beside her car, and it looks like she's having trouble."

The two turned to watch as Norma lifted the hood and glanced into the engine compartment, then shut it and began fumbling through her purse as if searching for a cell phone. Cole wheeled his truck around in a tight circle and pulled up beside her before she could retrieve it.

"Got a car problem?" he asked with a friendly smile.

"My water pump's been making a strange noise for some time, and I should have had it checked out," she ruefully replied. "It looks like it finally broke, and now all of my coolant has leaked out. I'm going to call a friend to come get me, and then have a mechanic from Foster's Auto Repair pick up my car."

"We'll give you a ride home, Ms. Patton," Mandy volunteered, climbing from the front seat into the crew seat behind. "You can ride up front with Dad."

Norma locked her car and stepped up into the truck, quipping, "I want to point out that this is the first I've been hauled home by the sheriff."

Cole countered, "Are you being completely truthful with the law? Remember that I can pull up your record at the courthouse and check out that statement."

"I have a clean rap sheet," she laughed. "Otherwise, the Courtland County School Board wouldn't have given me a job teaching and coaching your daughter and her friends."

"In some of the inner city schools around DC not far from where we used to live, quite a few of the students got into serious trouble," Cole wryly observed. "I'm glad we have teachers like you getting kids off to a good start at New Court High."

"And I'm glad we have parents like you working with us," Norma replied. "Young people like your daughter make my job fun."

"You hear that, Mandy?" Cole inquired. "That's quite a compliment. For the record, no teacher ever said anything like that about me."

"I have a feeling that you weren't as bad as you let on," Norma laughed. "People around this town have memories like elephants, and if you had been some sort of juvenile delinquent in your high school days, I don't think they'd have elected you to wear that star."

When they arrived at her secluded home on Upper Carter Creek Road, Norma got out of the truck, flashing a grateful smile. "Thanks for the ride home, Sheriff. Mandy, I'll see you in school tomorrow."

"I thought we were on a friendly first name basis now, Norma," Cole replied. "Call on us if you need a ride to work in the morning."

Chapter 9

"Let's get ready to rumble!" Connie announced in her deepest voice when she heard Cole answer the phone on Wednesday morning.

"What's this all about, Connie?" Cole replied, setting his coffee cup on his desk and shifting the phone in his hand. "You got a bad head cold? You sound like Kermit the Frog."

"Watch it, Sheriff," she cautioned. "You may not get to hear the latest news if you don't play nice. I'm calling to tip you off that we may have Armageddon about to start right here in Courtland County."

"Ok, now you have my attention, and I'll behave. What's the crisis du jour?"

"A Chicago based company trading as WindEnerG, Inc. has just submitted a request to the Courtland County Board of Supervisors for approval to build a wind farm. They want to put it on the top of Indian Ridge on land leased from the Goode family. The number and type of wind turbines would be similar to those planned for Poor Mountain in Roanoke County."

"Holy Moses, that's news to me. It's hard for me to imagine any sane person wanting to stir things up around here with a controversial project like that. Every time I pick up the Roanoke paper, I read another letter from some Bent Mountain resident protesting the construction of four-hundred forty foot bat-choppers in his back yard."

"Why in the world do you think the Goodes would lease their land on Indian Ridge for development of a wind farm?" Connie inquired.

"I'd say that the Goode family will get a big chunk of change if the project goes forward, for one thing," Cole replied. "And they might also rationalize that they are doing the environmentally friendly and politically correct thing by helping to produce clean, green electric power.

"But neither of those is the real answers, is it? You and I both know that the Goodes will be sticking it to the Dillons if those huge machines are builr on the ridge right above Dillon land, while the Goode family will never have to look at them from their property on Barkers Creek."

"Bingo!" Connie responded. "And suddenly the longstanding bad blood between the Goodes and Dillons escalates further to become a real feud."

"Not a pleasant thing to contemplate if you're sitting in my seat, charged with keeping the peace," Cole agreed. "Do you think there's even one chance in a million that the Courtland County Board of Supervisors will approve the request?"

"That's a little hard for me to say, sitting here in my office," Connie answered. "My first response is no way. But then I start to think about the county tax revenue and new jobs a big project like that would bring, and the tendency of the current board to approve any and all proposed developments creating growth, and all at once I'm not a bit sure.

"Approval could end up being punted to county residents in a referendum. If the project should go forward, regardless of how it's approved, it won't sit well with the Dillons. As principal land owners on Indian Creek, it's their view which will be degraded."

"I suppose that I ought to thank you for the heads-up, Connie, but you certainly haven't helped to brighten my morning."

"Bad news travels fast, and if I hadn't called, you'd have heard it from someone else around town before lunch," Connie replied.

"Not much goes on around New Court that everyone doesn't quickly find out about, even small stuff, like the sheriff giving a ride home to a pretty high school teacher."

"How the heck . . ." Cole was unable to finish his question before hearing Connie's laughter, followed by a click.

*****

The two boys didn't waste a second after hearing the freedom bell ring, racing through the door of New Court Middle School on the double and riding their bikes to Buddy's house to pick up a pair of binoculars. In no time flat, they were on the way down Carter Creek Road past the outskirts of town and beyond.

"I wish there were a lot more teachers' meetings so that we could get off early every day," Mikey mused as they quickly pedaled along, dodging the potholes on the quiet country road. "But I can tell you, there are a lot of things I'd rather be doing this afternoon than this. Why in the world do we want to go back and get mixed up again with that psycho with the shotgun?"

"Haven't you heard that when you get thrown off of a horse, you've got to get right back in the saddle, or you'll end up being afraid to ride?" Buddy replied. "This is the exactly same thing."

"But when a horse bucks you off, you know he didn't start out intending to hurt you. If that goon runs into us again after the last time he got on us, there's no telling what he might do. No one's going to be around to help us. Your old man and mine don't even know where we are."

"Relax! We're not going back on the psycho's property again," Buddy said reassuringly. "We're going to be doing our reconn from the top of Rock Hill on Old Man Meyer's land. But we're still proving that we're not scared of him. That's the important thing."

He glanced at his friend, sensing that that he was still worried. "The only reason no one knows we're out here is because that's the way we want it. Dad would kick both of our tails if he found out what we're up to."

"I still say this is a really bad idea from the get go," Mikey commented, glancing at the sun as it dipped lower in the western sky.

The boys turned off of the lightly traveled state highway to continue along a private gravel road, pedaling across an old timber bridge with a faded wooden sign warning any errant motorist, "Weight Limit 1 Ton."

They down-shifted when they reached the foot of Rock Hill to begin a long climb, but halfway up the twisting trail, the grade became too steep for them to make it, even in granny gear and standing on the pedals, so they got off and began pushing their bikes. By the time they made it to the top and were able to look out toward the winding silver ribbon of Carter Creek in the distance, both were panting like long-haired dogs on a hot summer day.

“You can see where Meyer’s pasture stops, and Psycho’s woods begin on the creek bank,” Buddy exclaimed. “That’s where he jumped us.”

“Let me have the first look with the binoculars,” Mikey requested. He scanned the landscape for several minutes before commenting, “There’s a gravel road on his land that ends in a clearing next to a log house and a couple of big sheds. It looks like he keeps cars and trucks parked under one of them.”

Mikey was preparing to hand over the binoculars when he caught a glimpse of several men emerging from the house. “Hold on a minute. I can see the man who had the shotgun, and he’s with a couple of other guys. It looks like they’re carrying some boxes out of the cabin and loading them into the back of a truck.

“Uh-oh! They’ve stopped now, and they’re looking in our direction. You don’t think they can see us up here spying on them, do you?”

“Keep your head down,” Buddy cautioned. “They might have seen sunlight reflecting off one of our bike mirrors, but I doubt if they can tell who we are from that distance.”

“I hope you’re right,” Mikey replied. “They’ve gone back to work now and aren’t looking this way any more. The one in the big hat got into the truck and is backing out from under the shed.”

Suddenly, Buddy sharply warned him, “Freeze! A snake just stuck his head out from under a rock behind you. If you step back, you’ll put your foot right on top of him.”

“What should I do?” Mikey asked in a panic

"Don't move! I can get a good look now—it's a three-foot rattle snake that's come out of a crack and is slithering over into the sunlight. It's not coiled up like it's about to bite."

Mikey backed up cautiously as soon as the snake was past him, handing the binoculars back to his friend. "You can stick around if you want, but I'm out of here now. The men we've been watching don't scare me as much as that snake."

"It's time to go," Buddy agreed. "You were pretty cool, standing there like a statue waiting for that rattlesnake to move on."

"I didn't have a hell of a lot of choice, did I?" Mikey shot back. "If you ever decide to come back here again, you'll be by yourself."

"But we did what we had to do," Buddy rationalized. "We proved that we aren't afraid of Psycho."

"I reckon so," Mikey grudgingly agreed. "But I sure hope he and the other two couldn't make out who we are when they were looking this way. He might do something to get back at us."

*****

"What were you up to this afternoon?" Cole asked, glancing across the dinner table at his son. "I hear school let out early. Floyd Manning told me he passed you and your sidekick riding your bikes way out Route 615 near the Meyer farm."

"Yeah, we were just riding around on our bicycles all over the place," Buddy replied, squirming in his seat.

Mandy suddenly spoke up, redirecting the conversation to cover for a brother obviously hiding something from his dad. "This afternoon our team went ahead without Coach Patton and held volleyball practice on the outdoor court behind the school."

Buddy exhaled in relief as Cole turned to his daughter. “You girls need to practice as much as you can if you’re serious about winning the district championship.”

Then he glanced at his son with a faint smile and a father’s unspoken, all-business message: I know exactly what you boys were up to. Don’t ever go against my orders again.

Chapter 10

"How'd you like to attend the Roanoke Symphony concert at the Jefferson Center in Roanoke this evening?" Connie asked, after hearing Cole pick up the phone on Friday morning. "You get to be my date."

"Is this another Rent an Escort solicitation?" Cole inquired, deadpan. "If so, it's the third one I've gotten this week, and, like I told all of those other ladies, I'm not available for personal services."

"Nope, this is legit. I received two complimentary tickets for helping to publicize the concert. We can have dinner in the Regency Room at Hotel Roanoke."

"Thanks for the invitation, Connie. I happen to be open this evening and would love to go with you. Dinner's on me, of course. I can pick you up around six, if that works for you."

Cole put down the phone, feeling good about the start to his day. The prospect of a good meal and an orchestra concert in the company of a very attractive lady put everything on his calendar into a better perspective—even the certainty of an unpleasant run-in with hot-tempered Luke Harkins when he would be served with his estranged wife's restraining order later that morning.

But the rest of his work day turned into a happy surprise, made more enjoyable by the fact that Harkins was loaded on moonshine whiskey and in no condition to react when his wife's papers were handed to him. In fact, Cole's day was downright pleasant, or so it seemed until Vernon and Junior Goode strode through the office door, both clearly upset.

"Sheriff, you've got to do something about those Dillons. They came onto our property last night and used a chain saw to drop some big poplars across our road. Those trees would have been worth good money when the land is cleared and the timber is sold to a logger, but now we'll have to cut them up just to get them it out of the way."

"How do you know it was the Dillons who did it?" Cole calmly inquired.

"You know plain well that that if anyone else had been running a chain saw on the mountain at night, the Dillons would have been on the phone with you raising hell. They're upset about us leasing our land for a wind farm on top of the ridge, and they're doing this mischief to send us a message."

"But you have no proof it was the Dillons who cut those trees, do you, Vernon?"

"It sure as hell wasn't beavers or woodpeckers. There's tire marks and footprints in the dirt up there. You need to go investigate for yourself, Sheriff. That's the job we elected you to do."

Cole allowed the two men to vent, knowing their family had voted for him in the last election, then promised, "I'll send one of my deputies out to look around and collect any evidence that may tell us who vandalized your property. We'll get back to you when we know more."

Cole followed the elder Goode outside, speaking to him not as the sheriff, but as a friend. "Vernon, how did relations between your family and the Dillons ever become so toxic? I know that there's been bad blood for a long time, but no one around here seems to know what caused the feud or even when it started."

"I know what triggered it, and Bayse Dillon knows, too," Vernon replied sternly, looking Cole squarely in the eye. "It's no one else's business, including the sheriff's. We'll keep all of that to ourselves. There's no way to ever mend fences between the two families after what happened."

*****

"You look like a million dollars," Cole commented as Connie answered the doorbell, her dark hair up, looking like a fashion model in a spectacular black cocktail dress and stiletto heels which lifted her to his height. "Even better than that," he added, drawing her appreciative smile.

"You clean up pretty well yourself, Sheriff," Connie replied. "Thanks for the nice compliment. I don't hear that from you very often." She slipped back inside to retrieve her coat, and then shut the door, taking his arm to walk down the steps and along the brick paved walkway to the car.

Cole detected the faint scent of an expensive perfume as they stood close together, recalling that the same exotic fragrance had been one of Jennifer's favorites, but cutting off that thought before it could go any further.

He had dated only a few times in the years since he had lost her, still feeling guilty when enjoying another woman's company. Friends had told him it was time to go on with his life, but that was proving to be much easier said than done.

During the long drive toward Roanoke, Connie hesitantly brought up a subject that the two had discussed several weeks before. "I hadn't planned to get into any unpleasant matters this evening," she said apologetically, "but I think you'll be interested in the latest discovery in Megan's investigation of the Kruger/Helfey deaths.

"Megan has declared a jihad. I told you that she uncovered records of two other female couples in this part of the state who died under mysterious circumstances. Now she's convinced that she's found still another, dating back to May, 2004, in Bland County. Maybe it's time to transfer Megan from my payroll to yours."

"I'd like to get into this with her sometime very soon," Cole answered. "It's beginning to sound more and more like a psychopath has declared open season on gay women."

"I think Megan may be able to help get to the bottom of this," Connie commented. "She's the proverbial dog with a bone when she takes on an investigative reporting assignment."

Cole and Connie returned to small talk, arriving at the Hotel Roanoke for dinner, then departing afterward for the Jefferson Center just in time for a thoroughly enjoyable musical program. Afterward, they returned to New Court along a deserted highway, holding hands.

Cole pulled into the driveway at Connie's house, walking beside her up the steps onto the porch and taking the key to unlock the door.

"Can you come in and stay for a while?" she asked softly, standing before him with her face expectantly tilted upward.

“Thanks, but I guess I need to get home and check on the kids. I appreciate your getting the tickets to the concert. I don’t know when I’ve had a nicer time.” He gently slipped his arms around her and kissed her cheek.

She pulled away, clearly surprised and hurt. “Your wife’s been gone for three years, Cole,” she said, trying to hold back the tears filling her eyes. “Why do you feel guilty getting close to me? I won’t keep going out with you and have you treat me like a sister.”

Cole was taken back by her frankness, and he started to apologize. “Connie, I swear to God I wasn’t thinking anything like that when I kissed you. You’re one of the most desirable women I’ve ever met. It’s just that I was married for so long to Jennifer, I seem to have forgotten how to be single again.”

“You don’t act as though you’re the least bit attracted to me, Cole, and I’m not begging you to be,” Connie replied, spinning on her heel. “I hope you know that you’ve spoiled everything between us.”

Chapter 11

"Bring him on in and we'll lock him up in Cell 4," the jailer on duty instructed Deputy Jake Johnson, as he forcefully dragged an unruly, bleeding man through the door. "We'll put his girl friend in Cell 8 back in the women's wing. Looks like they tore each other all to hell before you got them separated, judging by the scratches on his face. He looks like a peeled tomato."

"Yeah, and they'd still be at it if I hadn't come by and busted up the fight. I'll call one of our EMTs to come over and take a look at their injuries, but I think it's mostly superficial cuts and bruises. The woman probably has a few loose teeth where he punched her in the mouth.

"Meth addicts stay on it for a couple of days and get so strung out there's no telling what they'll do to each other. These two lovebirds don't look as bad as the truckers I arrested last week who'd gotten into a knock-down, drag-out brawl after some macho argument.

"Apparently this fracas started when he found out his woman had used the last of their ice, and he went postal on her, with her giving him back as good as she got. I had to tase him before I could restrain him and get the handcuffs on. I felt like I was wrestling a gorilla. Meth makes these freaks a lot stronger and harder to handle."

"Our society's got a big problem," the deputy replied. "This court house will continue to have a revolving door until we cut off the supply of drugs on the street. We bring them in for prostitution, robbery, or assault, the judge sentences them to three to six months in jail, and then they're outside again looking for a dealer. The next thing you know we have them back with us at the free Courtland County Bed and Breakfast.

"The boss is on a crusade to clean up the source of drugs in this county," Jake commented. "He's convinced that there's a major lab operating somewhere around these parts, and knowing Cole, he ain't going to let us get a moment's rest until we kick down the door and put them out of business for good."

"I assume you read these two their rights when you arrested them," the jailer interjected. "Most of the prisoners won't open their mouths without an attorney present once you've done that."

"That's still not going to keep me from interrogating each of them separately and leaning on them for information," Jake replied. "I'm going to use every trick in the book to try and find out where they're getting that stuff. All we need is for one of them to slip up and give us a lead to the source."

"Keep playing one against the other," the jailer suggested. "If you can get them going back and forth trying to even the score, there's no telling what information they might let slip out."

*****

"The Courtland County Board of Supervisors is hereby in session," Chairperson Molly Harper proclaimed to the restive crowd gathered in the Circuit Courtroom on Wednesday evening, glancing at the other four supervisors seated on either side of her in elevated seats near the front.

"There's only one item on the agenda tonight. That will be the initial hearing of a proposal by WindEnerG, Inc. based in Chicago, Illinois, to construct a wind farm consisting of up to eighteen turbines near the top of Indian Ridge. The turbines lineup would front Old Ridge Road on a tract of land owned by Vernon Goode, Sr. and family.

"The Board is well aware that many county residents have strong and conflicting opinions regarding this matter, but tonight we will run this meeting in a civil and businesslike manner according to Robert's Rules, and anyone who cannot conduct himself or herself accordingly will be escorted from the room. With that caveat, we'll get started."

Cole sat with Tank near the back of the courtroom, seeing members of the Goode family clustered on the left side of the room, and across the center aisle, the Dillons and other residents of Indian Creek Valley, including his mother-in-law, gathered on the right.

Cole also noticed that Connie Balfour and one of her reporters were seated near the front, together with a contingent of out-of-town reporters from the *Roanoke Times* and all three of the Roanoke-Lynchburg television stations. Behind them he spotted representatives of the Appalachian Trail Conservancy and Federal Aviation Administration.

Connie turned her head to glance about the room, making momentary eye contact with Cole, but looking away with no sign of recognition. Her coolness gave him an uncomfortable awareness that things had suddenly, and quite likely permanently, changed between the two of them.

His attention was redirected to business when Molly spoke again. "Mr. Sanders, as the WindEnerG representative who is now petitioning to build the wind farm, we're ready to hear your proposal explaining and justifying the request for approval. The floor is yours."

Cole watched Bayse Dillon shift in his seat as though wanting to stand and stop dead in its tracks any discussion of eighteen four-hundred foot wind turbines on the hill overlooking his back yard. His middle-aged son, Boyd, reached out to gently place a calming hand on his father's arm, and Bayse settled back to listen, still wearing a frown.

Jack Sanders proved to be a good project engineer and an effective speaker, making his case for electric power generation utilizing solar energy, pointing out that the greenhouse gases inherent in the combustion of fossil fuels are non-existent with wind turbine generators, reducing the threat of global warming. His message was clear: building wind turbines is the right thing to do for the future welfare of our country and the entire world.

"I think you'll look back ten years from now, and see the turbines spinning on the top of Indian Ridge the same way the Dutch look at their windmills along the Zuyder Zee, just part of the beautiful landscape in your world."

Jack knew he had scored a split decision with his presentation, half of the room calmly and contentedly sitting back, the other half clearly upset and waiting for a turn to stand and unload.

Molly deferred to the powerful senior member from her Indian Creek District in opening the meeting for questions. "Mr. Dillon, do you have a question?"

Bayse stood and drew himself up to his full six-foot four-inch height, asking in a booming voice, "I want to know why Vernon

Goode isn't trying to build these goddamn mechanical monsters up on his ridge on Barkers Creek where he's got to live with them, not on top of Indian Ridge right above my property."

Vernon didn't wait for Bayse to sit or for Molly to recognize him, standing to answer Bayse in an equally loud and emotional voice from across the center aisle. "Because the land on top of Indian Ridge is mine, and I can do any damn thing with it that I please, as long as it's within the letter of the law.

"You well know that I don't need approval from you or any other member of the Dillon family to build those turbines on my property, and none of your behavior here today will have any bearing on my plans or this petition."

Cole and both of his deputies moved into position, preparing to escort Bayse and Vernon from the room, while Molly futilely tried to regain control of the unruly crowd, finally giving up to adjourn the meeting.

Cole overheard his mother-in-law heatedly exclaim as she exited the room, "You tell 'em, Bayse."

He realized that over on Barkers Creek a name change might now be in order for bucolic Pleasant Valley Road.

Chapter 12

"I'm going to the football game with Covington High tonight," Mandy announced at the dinner table, reaching for another slice of pizza. "Beth and I are planning to sit with the other girls on our volleyball team."

"I'm going, too," Buddy chimed in, quickly banking another slice on his plate to be sure that he didn't get short-changed by his sister. "I'll keep an eye on her for you, Dad," he added helpfully.

Before either sibling could get in another word or serve themselves again, Cole grabbed the last piece from the box, announcing, "I'll be there to keep an eye on both of you. I happen to think that the Rockets can upset the Cougars tonight, and I don't want to miss a minute of it."

He didn't add that another reason for him and his deputies to attend the game would be to keep the peace, discouraging illegal consumption of beer and pot, and preventing school rivalries from turning into fights between teenage boys overloaded with a volatile mix of school spirit, testosterone, and alcohol.

An hour later, each of the three was on his or her way to the municipal ball field for a traditional small town high school football game under Friday night lights. Mandy spotted her friends just outside the stadium and walked over to join them, noticing that almost everyone around her was decked out in blue and gold, suddenly remembering that Covington shared the New Court High colors.

"Hope you don't mind if Sarah sits with us tonight," Beth commented. "Mom wouldn't let her come with the friends in her class."

"Glad to have you join us, Sarah," Mandy replied in her usual friendly way, while aware that now she might be seeing a lot more of her brother than she had planned. "Let's go find seats close to the field, in front of the cheerleaders."

A short time later, Buddy, Mikey, and two other sixth grade boys, Zach and Zane Arnold, were also heading into the stadium, following closely behind the Marching Cougars, who had just gotten off of a Covington High School bus.

"Wouldn't you like to drop something in her tuba?" one of the Arnold twins asked, watching a well endowed Covington girl in blue and gold walking ahead of them with the oversize king of band instruments slung across her shoulder.

"Wouldn't I like to do *what*?" Mikey inquired.

"Put something like a golf ball down the bell," Zach answered. "I bet it would make some weird noises when she started to play the National Anthem."

Then he turned on his friend, cocking an eyebrow, asking, "What did you think I meant, Dillon? Your mind in the gutter again? You're always thinking about weird stuff."

Buddy stifled a laugh, suggesting, "Let's sit up at the top of the stands where we can see everything." He had no more than closed his mouth. when he recognized his huge strategic error, spotting pretty Sarah Jackson sitting next to Mandy and Beth on the first row of seats. "I just came up with a better idea. Let's go down nearer the field where we can watch the game close up."

Mikey spotted Mandy at almost the same time, quickly closing the deal. "Yeah, we need to be next to the field so we can take in all of the action. Let's sit over there on the second row near the cheerleaders."

The four boys made their way through the stands to settle into seats behind the girls' JV volleyball team, Buddy one row directly above Sarah. Everything seemed to be going his way until something happened that would prove even the best-laid plans of mice and men can sometimes go astray.

Sarah glanced behind her, discovering the boys, excitedly chirping, "Zach and Zane, I didn't know you were coming!" She turned to chit-chat with the twins for the remainder of the evening, while Buddy silently sat close behind her, invisible to the special girl for whom he carried a crush.

Both school bands took the field together for the National Anthem. Then it was time for the kick-off, and the beginning of a four-quarter slugfest. The Rockets and Cougars were both jacked up and evenly matched, rock-solid on defense but neither able to consistently move the ball on offense or to score once in the red zone.

The game was a hard fought low scoring nail biter throughout, the Rockets still clinging to a narrow lead, 7-6, as the clock wound down to the final minute. Ray Johnson, New Court High's star senior linebacker, kept his teammates fired up and the Cougars in check, making tackles from sideline to sideline, the pop of helmets and pads carrying into the stands with each of his ferocious highlight reel hits.

The Cougars lived by the mantra "go big or go home," playing for the win from their forty yard line in the closing seconds. Their quarterback rolled out of the pocket on fourth down, pumping the ball once to freeze the blitzing Rocket safety before launching a Hail Mary pass to a lanky wide out receiver who was streaking down the sidelines in front of the New Court bench. The fans on both sides of the field were on their feet as the boy went high into the air to take the perfectly thrown ball on his outstretched fingertips.

That's when Ray Johnson went helmet to helmet with the receiver under a full head of steam. The sound of the collision could have been heard all the way to the West Virginia line when the two came together, both boys spread out flat and motionless on the field with the Covington boy's head gear knocked loose and spinning across the grass. They lay together on the ground afterward for interminable seconds, the fans on both sides now standing in apprehensive silence, many of them saying a prayer.

The Rockets and Cougars coaching staff converged on the field and knelt beside the prostrate boys as both began to clear the cobwebs, Ray standing first and showing his good sportsmanship by extending a hand to help his opponent to his feet. New Court fans came back to life and went wild as the game ended, and the Rockets notched their first win of the season.

Mandy and her friends were screaming and dancing when the sandy-haired Covington boy walked toward them to retrieve his helmet. His jersey was covered with grass stains and dirt, and blood from a cut on his forehead trickled past the black grease under each eye, giving him the look of a gridiron warrior. He glanced at her, and their eyes locked.

He stopped to give her a smile, shaking his head from side to side to acknowledge the hard hit he had taken, raising a hand in a silent gesture. Something about the boy's close cropped good looks reminded Mandy of a boy she had known in grade school, and she lifted her hand in acknowledgment, almost unaware of what she was doing.

She watched as the Covington player put his helmet under his arm, giving her one last long look before crossing the field to join his downcast teammates on the far sidelines, while New Court fans continued to celebrate.

Beth looked at Mandy, commenting, “Wow! Did you see that? That guy was checking you out. I thought he was going to walk over and start talking to you. If you're not interested, let me know, because I'd go out with him in a New York minute. I think he's really hot!”

“I never noticed anything after Ray tackled him and neither of them was able to get up off the ground.” Mandy replied, less than truthfully. “I was afraid both of them were seriously hurt.”

She quickly changed the subject, commenting, “We finally managed to win a big game, didn't we? Look at the New Court fans out on the field trying to tear down the goal posts.”

“Yeah, we finally came out ahead at the end for once,” Beth replied. “But that's not what you're thinking about right now, is it? You're still thinking about that boy on the other team, and the way he stared at you. Isn't that right? Be honest with me.”

Mandy was relieved to see her dad walking toward them, ending Beth's interrogation. “I told you kids that New Court would pull this game out tonight!” Cole exclaimed. “You won't see tougher defense by any high school football team in this end of the state. Ray Johnson is going to be playing for some big university next year on a full scholarship. He may even have a future in the NFL.”

Cole glanced around and saw Buddy and Mikey, as well as Beth and Sarah Jackson. “I’ve got room in the car to give all of you a lift home,” he volunteered. “Who wants to ride with me?”

“We’ll take you up on that,” Mandy replied, without even bothering to ask the other two girls.

“Mikey and I would rather walk home,” Buddy countered. After getting the cold shoulder from Sarah throughout the game, he wasn’t about to stick around her for a minute longer or pay her the least bit of attention.

“Let’s get out of here, Mikey,” he said, turning away to conceal his hurt feelings, not realizing that all of the while his dad was reading him like an open book.

Chapter 13

Irv Sutton nervously ran a hand across his two-day stubble, checking his watch to confirm his deliveryman was running late and knowing that was a bad sign. He was relieved when he finally heard the sound of gravel crunching under tires and saw a small truck approach the sturdy locked gate blocking the road. The vehicle came to a stop, and a dark-skinned man wearing a denim jacket and wide-brimmed hat lifted a hand from the steering wheel to greet him.

"You're an hour late, Pancho!" Sutton exclaimed. Where the hell have you been?"

"Sorry, Boss." Carl Viello replied through the open window. "There was a Virginia trooper following me coming up 220 around Martinsville, and I pulled off at a restaurant and ate a long breakfast to be sure he had moved on before I got back on the road."

Sutton unlocked the gate for the truck to enter, swinging up into the passenger seat to silently ride along for the remaining quarter mile drive to his compound, where the driver pulled under a metal roofed shed to park out of sight.

The two men carried cardboard boxes into a nearby concrete block building, stacking them on the floor against the wall. Sutton paused to comment, "It looks like your smurfs are good shoppers. There's enough pseudoephedrine in this stash of cold medicine for another big production run."

"There are a lot of people hanging around without jobs who're glad to make a few bucks buying over-the-counter medicine for me at the local drugstores," Viello replied. "Some of the smurfs are dumb enough to turn right round and spend what I pay them to support their own habits."

He stacked the last carton on the floor, asking, "When will we be ready to cook another batch?"

"Two nights from now, a cold front will be coming through with high winds, according to the weather forecast. That will carry the fumes out of here, and keep this place from stinking like a chemical plant. I doubt anyone could ever figure what we're doing out here in the middle of nowhere by looking at these buildings, but the smell is a dead giveaway. One of the neighbors could get a good whiff, and he'd know for sure that we aren't in the livestock business."

"Do you think that outfit running the mobile meth labs is going to draw attention from the law and cause us problems?" Viello asked. "Knowing that the state troopers are on high alert looking for drug dealers is what had me worried when smokey came up from behind and glued onto my tail."

"It hurts, and it helps," Sutton answered. "The law enforcement people may be looking harder, but they're hunting in the wrong places. As long as they're concentrating on small mobile labs in the back ends of stolen vehicles, they won't be beating the bushes looking for a big operation like this one, and that gives us an edge.

"Other than those two kids who floated down here on a raft and later came back to spy on us, and the county sheriff who drove out here with his deputy to hassle me, we're still flying under the radar. That's the way I plan to keep it."

"So we'll have another batch cooked and ready for me to deliver this weekend?" Viello asked.

"Yeah, there should be enough for you to supply our dealers at some of the truck stops around these parts, maybe even enough for others working the beer joints. Be sure to drive different vehicles while you're running your delivery routes, so surveillance cameras won't spot the same car showing up all over the place."

Sutton went back to work, and Viello rolled his eyes in annoyance. He had been dealing drugs and dodging the law all over the country since he was a kid, and now an ignorant Virginia redneck who called him Pancho was trying to tell him how to do his job. He muttered a Spanish obscenity under his breath and walked away.

*****

Jane Barker entered the dining room carrying the sheet cake she had baked and decorated, joining Cole, Buddy, and Beth Jackson in singing, albeit off-key, "Happy birthday to you, happy birthday to you, happy birthday dear Mandy, happy birthday to you."

"I remember the day I turned sixteen like it was yesterday," Cole reminisced. "Kids think that life doesn't really start until you finally get a driver's license."

"Now you'll be able to get in the car and come out in the country to visit me," Jane added cheerfully. "We'll drive all around the county together."

"It doesn't seem fair that she'll be driving now while I still have to wait three and a half more years," Buddy complained. "Dad, we need to get an ATV so I can wheel around off the main roads with my friends."

"Don't wish your life away, young man," Jane replied. "I'll give you my driver's license if you'll let me take your place and go back to being a youngster again. I had a lot of fun riding my bicycle when I was your age. Anyway, let's give Mandy a chance to blow out her sixteen candles, and after we enjoy her birthday cake and ice cream, she can open her presents."

"I suppose I'll need to update my Facebook page and tell all my friends that I'm over the hill," Mandy laughed. She began to tear the brightly colored wrapping paper from her birthday gifts one by one, discovering a wristwatch from her dad, a favorite CD from Buddy, a sweater from Grandmom, and a New Court High gym bag from Beth.

"I don't think I deserve to get so many nice things for my birthday," Mandy commented.

"There are four people in this room who disagree," Jane replied, giving her granddaughter a hug.

"Do you suppose that boy on the Covington football team is on Facebook?" Beth inquired. "If he is, you could friend him and let him know that you've turned sixteen.

Mandy gave Beth a quick look telling her please don't go there, but it was too late. "Who's the boy on the Covington team?" Cole queried, with a typical father's curiosity about the boys in his teenage daughter's life.

Beth clammed up, but Buddy chimed in. "Beth's talking about the guy Ray Johnson put the hurt on near the end of the game on Friday night. He was so woozy when he finally got up that it looked like he was making eyes at Mandy."

"I saw Ray lay him out, but I certainly didn't see him looking at your sister afterwards."

"It's good you got me keeping an eye on her, Dad," Buddy replied, as if he and Cole were the only two adults in the room. "You're starting to miss a lot of things these days."

"Buddy, that's enough," Jane intervened. "If boys pay attention to Mandy and Beth, that's only natural for pretty girls their age. Your mother was only two years older when she started dating your father. And just for the record, I don't think either your sister or Beth needs a twelve year-old boy for a chaperone."

"I'll be thirteen in March."

"Whatever."

"Thanks, Grandmom," Mandy sighed in relief. "You and I will definitely be driving around a lot from now on, without my immature brother riding along."

Cole added a final comment. "That's well and good, as long as you have a job and pay for the gas. But if some football player in Covington tries to get in touch with you, be sure to tell him that your father the sheriff is looking forward to making his acquaintance."

Cole and Jane moved into the kitchen to load the dishwasher and put the left-overs back in the fridge. "What's the latest with you and your neighbors here on Indian Creek Road regarding those wind turbines, Mama Jane?"

"You'll find out on Sunday when you read the *Courtland Tribune*. I helped collect money to run a notice in the paper protesting the project. It will come up for a vote by the Board of Supervisors in November, and I'm really worried that it will be approved then."

"Have you considered getting Connie to champion the opposition? Her editorials carry a lot of weight around here."

"Connie's in our camp, but she has political problems of her own. She can't afford to take too strong a position on this matter and alienate a lot of her readers if the *Trib* is to stay in business."

Jane covered the remains of the birthday cake with plastic wrap, slipping it into the refrigerator, then turning to Cole. "Did you and Connie have some sort of falling out? I started to tell her about something nice you'd done for me, and she got a strange look on her face as if things were not right between the two of you."

"It's nothing I did, Mama Jane, it's what I didn't do the last time we went out together. Connie wants a serious relationship, and somehow, I find that I'm still trying to be faithful to Jennifer."

Jane hugged her son-in-law, resting her face against his chest. "You're like a son to me, Cole. The day you and Jennifer were married, I think Wesley and I were as happy as the two of you.

"You gave her a wonderful life and the two finest children in the world. You were there with her every step of the way throughout your marriage. But Jennifer's gone now, and we both must find a way to accept that, as sad and difficult as it is.

"What I'm saying to you is this: I don't think Jennifer would expect you to live the rest of your life alone. You shouldn't feel guilt in sharing your life today with Connie or any other woman you may come to care for. It won't ever change the relationship between you and me, or my deep affection for you."

Cole held onto Jane, trying to find a way to wipe his damp eyes without letting her know that her son-in-law the sheriff was very close to losing control of his emotions.

Chapter 14

"I appreciate your coming here to meet with me today," Cole commented, sliding a mug of coffee in front of Megan Porterfield before taking a seat across the table from her in his office on Wednesday morning.

"Connie has told me about some of the work you've done in digging into the deaths of Susan Helfey and Diane Kruger. She said that you are a very tenacious reporter. I picture you like a tough old snapping turtle—once you get hold of something, you don't let go 'til it thunders."

"That's probably a pretty accurate description of my personality, Sheriff. I find it very frustrating that someone is walking the streets today scott-free, thinking that he's successfully pulled off the perfect crime. I'm not going to back off one bit until I find out what really happened to Susan and Diane, and can identify the person responsible for their deaths."

"Connie said that you've found a common pattern between the Helfey-Kruger murders and those of three other female couples who died around these parts under unusual circumstances."

Megan slid a folder across the table to Cole. "Here's what I've discovered so far. In 2008, there was the suspicious house fire on

Upper Carter Creek Road here in Courtland County that killed Diane and Susan.

"Looking back over the past six years, I've found out that Carlene Martin and Barbara McCoy, two middle-aged women who were living together as a couple in Giles County, died in a mysterious automobile accident back in 2002.

"In 2004, two women about their age, Kathy Dickenson and Mary Tolliver, who were sharing a home in Bland County, died in an equally unlikely car wreck in broad daylight under perfect weather conditions.

Megan paused to dig an old newspaper clipping from the folder, continuing, "Sally Barnes and Betty Crowell, a couple who had lived together for many years, were victims of a freakish house fire in nearby Monroe County, West Virginia, in 2005. The cause of that fire was never clearly determined.

"Look at how little time and effort was spent investigating all of these earlier so-called accidents, and the miniscule amount of publicity that resulted, almost as if the loss of these women's lives was not newsworthy. It's enough to make you sick."

Cole hefted the thin folder of papers, sliding it back to Megan. "Don't let that snapping turtle streak in you let up because you're frustrated and impatient. You and I know that there's no such thing as a perfect crime. Somewhere there's a damning piece of evidence or a reluctant eyewitness who hasn't yet made up his or her mind to come forward. Get out there and help find them."

"There's one clue I'm looking at now," Megan continued. "All of these deaths occurred during the early part of May. I'm wondering if there is any connection to the spring equinox, the Easter season, or some pagan holiday. I still have more work to do."

Cole and Megan wrapped up their discussion, and she walked to the office door. "Give Connie my best," Cole asked.

"Maybe you'd like to call and tell her yourself, Sheriff," Megan replied, smiling. "I have a feeling that she'd like to hear that come directly from the horse's mouth."

*****

"Looks like all three of us are signed up to run in the Goblin Gallop tomorrow morning," Cole observed on Friday evening at the dinner table. "It should be another big money maker for Camp Hope."

"The whole volleyball team is running the 5K," Mandy replied between bites of the Colonel's fried chicken, "We've decided to paint our faces and try to look like a bunch of zombies coming out of the graveyard."

"Mikey and I both signed up for the 5K, too," Buddy chimed in, reaching into the cardboard bucket for another drumstick. "We're both dressing up like professional wrestlers. I'm The Undertaker, and he's Stone Cold Steve Austin."

"I'm in for the shorter distance myself," Cole added. "No way I'd ever be able to make it six miles. I suppose I could go as an out-of-shape county sheriff. Come to think of it, that's what I am."

An hour later, the three were settled in the family room, Cole watching the evening news on the family's new flat-screen TV, and Mandy and Buddy absorbed with their laptop computers.

Mandy checked her email, finding a dozen new messages, half of them from Beth. Only two caught her attention. One was from Melinda Moore, and the second from someone with the handle Wideout24.

She opened Melinda's message first. "My cousin Barbara, who goes to Covington High, posted a message on Facebook saying one of their players is trying to find out more about the tall red-haired girl who was sitting in the stands behind the New Court High football team during the game last Friday night. I hope that you won't be mad at me for giving Barbara your name and email address."

She started to open the second message when she suddenly realized that Buddy had closed his laptop and was standing beside her looking over her shoulder, inquiring in a loud voice, "Who's Wideout24?"

Mandy put her finger to her lips, wheeling around to give her brother a light kick in the shin. Cole glanced up from the TV, turning in their direction to comment, "You kids don't have to be so quiet. Go ahead and talk all you want during the commercials. What's the big news you're both checking out?"

Buddy knew that he was holding the black queen of spades in a family game of Hearts, but he decided not to drop it on Mandy. "Nothing very interesting, Dad," he replied. "She's just looking at a bunch of dull girl stuff."

Mandy closed her computer, put it under her arm, and headed for her room, hearing Buddy whisper, "You owe me one."

Inside, with the door closed, she read the short message. "Hi. I got your name and email address through a friend here at school. I'm the Cougar receiver who got clocked in front of the New Court High bench near the end of the game. I waved at you when I came over to pick up my headgear, and saw you wave back. I'm hoping you'll reply to this email. My name is Dave Barnett aka Wideout24."

Mandy hesitated for a moment, then clicked on reply, keying only a few sentences before hitting the send command. "Hi, Dave. Glad you weren't hurt during the game. It's really nice to find out who you are. Maybe we can chat again. Mandy Grayson."

She shut down her computer, and sat silently contemplating what she had just done. Maybe it had been a huge error in judgment for her to reply to a boy living in another town who she knew absolutely nothing about. But somehow it didn't feel like a mistake; it felt more as if she had just started out on an exciting new adventure.

Chapter 15

Saturday morning dawned bright and clear, as Buddy rushed about in a black t-shirt and shorts, transformed into a poorly executed imitation of The Undertaker. A short time afterward he, Mandy, and his dad were on their way across town for the race, pulling into a nearly-full parking lot across the street from the courthouse.

Cole looked over the large crowd milling about on the lawn in front of the historic old building, attaching his race entry sheet to his t-shirt with safety pins. Most runners were wearing the official orange and black t-shirts with the Goblin Gallop 2011 logo on the front and the figure of a ghost stenciled on the back. Others were dressed in Halloween gear as simple as a witch's hat or as elaborate as rental-company costumes for Dorothy, the Scarecrow, the Tin Man, and the Cowardly Lion on the yellow brick road to Oz.

The anticipation of the start for the dual 5K and 10K events had everyone excited, contestants jogging up and down the road, or stretching to loosen tight muscles and burn nervous energy. Cole recognized many of the people in the crowd as natives of Courtland County, but he also saw a number of strangers who had apparently come from communities such as Roanoke, Salem, Blacksburg and even towns in nearby West Virginia.

As the clock counted down toward the 9:00 start time, the serious runners moved as closely as possible to the front of the pack, while the fun-runners dropped in behind them. Cole found himself at the very back.

Looking toward the front row, he spotted Connie Balfour in black Nike running shorts and a faded orange Goblin Gallop 2007 t-shirt, looking every bit the athletic road-racer he knew her to be. Standing close to her was a clean-cut man who looked like another competitive runner.

His study of the two was interrupted by the starter's bullhorn command: "Runners to the start line. On your mark; Get set; Go!"

The loud report of the starter's pistol launched the pack forward, quickly sorting out the hares from the tortoises. Cole could see Connie quickly move ahead with the leaders, her long, easy stride marking her as a race finalist contender.

He maneuvered into a slower group loping along at a pace he thought he could maintain for three miles, finding himself directly behind Mandy and her friends, beside Norma Patton. It quickly became apparent that Norma had been training for the event, breathing easily and chatting with him as if they were walking in the park, while he did no more than nod in reply, conserving every bit of his wind in order to make it to the finish line.

The pack of runners began to string out in clumps along the road, conditioned athletes loping ahead swiftly and easily, beginners laboring up hills with choppy strides, breathing hard, grasping for paper cups of water offered by volunteers at aid stations along the way. Cole tried to take his mind off the grind by silently counting his foot steps from one to one-hundred, repeating the cadence again and again.

His lungs were burning and he was straining for air when he glimpsed the 5K finish line ahead. That was when a balding older man pulled out from behind and began coming around to pass him. Such an insult to his manhood was too much for Cole to endure, and he dug deep for his last molecules of oxygen, responding with a final desperate kick, catching up to the old-timer, running neck and neck, down to the wire.

He visualized two old codgers stumbling along side by side at a geriatric pace down the hallway of a retirement home, flailing at each other with their canes, as he edged ahead to cross the finish line a half-step in front of his challenger.

"Good race!" the man congratulated him, as they stood together, bent over and gasping for breath. "I almost got you there at the end, didn't I?" he chuckled.

"You sure did," Cole replied, extending his hand in a gesture of good sportsmanship. He glanced toward Norma, sensing that she was struggling to keep laughing. "I'm going to get into shape before I enter another one of these races, and someone like you runs me into the ground."

Norma added her congratulations. "Way to go, Sheriff. I'm relieved to see that the EMT's won't be giving you a ride in the ambulance today. You were breathing pretty hard coming up that last hill."

"Promise me that you won't tell the kids how much I struggled today," Cole pleaded. "They already think I'm over the hill."

"My lips are sealed," Norma replied with a laugh, throwing an arm across his shoulder to give him a friendly, encouraging pat on the back.

Cole looked toward the 10K finish line and saw Connie and her male buddy coming in on the dead run, Connie earning a round of applause from a group of friends for once again winning the race with the best women's time.

Connie glanced toward Cole at exactly the same moment, spotting him standing next to Norma. She turned to walk away with the young runner, and all Cole could do was stand and watch, knowing he was far deeper in the doghouse with her than he had ever been before.

*****

Mandy sat at her desk on Saturday evening uploading to Facebook the photos she had taken before the Goblin Gallop early that day. She realized that the zombie look she and her friends had attempted to achieve with mascara and eye shadow had missed the mark, and that they all looked more goofy than supernatural. Still, she was pleased with the pictures—they captured the excitement of the race and the fun of a morning spent with her best friends.

She was about to turn off the computer, when she decided to check her email one last time and discovered a new message. Her heart jumped as she saw the address she'd been waiting for.

"Hi there, Red. Glad you answered my message. I haven't had much time to get back in touch. Friday night, we played Clifton Forge at home and beat them 27-7. I managed to pull in a long pass and score the final touchdown near the end of the game. Today I worked at Safeway. I just got home. What have you been up to? Do you have a picture you can send me? WO24."

She read the message again, hesitant about returning serve and keeping the ball in play, but realizing that she didn't want the game to end. Then she keyed in her reply and hit the return.

"I'm glad you scored a touchdown last night, since you weren't playing us. Sounds like you have a busy life, between school, football, and working a part-time job. What year are you in? I'm a sophomore. This morning some of my JV volleyball teammates and I ran the Goblin Gallop 5K here in New Court. I'm attaching a picture of us made up to look like zombies. I'm the tallest of the living dead, the third girl from the left. Maybe you could have picked me out without that clue. Mandy."

Chapter 16

"I know that closed meetings of the Board of Supervisors don't sit well with county citizens, but this time I see no alternative," Chairperson Molly Harper proclaimed, addressing the other four members, Ted Newly, Vince Johnson, Boyd Conner, and Marvin Clark.

"The open meeting three weeks ago ended in a hateful shouting match, and I think things would have gotten completely out of hand if we hadn't adjourned when we did. I wouldn't have been surprised to see Bayse Dillon and Vernon Goode duke it out right here in the room.

"Today, I want to discuss that same controversial WindEnerG request to build wind turbines on the Goode property atop Indian Ridge and find out where each member stands. A vote to approve or disapprove will be made at a future meeting open to the public, but one where there will be no surprises. I'd like to invite each of you to explain and justify your position. Who wants to lead off?"

Vince Johnson raised his hand. "This may be a short meeting, Molly. All of us know that as the representative for the Indian Creek District, you and the Dillons would rather see a nuclear power plant built on that mountain than a cluster of wind turbines. When it comes to a vote, you are definitely going to say no.

"As the representative for the Barkers Creek District, with half of the voters being connected in one way or another to the Goode family, I support the project. It provides the highest use of the property and the biggest financial return to Vernon Goode. It brings new jobs and tax revenue to Courtland County. And it's the environmentally friendly way to produce electric power. That leaves our three associates sitting on the fence."

"I'm not on the fence," Ted Newly chimed in. "I stand with Molly. Those wind turbines don't belong on the top of Indian Ridge. They may be out of sight of the Appalachian Trail, but they'll be in view for half the residents of Courtland County, and they'll spoil the beauty of one of the most scenic environments in the world. If wind turbines go in on top of that ridge, who's to say that we won't be back here next year deciding whether to approve a wind farm on top of Painters Mountain?"

Boyd Conner glanced at the man beside him, then spoke. "Marvin and I don't like being the swing voters, but we've both given this matter a lot of thought, and we've weighed all of the pros and cons.

"Vince stated the reasons why we favor approval of the project. We believe wind turbines would be an asset to Courtland County, providing new jobs and additional tax revenue, if all of us can just get past the NIMBY attitude. The wind farm would demonstrate a progressive mindset for the Board of Supervisors as we continue soliciting other industries to build their new manufacturing plants here."

"Is Boyd really speaking for you, Marvin?" Ted asked. "You're the last person in the world that I would expect to champion those enormous windmills right above beautiful Indian Creek Valley."

Marvin shifted in his seat, staring at the table before answering, "There are a lot of trade-offs involved in developing a healthy county economy, Ted. Sometimes we have to compromise our pristine natural beauty for industrial development and commercial growth. I think that this is one of those times. I vote yes."

Molly glanced around the table. "Now we know. The Board's current position is three to two in favor of approving the WindEnerG petition. I'll go ahead now and post the date for the next public Board meeting as four weeks from now, and at that time we'll bring this matter to an official vote. This meeting is adjourned."

She turned to Ted as they started to leave the room, shaking her head and speaking in a resigned voice. "Heaven help us now. It's like the Mason-Dixon Line is about to be redrawn right up the middle of Main Street."

He replied with a wry smile as he switched off the lights, "Amen. I'm going home to get my great granddaddy's Confederate Army revolver and saber out of the trunk, and tell Mabel to start digging a trench across the front yard."

*****

Buddy and Mikey entered the darkened New Court American Legion Hall, taking in the elaborate orange and black Halloween decorations and checking out the large crowd of teenagers inside. The rhythmic beat of a hip-hop dance tune reverberated from speakers around the room, adding to the bedlam.

"I see Sarah Jackson standing over on the other side of the room," Mikey observed, knowing she had pointedly snubbed his friend throughout the football game. "You think she's so good looking. Why don't you walk over and talk to her?"

"Why don't you take a jack-o-lantern and stuff it up where the sun don't shine," Buddy fired back. "I don't think Sarah's so hot. There are a lot of girls in our class that are way prettier."

Mikey punched him in the arm, laughing aloud after getting exactly the response he had expected. "Let's see if we can get a ping-pong table. I bet I can beat you two games out of three."

"Ya think?" Buddy countered sarcastically. "I can't even remember the last time you beat me. Oh yeah, it's coming back to me now. You made me wear a blindfold and use a frying pan."

"Is your sister going to be here tonight?" Mikey inquired as the two boys crossed the room.

"Mandy's already somewhere around here with her friends," Buddy replied. "But you may have waited too late to make your move on the older woman. She and one of the guys on the Covington football team have started swapping emails. She thinks it's a big secret, but I'm on to her. Dad is the only one who doesn't know."

"You think he'll bust up her hot-line when he finds out?" Mikey asked in a somewhat hopeful voice.

"No telling. Maybe you've still got a shot with her if you can find a kitchen stool to stand on. She's at least a foot taller than you."

Buddy and Mikey spent the rest of the evening on the ping-pong and pool tables, with occasional breaks to play the array of flashing, clanging, and buzzing pinball machines, stopping from time to time to munch on snacks provided by their Legion Hall hosts.

At 10:00, they left together, walking toward home in plenty of time to make their 10:30 Halloween night curfew. Trick-or-treaters had deserted the dimly lit streets hours earlier, leaving only a few teenagers still walking about, and an occasional car cruising slowly by, in no hurry to get anywhere.

The two boys were passing Foster's Auto Repair when Mikey noticed something out of the ordinary. "Look over in the alley behind the building," he said softly. "It looks like there's a truck parked in the shadows almost out of sight with a man sitting in it. I wouldn't have noticed if I hadn't seen the light from a cigarette."

Buddy stopped to look, replying, "I don't see anything. You sure you're not looking at the reflection from a streetlight."

Mikey walked back and studied the scene again. "I'm positive I saw some guy parked there a couple of minutes ago, but I can't see anyone now. Let's clear out of here and head for home."

The two were turning off Main onto Wagner Street, toward their neighborhood when they saw the headlights of a vehicle coming up from behind. Both boys had moved off the paved roadway onto the gravel shoulder to allow it to pass, when they realized that it was slowing to pull in behind them.

Buddy turned his head to look back, now able to tell that the vehicle was a old pick-up truck. He stared through the windshield into the dark cab, hoping to recognize the driver as a family friend, but unable to make out the person behind the wheel. Then he saw what the man was wearing, and it made his blood run cold: a camouflage cap. "Run, Mikey! It's Psycho."

The boys were frozen in their tracks when they heard another vehicle speeding toward them, its tires screeching against the pavement as it came to a hard stop just behind the pick-up. The truck pulled out, peeling rubber as it accelerated, followed by a dark-colored car drafting it like a NASCAR racer setting up to pass. Both were quickly gone up the road and out of sight, leaving the boys alone once again.

"Let's get out of here before they come back!" Mikey exclaimed, sprinting off as fast as he could, Buddy matching him stride for stride. The boys raced side by side toward the Grayson house covering five blocks faster than ever before.

"We're almost there," Buddy called out. "I see our porch light. No way Psycho can catch us now."

"You sure it was him?" Mikey asked, struggling to keep up.

"All I saw was a camo cap, and then I took off," Buddy yelled back.

Both boys were gasping for breath as they bounded up the porch steps two at a time and burst through the front door into the house, Buddy stumbling over his own words as he excitedly related what had happened to his dad.

"You couldn't see who either driver was?" Cole asked. "All you can tell me is that one vehicle was an old pick-up, and the other a dark late model car?"

"Yes, sir," Buddy answered. "But I'm sure the man in the pick-up was wearing a camo cap. He scared us so badly that we took off and never looked back. Would it be OK if Mikey stays here tonight?"

"No problem," Cole replied. "Just be sure to call his folks and tell them. I'm going out for a little while, but I'll be back soon."

Cole slipped his pistol into a jacket pocket, and went out the door to his truck, spending the next hour cruising the streets of New Court and back roads of Courtland County in search of vehicles fitting the boys' description. He had no luck in spotting either the truck or car anywhere along the now-deserted byways.

He returned home to reassure Buddy and Mikey that everything was OK, although lacking certainty in his own mind. He had no explanation for what had happened, only an unsettling gut feeling that the Halloween trouble maker in a camo cap was indeed the man Buddy called Psycho, the one who had threatened his son before and now terrified him again as a direct challenge to his father, the sheriff.

*****

Maurice Jones could feel his heart pounding from adrenalin as he slowed his automobile and made a tight U-turn, allowing the truck he had been tailing at high speed to continue down the highway and out of sight. He had not expected his day to end in such an exciting way when the alarm clock had gone off early that morning.

He had rolled out of bed at 6:00 and driven to Tennessee in an old school bus, now painted blue and carrying the logo Grace Unification Church in bold black letters on both sides. The fact that there was no such religious denomination anywhere around had been checked out by his bosses. They were veteran coyotes who specialized in hauling illegal foreign nationals from south of the border to places in Virginia or West Virginia where people without green cards could find manual labor jobs and fit in unnoticed among the locals. People in Appalachia who were struggling to make a buck were always on the lookout for rock-bottom cheap hired help.

Maurice had taken the bus driver's job not by choice, but as a last resort. The chances of a fugitive from the law such as himself finding a legitimate job were slim and none. The cash he was paid after each trip between Knoxville and Roanoke provided barely enough to cover food and rent, with just a bit extra to mail home to his unemployed mother in Henry County. But the income from this work did buy him time in his quixotic quest to square himself with the law in Courtland County, redemption he felt necessary before turning himself in to the judge.

While returning to his motel room on Halloween night, he had taken Main Street, and by pure chance come upon a man confronting two frightened boys, one of whom he knew to be Sheriff Grayson's son. He knew the man by his battered one-of-a-kind pick-up truck. He was a local loose cannon with a mean streak, quick with his fists in an argument, with a reputation for dealing in illegal drugs.

Maurice had impulsively wheeled his car in behind the truck and flipped on his high-beams, interrupting whatever it was the man was planning to do to the boys, rousting him away from them and back onto the road in a bumper to bumper chase out of town.

He knew that he had put himself in a bad position by taking on a man who was never without a weapon, but he felt that helping the sheriff's son out of a tight spot justified the risk. His intervention would come out when he went to court, and with luck, the judge would cut him a break.

Maurice continued back to the motel and parked his car in the usual spot behind the building, out of sight from the road. The adrenaline rush was gone, and all he could feel was fatigue from a long, hard day, as he stretched out across the bed on his back.

The thought flashed through his mind that all he now needed before turning himself in was one home run. Somehow, he needed to help Sheriff Grayson shut down the drug business in Courtland County. Then his eyes closed, and he plunged into a deep, dreamless sleep, sawing logs until the morning sun came up and a ray of light squeezed past a torn curtain to brush his face.

Chapter 17

When he returned from lunch on Friday afternoon, Cole spotted a yellow post-it with a scrawled note reminding him to call Megan Porterfield stuck on his desk. He dialed the number and heard a friendly female voice, knowing instantly that it was not Megan on the other end.

"Connie, is that you?" he inquired hesitantly, aware that it had been a month since they had last spoken, on the night she had angrily walked away from him and closed the door in his face. "How are you getting along?"

"Fine, Cole," he heard her respond coolly. "Are you trying to reach Megan? I heard her phone ring and picked it up."

"I was returning Megan's call, but I'm glad to get you on the line. I saw you win the 10K race last Saturday, but didn't get a chance to congratulate you. How many times have you won the Goblin Gallop?"

"Several," Connie replied, her tone still frosty. "You seemed to be busy talking to a young woman."

“That was Norma Patton, Mandy’s teacher and volleyball coach. We happened to run together in the 5K. I didn’t hang out with her after the race.”

“You don’t need to explain anything to me. That’s none of my business.”

“Connie, I need to talk to you about what happened the last time we were together.”

“This isn’t the right time or place, Cole. You’ve had four weeks to get in touch with me, and there are five different ways you could have done so. I’d rather not provide any drama for the people that are listening in on this conversation. Do you want me to have Megan call you when she gets back to her desk?”

“Yes, please ask her to call me back.” Cole replied, struggling awkwardly to find the right words. “When can we get together and talk privately?”

“We’ll see, Cole. It may be a while. Have a good day.”

He was still at his desk when Megan called back, excitement ringing in her voice. “Sheriff, I’ve discovered something about the string of fatal accidents involving lesbian couples between 2002 and 2008 that I should have caught before. Do you have time for me to fill you in?”

“Shoot.”

“There’s a common denominator in the deaths of all four that I never dreamed of until suddenly last night when it jumped out at me. Have you seen a pattern?”

“I recall all of the women lived in this area and died in the springtime. I’ll take a swag that you’ve discovered all of them once lived in the same town, attended the same school, or worked for the same company."

"Nope, not even close," Megan responded. "We knew all eight died in May, but I've just realized that the accidents all occurred on the same holiday."

"The only holiday in May that comes to mind is Memorial Day."

"That's not the one, Sheriff. It's Mother's Day."

"All of them died on Mother's Day? Unbelievable! What are the odds of four unrelated fatalities randomly occurring on the same day over a six-year period? Slim to none?"

"Based on my college statistics class, I'd say your answer's about right."

"Connie has you figured, Megan. You are one helluva investigative reporter. Have you come up with a hypothesis as to why someone would be committing murders and disguising them as accidents on, of all days, Mother's Day?"

"I think some whack-job may be targeting and killing lesbians to get back at his mama for something that happened when he was growing up."

"That seems as logical as anything I could dream up. You know that I'll have to share your finding with the task force assigned to the Helfey-Kruger deaths, don't you?" Cole asked.

"I understand, Sheriff. I'm just asking that if and when an arrest is made, I'll be the first journalist with access to the task force, and I'll be given the chance to break the story. That only seems fair."

After agreeing to Megan's request, Cole called Virginia State Police task force leader on the Helfey-Kruger case, reporting what she had discovered. Detective Sam Manning was clearly grateful for a new lead in a long, frustrating investigation.

"I knew that Susan and Diane died on Mother's Day, Cole, but it didn't seem particularly significant to me. It's only when you put that one so-called accident in context with the other deaths that it hits you right between the eyes, and you realize that you're likely to be dealing with a serial killer and a string of hate crimes."

"That's the only logical conclusion, Sam. Somewhere around these parts, somebody has a macabre way of retaliating against his mother. We need to find him before he celebrates Mother's Day again. I think Megan has just given us a major break in the investigation."

He had little time to mull over Megan's bombshell before the afternoon parade of visitors started, led by Vernon Goode. "Sheriff, I've just about lost patience with your office. Just how much longer must I wait before you bring charges against the Dillons for trespassing on my property and vandalizing my trees?"

Cole kept his cool, hearing Vernon out and punching his card, then sending him away with the satisfaction of having unloaded his displeasure with the Courtland County Sheriff's Department once again.

Darlene called to him from the other room, "Old Vernon could write the book on how to beat a dead horse, couldn't he?"

"Yep, it gets kind of old, but I can't lose sight of the fact that the Goodes helped vote me into office, so I'll just let him keep whipping that dead animal all the way to the glue factory."

At 5:00, Cole closed his office door and went about a little private business, burning a CD with Rod Stewart's *Have I Told You Lately That I Love You.* Then he was out the door and down the street to the florist.

"Becky, I need your help. Which flowers give a man the best shot of getting out of the doghouse with a lady?"

"I think you need to go with the old stand-by, a dozen long-stemmed red roses," Becky laughed. "Here's a card."

Cole quickly scribbled, "Connie, I'm sorry. Give me another chance. The CD says it all—Cole."

"Would you send this disk along with the flowers?"

"Glad to do it. I take it that you want the roses delivered to Connie Balfour at her home?"

"As soon as possible. It's an emergency, Becky," Cole replied with a wink."

Cole left the shop, hearing Becky call to him, "I'll drop the flowers off on my way home in a few minutes. I hope they'll help you patch things up."

He picked up Mandy and Buddy, taking them to Bucky's Burgers for a favorite, if nutrition-challenged, dinner of burgers, fries, and milkshakes.

As the three sat in a booth, Mandy turned to her brother, asking, "What do you think Dad has on his mind right now, with that far away look on his face?"

"You're thinking about the Big Buckys we're all eating, aren't you, Dad?" Buddy inquired between bites. "These are the best hamburgers I've had in a long time."

"I don't know how you got promoted as far as the sixth grade," Mandy commented. "You seem to be so totally clueless."

"Go easy on him, Mandy," Cole interjected. "He's not the only one."

As soon as the family returned home from the restaurant, Cole slipped into his bedroom and closed the door to make a phone call. Connie picked up on the second ring, answering coolly, "Hello, Cole."

"Did you get my flowers?".

"Yes. The roses are lovely."

"And did you find the CD that I sent along with them?"

"Yes, but I haven't played it yet. Sorry, but I don't have time to talk with you now. I've got to run—a friend is here to take me to dinner. Thanks again for the beautiful flowers."

Cole hung up the phone, hoping that Connie had not sounded quite as distant as she had the last time they had spoken, but with no certainty that anything had improved. He left the bedroom to join Buddy in the living room, taking a seat beside him on the sofa in front of the TV.

"How are things going, Pop?" Buddy inquired. "You look like something's still on your mind."

"Things are going OK, son, I suppose." He hesitated for a moment, adding, "But you're going to find out as you get old like me that it's a lot easier to screw things up than it is to fix 'em afterward."

"I got some news for you, Pop. I may be only twelve years old, but I've already figured that out."

"Yeah, I probably doped that out myself by the time I was in the sixth grade. But somehow I forgot that bit of wisdom over the years, and now I have to go back and have it pounded into my thick head all over again."

"Does this have anything to do with something that happened a few weeks ago between you and Ms. Balfour?"

"Yep."

Buddy gave his dad the look of a worldly-wise bachelor, well schooled in the ups and downs of romance. "If she's anything like Sarah Jackson, you're a whole lot better off without her."

Chapter 18

"We're going to back down on meth distribution around here until things cool off," Irv Sutton told Carl Viello and Lew Fuller as the three finished another batch early Wednesday morning. "We're starting to get too much heat from the county mounties. It would be safer to move our operation into another town like Lynchburg, Danville, or Richmond until things cool down."

"It's not going to be easy setting up business in a new town," Viello commented. "You never know when you're working out a deal with a buyer if you're actually talking to an undercover cop. It's a good bet you're going to be caught up in a turf war if another dealer catches you moving in on him and trying to steal his business. That's when things get rough and bodies start turning up."

"You're worried about the heat around here?" Fuller asked. "Then why did you pull that stunt on Halloween night, running up behind the sheriff's kid, trying to scare the hell out of him? I found out that Grayson drove all over the county that night looking for the guy who threatened his boy."

"You should know why," Sutton retorted. "You were the one with the spotting scope who saw him and another kid up on the ridge spying on us last month. I figured that after I was through with them, they'd be afraid to come out of their house, and we'd never see them around here again. There wouldn't have been any problem if somebody hadn't pulled in behind me and screwed things up."

"You ever figure out who it was?" Viello asked.

"I have no idea," Sutton answered. "He had halogen headlights on high beam, and they made me blind as a bat. He could have been someone who's had a run-in with me before. There are plenty of people around here who have.

"He might have been some neighborhood watch guy who lives nearby and was trying to protect his part of town from drug dealers. Or it could have just been some ordinary citizen who drove up because he saw a stranger pull in beside a couple of kids. Hell, for all I could tell, the driver might have been Batman."

"Why did you run off before you found out?" Viello continued, not amused by Sutton's attempt at humor.

"I had a bag full of cash in the car, so I couldn't risk sticking around. The guy who was hassling me kept his bright lights in my rear view mirror to blind me until he peeled off and disappeared a mile down 301."

"I think you made a big mistake," Fuller commented. "You had that run-in with Grayson before, and he knows who you are and where you live. If his kid had been able to ID you, the sheriff and his deputies would have been out here with a warrant, and we'd all be locked up back in the Courtland County jail waiting to go up in front of Hard Time Janette."

"I had my hand over my face so the kids couldn't recognize me. I figured I could mess with their minds. It would have evened things up between me and Grayson for pulling that tough lawman crap on me back in September."

"Lew's right, Boss," Viello stated emphatically. "It was a stupid thing to do. Don't drag us in on your feud with the sheriff. This is a money making deal as long as we don't do something reckless. If you're hung up on fighting with Grayson, say so, and we're both out of here."

Sutton was not used to being hauled up by subordinates. "Both of you shut the hell up!" He angrily spouted a string of obscenities and threw the jug in his hands to the ground, grinding the shards into the floor as he strode out, slamming the door so hard it cracked the glass.

*****

"Thanks for inviting us over for dinner, Mama Jane," Cole said, standing behind her with his hands affectionately resting on her shoulders. "Looks like you've been working here in the kitchen all afternoon."

"It's good of you to come, son. I must confess that I find it a bit lonely eating by myself. I really look forward to having the three of you over for meals. It took no time for me to make a meatloaf and throw it in the oven."

Mandy and Buddy had hugged their grandmother and gone into the living room, giving Cole the opportunity to ask the question that was foremost on his mind. "Anything new from your end on the Dillon-Goode battle over that beautiful mountain top I'm looking at through the window?"

"I doubt I've learned anything that you probably don't already know. I ran into Junior Goode and his wife Janice at the grocery store yesterday, and they both were very friendly. I stopped to chat with Junior for a few minutes, asking about his father, and he said that Vernon was getting along fine.

"He came back to speak to me just as I was getting ready to check out, telling me that his father had a very high regard for me, and hated that I was one of the folks caught up in the wind farm battle. He came right out and told me that his father has no use for Bayse Dillon and his family, and takes great pleasure in upsetting them, but he regrets that others who live nearby are turning against him."

"Vernon knows how to restore peace in the county and placate the people in Indian Creek Valley," Cole observed. "He and his family could get along without the money they'll make for leasing that piece of land to WindEnerG. I wonder why he's willing to alienate so many friends and neighbors to get back at Bayse. It seems like a classic case of using a shotgun when a rifle would take care of the fox in your chicken coop without killing the hens."

"Do you think I should take this opportunity to talk to Vernon and try to find out what started the feud, or is that a really bad idea?"

"I have no idea how much he'll tell you, Mama Jane, but I don't think that he'll go off on you like he would on almost anyone else daring to bring it up. It's your call."

"I'm ready to take a chance on offending Vernon. I feel as strongly as Bayse about having to spend the rest of my life looking at eighteen towering machines up on that beautiful mountain top."

*****

Mandy waited until Buddy turned on the TV before slipping upstairs into the guest bedroom with her laptop in hand. She opened her email, finding the latest message from Wideout24.

"Hi Red! Thanks for your reply last night, telling me about your family. It's sad to hear that your mother died when you were only 12 years old. I don't think I could get along without mine. You never told me before that your dad is the sheriff of Courtland County. If he finds out that you and I are messaging each other, is he going to come to Covington looking for me? (Just kidding, I hope-)

"Friday night, we have our last game of the season against James River High. I'm hoping to get the ball thrown my way, so I'll have a shot at another touchdown pass for the season, and a better chance of getting picked for the all-district team. Does that make me sound like a conceited hotdog? I'll be watching my email and thinking about you—Wideout24 aka Dave."

"PS: Do you have a picture of yourself without the zombie look?"

Mandy clicked on return, and her fingers flew across the keyboard. "Dave, I don't think you're a hotdog. I watched you stand up right after getting knocked out in the game against us, trying not to let anyone see how badly you were hurt. I hope you'll catch a lot of touchdown passes when you play James River. And I'm pulling for you to make all-district.

"Your parents sound really nice. I laughed when you told me recently that your dad is a manager at the paper mill, and when people complain about how the town stinks like rotten eggs, he tells them it smells like money.

"My dad can be pretty tough when he's on duty as sheriff and has to confront people who break the law, but we never see that side of him. I promise that he won't be coming to Covington, looking for you. Maybe someday soon you'll get to meet him and find out how nice he really is. Hope I'll hear from you again tomorrow. Mandy."

"PS: I'm attaching a picture of me taken the night I turned 16. No zombie look this time."

She had just clicked send and was starting to shutdown her computer when Buddy pushed open the door, inquiring, "You sending another email to that football player?"

"Please lower your voice," Mandy appealed.

Cole was outside, nailing a loose board on the front porch, never hearing the conversation, but Jane was much closer, catching every word, storing that piece of information for an early future talk.

Peggy was no longer around to guide her coming-of-age daughter, but Grandmom was still there, ready, willing, and able to give Mandy any needed motherly direction.

Chapter 19

On Saturday morning, Norma Patton was leisurely enjoying a second cup of coffee when her housemate and fellow teacher, Emily Latham, flew down the steps to join her. The two had shared the rent and utilities on a small frame farmhouse on Upper Carter Creek Road since Norma had joined the faculty several years earlier, splitting expenses to save money.

"I overslept—I'm running late for an appointment to get my hair cut and colored," Emily explained as she grabbed a bagel from the counter and bolted out the door. She called back from the front porch, "Norma, the Platts just pulled in with their meat and produce. Come on out and see if they have anything that we need."

Norma slipped on a sweater and walked outside to greet Joe and Jerry Platt, two middle-aged brothers who lived on a remote tract of mountain farmland near Larkspur, running a small business selling home delivery organic fruit and vegetables, and free-range meat.

"Good morning, Ms. Patton," Joe called out, dropping the tail gate on the small truck to display his products. "Will you be needing anything from us today?"

"Not much, I'm afraid," Norma replied, smiling. "Emily and I are both on diets, and we normally have cereal for breakfast instead of bacon and eggs. But I would like to buy some of your sourwood honey if you have any left."

"Yes, ma'am," Jerry replied. "Let me slip a pint jar in a brown bag for you. Our bees don't produce the way they used to a few years back, and I doubt we'll have any honey left to sell when we come your way in a couple of weeks."

Norma fished in her purse for the exact payment, politely inquiring as she handed him the money, "How's your uncle?"

"Calvin's about the same," Jerry replied. "He's still the same cantankerous old man, pickling in his own vinegar."

"Grouchy as the day he was born," Joe added. "If he ever stops complaining about what the government's trying to put over on us, or what a sorry shape this country's in, we'll start to worry."

"Has he always been so miserable?" Norma asked. "Calvin's come by here to deliver produce to Emily and me, and we've never seen him smile or heard him say a cheerful word."

"He's been hard to get along with as long as I can remember," Jerry commented. "He went from bad to worse after his wife got fed up with his guff and ran off with a girlfriend quite some years ago."

"I'm sorry you two have to share your business with such a difficult person," Norma sympathized. "Y'all have a good day, and drop by the next time you're in our neighborhood.

The two men climbed back into their truck, waving to her as they backed out of the gravel driveway onto the road, continuing on their route around the back roads of Courtland County and beyond.

*****

Norma locked up the house after breakfast and was quickly on the road to Roanoke for a morning of browsing through the shops at Valley View Mall. She looked forward to seeing the Christmas fashions in store windows, once again leapfrogging the Thanksgiving holiday.

Norma needed to shop for one or two more outfits for school wear as the winter season approached. But most of all, she looked forward to having lunch with a very special person who had come into her life at the start of the school year.

Joe McCallister, a bright and likeable young man with an Ivy League education, had moved from Portsmouth to New Court in August, accepting a position as assistant principal and a teacher of English, history, and government studies at the high school.

He had literally bumped into Norma in a crowded hallway on the first day he reported for work, and the sparks had flown. The two were soon taking breaks together, and staying in touch by phone and email. But Joe's marital status and family situation back in Portsmouth posed huge stumbling blocks in their relationship.

Joe's estranged wife, Kristen, had taken a job when their son entered the first grade, and she soon afterward decided that she wanted out of the marriage. She had made their home a domestic battleground, and he had moved out reluctantly in order to spare Joe, Jr., emotional damage from constant bickering between his mom and dad. Kristen had filed for divorce soon after he left.

Custody of the boy caused an ongoing battle. Kristen wanted sole custody, and Joe was determined to help raise his son. Divorce proceedings had gotten uglier when Joe discovered that Kristen had been in a serious relationship with another man while they were still living as man and wife. She had countered with a trumped-up charge of adultery against him.

Joe knew that his behavior would be under close scrutiny until the divorce was final and custody of his son awarded. It would not be wise for him to be seen keeping company with another woman until that time. But that had not kept him and Norma from spending time together in out of the way places when opportunities arose.

On this fall morning, Norma entered the outskirts of Roanoke and took the entrance into the shopping center, carefully navigating through the maze of cars. She entered the Mexico Way Restaurant around noon, checking her watch to be sure that she was on time, slipping into a side alcove to wait. A few minutes later, Joe came through the front door, and she stepped out to greet him.

"Am I on time?" he inquired, wrapping his arms around her for an affectionate hug.

"Right down to the minute," she replied, as the two followed a young hostess toward a vacant booth in the back.

Both were glancing about the room when they unexpectedly spotted a fellow teacher, Joan Lawson, looking directly toward them. She raised her hand in a friendly greeting, returning to her lunch as if nothing were out of the ordinary. Norma and Joe knew they had blown their cover, relieved that it was only in front of a close friend.

The two spent the day together in out of the way places, driving up to the almost-deserted overlook atop Mill Mountain just after sunset. Joe slipped his arm around Norma and confided, "It's been a hard slog for me going through the divorce with Kristen.

I'll be so relieved when all of the legal maneuvering is over, and I finally get shared custody of Joey.

"I'm tired of having to avoid being seen with you outside of school. I want to be able come right out and tell our friends that we're in love, and plan to be married. We're not the type of people who sneak around."

"It won't be much longer," Norma reassured him. "But for now, I suppose we'll have to continue to keep it a secret that we're seeing each other, and I'll just go on living the life of a single gal. I've shared that old house on Upper Carter Creek Road with Emily for so many years that some people may be starting to think we're a couple."

After dinner at an Italian restaurant, Joe followed closely behind Norma back to New Court along a dark country road under an ink-black canopy studded with sparkling lights. He parked his car next to hers in front of the house, and walked beside her to the front door, where the two exchanged a long kiss, then a second, before Norma reluctantly turned to go inside.

Emily dropped the book she was holding, glancing up from her chair as the front door opened. "I'm so glad to have you home. Did you kids have a good time?"

"We had an incredible time, including two delicious meals, and a wonderful movie. We bumped into Joan Lawson at lunch, and now she's also in on the secret that Joe and I are dating. How was your day?"

"I've been running errands most of the time you've been gone. I came home after eating dinner at Bucky's. It's pretty quiet being here with no one to talk to when you're away. At times this old house creaks and pops, and the first thing you know, I start imagining that I'm not alone. It's a bit unsettling."

"I'm sorry you find it to be so spooky," Norma commiserated. "But to be perfectly honest with you, I've also been here by myself at night and imagined that I heard prowlers. A couple of months ago when you were out of town, I would have bet my life that I heard someone walking across the porch around midnight."

"Funny you should say that," Emily nervously replied. "I could have sworn that I heard those loose floor boards on the front porch creaking as if someone were tip-toeing around outside the window, just before you got back."

"We've both got to quit watching old horror movies," Norma laughed. "The next thing you know we'll be peeking under our beds to be sure no one's hiding there before we turn out the lights and crawl under the covers."

"Let's get off this stupid subject right now," Emily giggled. "I'll probably be sleeping with my bedroom door open and the bathroom light on all night, as it is. Please leave your bedroom door cracked, if you don't mind."

"No problem. I guess we're both paying the price for renting all of those slasher movies on Netflix."

Chapter 20

Marvin Clark and his wife Polly followed other parishioners out of Deliverance Baptist Church after the Sunday service, and walked to the back parking lot. "We could use a new car," she remarked, staring at their '95 Taurus, knowing that the odometer showed over 200,000 miles.

"It's a pity that things have been slow for our construction business for such a long time. I guess we'll have to keep nursing ol' Bluebell along for another year or two, although I'd love to be out shopping for a new Lexus."

"Maybe that's not just a pipe dream," Marvin replied, catching her by surprise with his remark as he opened the door for her. "There's a stretch of new road coming up for bids southwest of here that we have a shot at. We'd be in high clover if we could land that contract at the right price."

"Yes, but how do we get a decent margin when all of the road builders are hurting for business? I imagine we'd have to cut our profit to the bone and take the order at near-cost just to keep our crews working."

"Not necessarily, honey," Marvin replied. "There's a lot that goes on behind the scene when it comes to the awarding of government contracts. You can still land lucrative orders if you have the right connections with key politicians."

"What connections do we have that would let us price in a decent profit and still take that order away from our competitors?"

"It's a complex business situation with a lot of people giving and taking," Marvin continued. "I'd probably need to diagram it in order to explain it clearly, but here's a simple answer.

"A big Chicago outfit wants to build a multimillion dollar installation in these parts, but they need the approval of a few key players. This company is politically connected from Illinois all the way to Virginia. They have considerable influence in the awarding of new road contracts in our area.

"If the owner of a construction business happens to be a key player who can help this company win approval of their multimillion dollar project, he's in the cat-bird seat when the next lucrative road contract is awarded."

"Marvin, you can't be thinking about making any decision on behalf of the Courtland County Board of Supervisors where you have a potential conflict of interest!" Polly exclaimed in alarm. "You have far too much integrity to do something like that."

"I honestly believe that building a wind farm on top of Indian Ridge is in the best interest of the citizens of this county," Marvin said defensively. "I'm just following my own good judgment and conscience if I vote to approve the WindEnerG application to build that wind farm.

"Likewise, if have no contact with anyone involved in selecting the winning bid for that new road, and if our company just happens to be the successful bidder and gets a desperately needed contract, my conscience is clear."

"Be careful, sweetheart," Polly cautioned. "You're on a slippery slope."

*****

Cole was relieved to see that it was now 1:00 on Sunday, having pulled morning patrol duty so that his deputy could join his wife at church for the christening of their infant son. Now it was Jake's turn to take over, giving him the rest of the day off. He knew that Mandy and Buddy were both at Mama Jane's for the day, so on an impulse, he picked up his cell phone and called Connie.

The phone rang several times, and then he heard it go to voice mail.

"Connie, would you pick up? I know that you're screening my calls, but I'd really like to talk to you." Cole waited patiently without luck, then plaintively added, "Please call me back." He was just slipping the cell phone back in his shirt pocket when he heard his distinctive ring tone.

"Connie?"

He was relieved at her come-back, in the friendly tone of earlier days. "Who were you expecting, your sister?"

"Please don't start with that sister stuff again. How many more times do you want me to apologize?"

"I'm going to have to think about that."

"Can I come over and see you while you're thinking?"

"Bad timing—I'm outside washing my car right now."

"You didn't say no. I'm on the way. Over and out."

Five minutes later, Cole pulled up in front of Connie's house and parked his patrol car, spotting her standing in the driveway wearing blue jeans and a long-sleeved orange and maroon VT jersey, rinsing suds from her automobile with a garden hose. Cole was struck by how young and pretty she looked, long brown hair cascading down to her shoulders, jersey and jeans setting off a slim, athletic figure that would turn a man's head in any setting.

"Have you come here in uniform to arrest me?" she asked, as he started toward her. "You must not know much about Balfour women. I'm not going to let you haul me off to jail without a fight."

Cole continued walking toward her, playfully pulling out his handcuffs as he drew close. Connie caught him by surprise, pointing the nozzle directly toward him, the cold stream of water striking him full force in the chest, making him wince in the cool fall air as it drenched the front of his uniform from head to foot.

"Resisting arrest, are you?" he called out, rushing forward to grab the hose from her hands and turn it on her, soaking her to the skin. "Balfour woman or not, this is how we handle troublemakers around here."

"You brainless, overgrown, Neanderthal throwback . . ." Connie shouted, trying to string together more insults and keep from laughing, as he wrapped her in a bear-hug and kissed her hard on the mouth. She threw both arms around his neck to pull his face even closer, wrapping her legs around his waist as he swept her off the ground and carried her up the porch steps into the warmth of the house, still clinging tightly against him as they entered the living room.

"OMG, we're ruining my new carpet," Connie exclaimed, suddenly aware of water pooling around them.

"The rug's your problem, Smartie Pants," Cole replied, kicking off his soaked shoes as he continued to hold her. "I wasn't expecting a teenage carwash water battle with you when I came here, and I don't have any dry clothes out in my car. Since you started all of this, tell me what I'm supposed to do now."

"Wait just a minute," Connie replied, breaking out of his wet embrace to rush from the living room trailing water into her bedroom. She quickly returned, now dry and barefoot, wearing running shorts and a faded t-shirt, carrying a blanket.

"Wrap this around you and give me your clothes. I'll throw everything in the dryer. It'll be ready for you, dry and warm, in just a jiff."

Cole stepped into the hallway to slip out of his wet uniform and wrap himself in the blanket, leaving only his head and bare legs exposed, re-entering the living room to quip, "You're probably thinking that I look like one of General Washington's troops at Valley Forge."

"Nope, actually I was thinking more along the lines of a homeless man under the viaduct on I 581," Connie replied with a laugh, walking back into the hallway to gather up his wet clothing.

Cole stood awkwardly shrouded in the blanket and waited for her, unsure as to what to do. Then he heard the unmistakable voice of Rod Stewart filling the house with the song he had sent her, *Have I Told You Lately That I Love You*? Connie walked back into the living room and stood facing him. She reached out for his hand, then lead down the hallway toward her bedroom.

"After the way you treated me the last time we were together, I didn't care if I ever saw you again," she said softly. "I certainly never intended to renew our friendship. But do you know what turned everything around for me? It was that damn song that you sent me.

"I played it one time, and after that, I just couldn't seem to get it out of my head. I haven't been able to get you off of my mind since then. I wanted so much to see you again. You have no idea how happy I was when you finally called me, although I tried not to let it show."

Cole stood before her, slipping his hands beneath her shirt to cup her slender hips. "If that song made you forgive me and set everything right between us again, why in the world did you turn the hose on me when I drove up?"

"It's a Balfour woman's way of getting off to a new start with her man," Connie answered. "Anyway, that's my story, and I'm sticking to it."

Cole tightened his arms around her, feeling her warm skin soft beneath his light touch. "In my lifetime, I've heard some amazing excuses for doing crazy stuff, but I swear to God, your's wins first prize."

He rested his lips against her ear. "You have no idea how incredibly happy I am that you took me back, or how very much I love you."

She tilted her face upward to kiss him. "Show me."

Chapter 21

Tom McFarland turned off his computer for the day, slipped on his blue blazer, and left through the side door of New Court United Methodist Church, carefully locking the door behind. The sun had begun to set, and nearby street lights had already come on, splashing soft orbs of light on the pavement below.

He was walking toward his car, his mind subconsciously on autopilot, when suddenly he became aware of something that made the hair on the back of his neck begin to rise. A tall man was leaning against his car, waiting for him, and even in the dim light, Tom could tell that it was no one he knew.

He tried to shake off his growing apprehension, realizing that it was wrong for a Christian minister to fear a stranger. Assisting everyone in need went with the pastoral mission he had accepted at ordination, serving the Lord and His entire flock, not an elite minority with whom he might feel most comfortable.

Still, he could not help but remember that it had only been a couple of years earlier when two men had broken into a small church on Upper Carter Creek Road, searching for money and setting fire to the building to cover their tracks afterward, burning the historic structure to the ground. Tom knew this wasn't the 1960's, and that he wasn't living in Mayberry.

He tried to take control of the situation, calling out in the tone he projected from the pulpit on Sunday mornings, "Good evening. Is there anything I can do for you?"

The stranger stepped away from the car, glancing in all directions to be certain that the two were alone, and then inquired in an unthreatening voice, "You're the preacher here, aren't you?"

"I am," Tom acknowledged, sizing up the stranger as an athletic African-American man in his twenties, waiting for him to continue.

"Could we go inside and talk?"

Tom considered the request with uncontrollable misgivings. "We could do that, but I believe it would be more convenient if I were to simply unlock my car so we can sit inside and chat right here on the street."

Tom operated his fob to pop the door locks, permitting the man to slip into the passenger seat. When he took the driver's seat, he cautiously left his door slightly ajar.

"Can you tell me why you've come here this evening, and what you'd like to talk about?" The man's forthright answer confirmed his wisdom in not entering a dark, empty building, even a church, with a total stranger.

"I'm a convicted felon with an outstanding warrant for my arrest." Seeing a frightened look come across the preacher's face, he quickly continued. "But I want you to know that I didn't come here tonight to give you any trouble. I'm here to ask for your help."

Tom breathed a sigh of relief. The man was only asking for assistance, and suddenly he felt empowered as a minister. "Let me introduce myself. I'm Tom McFarland, pastor of New Court United Methodist Church."

"I already know who you are. I read the local paper whenever I'm able, and I've seen where you've helped people in trouble, people like me."

"And I'll also help you if I can," Tom replied. "But before we go any further, I suggest that you turn yourself in to the sheriff of your own volition. I'll see that you get a good defense attorney, and that you receive any other legal aid you may need."

"I'm not ready to do that until I know how hard the law will come down on me, and how much jail time I'll be facing."

"Then why did you come here to see me tonight? How can I or anyone else help you if you're not willing to take advice?"

"I'm here because of something Sheriff Grayson did. I was running drugs back in September, and I wrecked a stolen van over near Slate Bank while he was chasing me. He had his gun on me when I got out and started to run. He could have easily shot and possibly killed me, but instead he let me get away. I know some cops who would have pulled the trigger a half dozen times without even thinking twice.

"I've thought about what happened ever since that day. I can recognize Grayson and his kids from pictures in the newspaper. I tried to figure how I could pay him back for choosing to let me go, and then on Halloween night I got the chance.

"I happened to be passing through New Court when I saw a man in a truck pull in beside Grayson's kid and another boy like he was planning to harm them. I drove up hard behind this guy and scared him off. I stuck on his bumper for a mile down the road, giving the boys time to run home.

"I don't know whether that counts for anything, but I thought it might help me catch a break from Grayson when I turn myself in. For the record, I quit the drug business the day I cracked up the van."

"It sounds like you've started making good decisions," Tom affirmed. "I'm willing to go to bat for you if you really want to turn your life around. Specifically what were you looking for from me when you came here?"

"I want you to talk to Grayson. Let him know that I've gone straight. Tell him what I did for his boy, and say that I'm going to help him get the drug dealers out of Courtland County. After I balance up my account at the courthouse, I'll give myself up, stand trial, and serve my time."

"I'll tell Sheriff Grayson that you've decided to take your life in a new direction, and fill him in on everything you've told me. But I'm absolutely certain that he doesn't want you or anyone else acting like a vigilante. The best thing for you to do is to stay out of trouble and surrender to him as soon as possible.

"I'm going to pray for you, and this life change you're trying to make. Are you, by chance, familiar with the story of the Apostle Paul, and how he encountered Jesus and became a Christian on the road to Damascus?"

"I learned the story of Paul when I was a little boy growing up in a rundown house outside of Danville, going to Sunday school with my two sisters." A faint smile crossed the stranger's face as he added, "Maybe I'll look back and think about my conversion on the road to Slate Bank."

"I hope that someday you will," Tom replied. "Will you tell me who you are?"

"I didn't plan to do that when I came here tonight, but I expect Grayson will already know exactly who I am when you talk to him, since my fingerprints were all over the inside of that stolen van. My name is Maurice Jones."

"Let's have a moment of prayer together before you leave, Maurice," Tom proposed, bowing his head and reaching out to take the stranger's hand.

Tom had started to pray when a Courtland County Sheriff's Department patrol car slowly cruised by, turning around further down the street and coming back to stop beside them. Tom recognized a newly hired young deputy behind the wheel.

"Everything OK, Pastor?" the deputy inquired, carefully sizing up the stranger in the passenger seat.

"Everything's fine, Robert," Tom replied, knowing that he would later have to face Cole Grayson's displeasure for his failure to report the fugitive sitting beside him. "We were preparing to have a moment of prayer together."

"Then I won't bother you any longer," the deputy offered. "Y'all have a blessed evening," he called out, rolling up his window and slowly pulling away.

Silence settled in about them as the cruiser disappeared around the corner. "Let's have our prayer now." Tom suggested. "Lord, watch over Maurice. Allow me and Sheriff Grayson to act as Your Hands and help guide him safely home. In Christ's name we pray. Amen."

Maurice opened the car door and stepped out into the shadows. "Thank you for your words. I owe you one for not outing me to that deputy. I'll see you again, but before then, there are some things I have to do to square things with the law."

"I'll be praying for your safety and salvation," Tom replied. "Remember my advice. Don't wait long before turning yourself in."

*****

Cole was sitting back in a recliner watching a rerun of *Unforgiven* when the phone rang and he found himself on the line with Tom McFarland. He tried to split his attention between his pastor and the flat-screen TV until he realized what Tom was saying, and then he quickly hit the mute button.

"Well, I'll be damned! Pardon me, Tom, I didn't mean to let that slip out. So Maurice Jones came to see you? Why didn't you just tell him to turn himself in right now and face the music? I don't want or need his help. He won't get any points with me or the judge for what he's trying to do."

"I gave him that advice, Cole, and he's planning to come in when he feels the time is right, but first, he's determined, in his words, 'to balance up his account at the courthouse' by helping you clean up the drug business around here.

"He also told me that on Halloween night he stepped in to run off a man who was threatening your son. He wanted you to know that. Cole, I think the young man really stuck his neck out trying to protect Buddy."

"That solves one mystery," Cole confessed. "Buddy and one of his friends were walking home from a party when an unidentified man pulled up beside them in a pick-up truck and scared the living hell out of both of them. There I go again with the bad language, Tom. Pardon me.

"Anyway, about then a car wheeled in behind the truck, and both vehicles took off down the highway. Buddy and his pal sprinted all the way home to tell me, and afterward I spent some time out on the back roads around here looking for the men they saw. I'm glad to finally learn what went on."

"If Jones comes around again to see me, I'll let him know that you're now aware of his Good Samaritan act," Tom commented. "I'm confident that's he's keeping it real when he says he's trying to get his life back on track."

"Tell him I'll try to get him a break if he turns himself in," Cole replied. "He's balanced up the score with me personally. As far as his account with the legal system, that's another matter. I'm willing to help him, but be sure he understands that acting like a sheriff's department volunteer won't win any points with me."

"I'll pass that on if I get the chance," Tom concluded. "I suspect that you want to get back to whatever program you were watching on TV. I heard a lot of shooting in the background when you first picked up the phone, and I'm sure you don't want to miss any of the action."

"It's too late for that now, Tom. I've just watched the ending of a typical Eastwood western, and everyone's been shot dead except Clint. Thanks for the call. I'll see you in church on Sunday morning."

Chapter 22

"Let me have your attention, please," Chairperson Molly Harper repeatedly called out to the noisy, agitated crowd filling the Circuit Courtroom on Wednesday evening, banging her gavel on the desk top again and again. As the room quieted, she continued. "The Courtland County Board of Supervisors is now in session.

"We're here tonight for a Board vote on the WindEnerG request to build a wind farm consisting of up to eighteen turbines fronting Old Ridge Road on the Vernon Goode property atop Indian Ridge. This matter was discussed at the October 12 Board meeting but never brought to a vote due to a disruption by attendees, causing the meeting to be adjourned.

"Sheriff Grayson and his deputies are here tonight to see that nothing like that happens again. Anyone out of order and acting up will be immediately removed from the room. With that, I will now ask the representative for WindEnerG to present the application."

Cole leaned against the back wall, watching the meeting proceed and sensing the hostility ratcheting upward between the Goode and Dillon factions. The charged atmosphere seemed ready to flash-over by the time the developer's attorney wrapped up his pitch, people throughout the room raising their hands for permission to speak.

Molly took charge again, looking over the crowd, and speaking in a strong voice. "All properly submitted endorsements of and objections to this proposed wind farm have been carefully reviewed by the Board. There are many conflicting opinions by people who claim to be experts on the environmental impact, but nothing we've studied seems to be an insurmountable obstacle which would prohibit construction.

"I will tell you openly that most of the communications to this Board have been from citizens opposing the wind farm. Many have expressed strong personal feelings and opinions unsupported by scientific evidence or data. Some of the feedback we've received is just angry ranting by people unwilling to reveal their identity.

"Tonight, the Board will hear anyone who wishes to bring new insight or information to the discussion, either pro or con, but not unless it is supported by facts. In that context, is there anyone who still wishes to speak?"

Bayse Dillon was the only person to raise his hand again, and when Molly gave him the floor, he spoke in a deep, emotional voice. "I don't have any new scientific facts the Board seems to need in order to deny this permit, but I do have what you call an insurmountable obstacle facing the project.

"Those giant turbines the Board seems ready to approve on Indian Ridge right above my home place will have to be built on top of the mountain at the end of a narrow, twisting gravel road. Some of the pieces can be taken apart and hauled up the mountain on heavy duty flatbed trailers. But none of you public spirited folks in this room seem to have a clue that each one of those three huge blades for each turbine must go up the mountain in one piece. They can't be taken apart and crated up for hauling like something you'd buy at Home Depot.

"Each blade is about a hundred and fifty feet long, almost too big to fit out front on the courthouse lawn. They're fragile, and they can't be bent around going through sharp turns or by sudden changes in grade during the haul without ruining them. What you need to handle them is a very long, specially designed flatbed trailer, and a road that has been built with a constant grade and wide turns, almost the same way VDOT builds the interstate highways in Virginia.

"The special purpose trailers are available, but the existing road running up the side of the mountain to the top of Indian Ridge is no good for hauling those blades, and that means you need a very expensive new roadway. But the big point I'm trying to make is that Vernon Goode's property does not include a suitable right of way, and any new road would have to be built on my land.

"All of you realize that this so-called wind farm is a private enterprise, not a government project, and you should already know that there is no eminent domain law on the books that can be used to condemn my land and force me to sell it for such a purpose.

"I tell you there's no way in hell to get those enormous turbine blades to the construction site without my consenting to sell a sizeable tract of my property for a new road. And I'll give you my personal opinion that a wind turbine with small enough blades to be suitable for hauling up the old road wouldn't generate enough electric power to light up your Christmas tree.

"I invite the Board to go ahead now and vote to approve that permit, and wish the WindEnerG folks in Chicago good luck on recovering one farthing of the millions of dollars they're about to stuff down this rat hole." With that, Bayse dramatically nodded to the Board and settled back into his seat.

A hush settled over the room until Molly broke the silence by asking, "Does anyone from WindEnerG wish to offer a rebuttal?"

Both the company attorney, Mark Winestein, and the project engineer, Jack Sanders, stood, and Sanders spoke. "We anticipated Mr. Dillon's unwillingness to sell us the required strip of his land on the north side of the mountain. We're already negotiating with property owners on the south slope of the mountain for the right of way for a new road. We do not agree with Mr. Dillon that his refusal to cooperate with us constitutes an insurmountable obstacle or showstopper, and we still request approval to build the proposed wind farm."

The room began to buzz again with private conversations until Molly gaveled the meeting to order. "I'll read the precise wording of the request for a permit, and afterward we'll take a vote by the Board, using a show of hands."

She quickly ran through the legalese, then polled the Board. "All in favor?" Vince Johnson, Boyd Conner, and Melvin Clark raised their hands.

"All opposed?" Molly then raised her own hand, joined by Ted Newly.

"The Board vote is three to two, approving the construction permit for a wind farm on the Goode property," Molly announced. "The meeting is hereby adjourned. Sheriff Grayson, please see that the crowd remains orderly as we leave the courthouse."

Cole could hear angry comments muttered by opponents of the project as the room emptied, one theme predominant: Vince Johnson, Boyd Conner, and Melvin Clark sold us out. None of those three will be back on the Board after the next election. He overheard his mother-in-law consolingly whisper to Bayse, "I'm as sick about this as anyone. You certainly did everything you could."

Cole followed the crowd out to the parking lot and watched carefully as they drove away, knowing that although the meeting was over, the hard feelings were likely to get even worse as the project got underway. They would reach a boiling point when eighteen steel and fiberglass giants stood on the spine of the pristine mountain, their spinning arms stretching four-hundred forty feet upward to the sky.

He was deep in thought when he heard a soft voice comment, "Aren't you glad you didn't have any unruly folks to deal with today, Sheriff? You didn't have to taser a single one of them."

Cole spun around, realizing that Connie had walked up unnoticed, now standing only an arms length away. She was wearing a brown tweed coat, pencil skirt, and heels, her brunette hair up, far more formally dressed than he was accustomed to seeing her during working hours as editor of the small town *Tribune.*

"You look incredible," Cole said, stepping in to face her. "But why come so dolled-up to cover a Board of Supervisors meeting that might have turned into another Carroll County Courthouse shoot-out? It probably would have been smarter for you to have worn a bulletproof vest and a helmet."

"If I were wearing body armor, then you wouldn't be standing so close right now, paying me nice compliments, wanting to put your arms around me."

"You must be clairvoyant," Cole answered, wrapping Connie in his arms, lifting her so that she was on tip-toes as he held her in a long kiss.

"Got any idea now how much I love you?"

"A bunch. Remember, you just told me that I was clairvoyant."

"You're starting to scare me, but in a very interesting way. Do you plan to show me more of your ESP talent when I come over tonight?"

"Only if you ask. Are you suggesting that I revise the program and add a mind reading performance?"

"I'll take a pass on the ESP act tonight, Ms. Balfour. Use your imagination and come up with something spectacular."

Connie winked, and seductively flicked Cole with one end of her gauzy scarf. "Be careful what you wish for!"

"I've never been cautious a day in my life. I'm just an old country boy who's always been ready to take my chances and go for it."

Chapter 23

Buddy bounded into the house, followed by Mandy and Cole, smelling the unmistakable aroma of turkey baking. Jane greeted them at the door, cheeks flushed from standing in front of a hot stove.

"Good timing," she exclaimed. "We won't eat dinner until 1:00, but I can use some help getting everything together. Mandy, how about grabbing an apron and helping me get that pumpkin pie ready to go in the oven?"

She turned to Cole, and commented, "I don't know what I'd do if y'all weren't around to fix the things that keep breaking here. This time it's the back porch light that's quit working. I tried replacing the bulb, but that didn't do the job, so I decided to just leave it alone until my two electricians could check it out."

"OK, apprentice electrician," Cole called to his son. "Mama Jane's given us a work order. Grab the screwdriver and voltmeter out of the truck, and let's see if we can find the problem and get her porch light back on."

Jane watched the two leave the room, joining Mandy in the kitchen for the grandmother-granddaughter talk she had been planning for some time. "Tell me about what's going on at school, now that volleyball season is over."

"Not much, Grandmom. We're out of school for the Thanksgiving holiday from now until Monday, and then we can look forward to the Christmas break."

"The Christmas season is always so much fun. I remember from back in my high school days when I was your age that there was always a winter formal. Are there any plans for something like that this year?"

"Yes, in January, but it's not a formal, although there will be a band."

"Is there any special boy at school that you'd like to go with?" Jane continued to add fresh vegetables to her tossed salad, while closely observing her granddaughter from the corner of her eye.

Mandy set the pumpkin pie in the oven and nervously faced her grandmother. "Grandmom, if I tell you something, will you keep it a secret until I'm ready for everyone to know about it?"

"My lips are sealed."

"There's a boy in Covington who's been exchanging emails with me. It all started after a football game back in the middle of October, the night New Court played Covington. My friends and I were sitting on the sidelines, and one of their players got tackled right in front of us. He and I looked at each other, and he waved at me, and I waved back, but that was all that happened. Two weeks later he managed to find out my name and email address through a friend, and he sent me a message. That's when I found out his name is Dave Barnett."

Jane continued chopping a stalk of celery, her face expressionless, waiting for Mandy to continue.

"I answered his message, and something clicked between us. We started emailing each other, and now it's at least once a day, sometimes much more often than that. He's a junior at Covington High, and he's the best receiver on their football team. He works part time at a Safeway."

Jane diced a tomato to add to the bowl, realizing how many communications and how much personal information had now passed between her granddaughter and this young man. "I don't suppose you'd have a picture of him to show me, would you?"

"I'll be back," Mandy replied, leaving the room long enough to retrieve her purse and pull a photo from it. "This is Dave. My best friend Beth thinks he's really cute."

Jane took the picture, observing a smiling, athletic boy with sandy blonde hair in a buzz cut, wearing khakis and a gray t-shirt stenciled with the logo *Covington Cougars Football.* "I think Beth's right," she replied. "He's a very nice looking young man. Who all knows about Dave besides Beth and me?"

"Buddy knows, but I haven't told Dad. I don't know what he'll say when he finds out that I've been chatting on the net for weeks with a boy in another town that I've never actually met in person.

"Dad thinks I'm still his little girl, and he keeps a close eye on the kids I hang out with, like he's afraid I might make some poor decisions and get mixed up with the wrong crowd. He's run into a lot of bad situations in his work that started when women connected with strange men on the internet. He told me that the prisoners in the jailhouse are always trolling for girlfriends."

"I think you underestimate your dad's confidence in you and your judgment, Mandy. He may have some trouble accepting the fact that you're growing up to be a young lady now and not his little girl, but he deserves to know what's happening in your life, help you make the right decisions, and share your friendships.

"You really need to talk to your father. I'm here if you need my support. And I think it's time for Dave to drive over to New Court to meet you and your family face to face."

"He's told me that he wants to do that, Grandmom. I just didn't want him showing up at the front door until I got up the nerve to tell Dad all about him. Dave's a little nervous about meeting Dad for the first time, knowing that he's the county sheriff."

"Don't delay in having a conversation with your dad, Mandy. You and Dave have done nothing wrong, but if you continue to communicate with this boy and keep your father in the dark, he may be resentful when he finds out. I know that I would be hurt."

"You always know the right thing to do, Grandmom. If Mom were still here, I'm sure that I would have told Dad long before now. Thanks for giving me your advice."

Jane wrapped her arms around Mandy. "You just keep coming to me whenever you need someone to talk to. I feel like I have a little of your mother back with me every time we have a heart-to-heart like this."

She swallowed the lump in her throat, adding, "Please call those two electricians to dinner. Tell Buddy that he needs to go upstairs and wash his hands, and let your father know that the turkey's ready for him to carve. If the porch light isn't fixed by now, it can wait until another day."

Mandy leaned out of the back door, calling out, "Dad, Buddy! Soup's on! Grandmom says to come and get it!"

*****

It was late when Cole, Mandy, and Buddy got home. "I swear, I don't think I'll be ready to eat another meal for a week," Cole sighed contentedly as he settled down on the sofa. "Your mother was a terrific cook, but I believe that when it comes to a turkey dinner with all the trimmings, her mama wins the prize."

Buddy disappeared upstairs to his bedroom, while Mandy sat down on the sofa next to her father, resting her head on his shoulder. "Dad, can we talk about sometime really important, something I should have let you know about weeks ago?"

Cole slipped his arm around her, and Mandy opened up to tell him everything about Dave Barnett.

She had been unsure how her father would react when he first learned of her secret boy friend, and she was surprised that he did not interrupt her until she had given him every detail. "I told Grandmom about Dave before dinner, and she insisted that I tell you right away. Here's a picture that he sent me last week."

Cole studied the picture, then handed it back to her, speaking for the first time. "This is the boy that Buddy tried to tell me about, the one who got tackled in front of the New Court bench?"

"Yes, Dad."

"And you've told me everything that's gone on between the two of you?"

"Yes, sir."

"If he wants to continue communicating with you, he needs to come to New Court so I can meet him. There's nothing new here, Mandy. This is Grayson and Barker family standard operating procedure. Your grandfather put me through the same drill when I started dating your mother."

"Do you want me to tell him that?"

"You bet I do. Tell him we'll all go out to dinner when he comes. Assuming he passes muster, I want him to tell me what it's like being the wideout receiver and taking those really hard shots. When I was a running back in high school, I never had to go up against a future NFL defensive back like Ray Johnson."

Mandy kissed Cole on the cheek as she got up from the sofa. "I love you, Dad. Grandmom gave me good advice. I never should have waited so long to tell you about Dave."

Cole smiled lovingly, and answered gently, "You're absolutely right."

Chapter 24

Megan Porterfield drove her pride and joy Mini Cooper into the small community of Sweet Chalybeate, West Virginia, on Monday morning, turning onto a narrow gravel road winding a hill toward a small, rustic home situated near the crest.

As she turned off the engine, a Heinz 57 with big head and short legs waddled down the hill to check her out. Megan could see as the dog got closer that he was both old and almost blind with cataracts, wagging his stubby tail to greet her.

A slender woman in faded jeans and sweatshirt called out to her from the front porch above, "Roy won't bother you. He's had a gentle disposition since someone dropped him down by the highway as a pup and I adopted him. You can take one look and tell that was a long time ago."

"Thanks for the tip-off, Darlene," Megan called back. "Nice to meet you, Roy," she said, bending to scratch the dog between the ears. "You seem like a friendly soul, and that's the kind of dog I like."

She closed the sun roof to keep out the yellow jackets swarming overhead, picked up her canvas tote, and started walking up the hill. “Looks like I parked near a nest of your pet bees down here. They’re all over the place.”

“You need to watch out for them, or they’ll eat you up,” the woman cautioned. “I spotted where they’ve nested in a chipmunk hole in the ground, and I’ll come down there this evening and fill their tank with regular. Gasoline’s an old-timey way of getting rid of yellow jackets, but it still works better than any of the insecticides you can buy.”

Megan was out of breath by the time she joined Darlene, and the two were comfortably seated side by side in lawn chairs on the front porch. Megan fished a notebook from her bag and began the interview.

“I realize that it’s hard for you to talk about your sister’s death, but I really need to hear every detail you can recall about what happened to Sally and her partner, Betty Crowell, just before they died in that house fire on Mother’s Day, May 8, 2005. I’m a newspaper reporter, but what I learn from you could possibly help to break this case and lead to an arrest.”

Darlene took a deep breath, and spoke hesitantly. “I have as much trouble talking about Sally now as I did right after she died six years ago. She was the best sister anyone could have, and I miss her and Betty more than anyone will ever know. Those two were the perfect couple.

“I don’t recall any unkind words passing between them, or any disagreements that they didn’t quickly put behind. They ran a little nursery, Mountain Blossoms, outside of Slate Bank, and although they never made much money, it was enough for them to get by, and they were happy as a couple of larks.”

“Did anyone ever make trouble for them because of their lifestyle?”

"Not to my knowledge. That's not the nature of folks living in these parts. People around here tend to mind their own business."

"Can you recall any business dealing they had with a customer or supplier that might seem out of the ordinary, looking back?"

"I can't recall Sally telling me of anything like that. Everything seemed to be going along fine at the time of their deaths, their small business starting to grow just a bit and bring in more money. She and Betty were fixing up another old greenhouse that was already on the premises when they bought their florist business, and they had just hired a couple of general carpenters to work for them part time. The renovation was almost finished at the time of the fire."

"Do you know who the men were? Maybe the Mountain Blossoms business files would show to whom Sally and Betty wrote checks."

"Most of those files were lost in the fire. I doubt there's any record left as to who did the work. But I'd be happy to look around to see what I can turn up and let you know."

"Please do. There might be some significance in the fact that the work was done just before the fire, or then again, it might mean nothing at all. But right now, it seems like the only lead we have to work with."

"I'll get right on it, Megan," Darlene promised.

"You'll be seeing a lot of me in the days to come, and together we're going to find out what happened in 2005. One last thing: I understand the fire started when an old electrical heater ignited a window curtain during the night, and then the home went up like a tinder box before Sally and Betty could escape. Is that right?"

"Yes, that's what the fire marshal told us after his investigation. But it struck me as strange that Sally would have been using a heater on such a warm night. She always watched her pennies, and it wasn't like her to waste electricity."

Megan said goodbye and walked back to her car, quickly stepping inside to avoid the yellow jackets angrily buzzing around her head. She had just closed the door when she saw Darlene running down the hill, waving an arm to get her attention, Roy stumbling behind, struggling to keep up.

"Hold up a minute before you leave," Darlene called out, stopping beside the car. "Something just came back to me. I remember now Sally telling me the two carpenters were brothers and worked out of Pearisburg. She said the older one reminded her of Jay Leno."

Suddenly Darlene let out a scream, swatting at her legs with both hands, retreating a short distance and calling out, "Several of those bees got up my pants legs and ate me up! Roy, get over here right now, before they sit on you."

Roy failed to move quickly and paid the price, yelping in pain as the yellow jackets swarmed in to repeatedly sting exposed skin. Seeing the confused dog frantically turning in circles and not knowing what to do, Darlene rushed back to the yellow jacket nest, scooped him up in her arms, and ran up the hill toward her house. A few angry bees followed, continuing the attack.

Darlene made it up to the front porch before stopping to set the old dog down and raise her arm in a friendly goodbye. Megan returned the wave, driving away with a growing respect for Darlene. She had watched the woman willingly take the punishment of a swarm of angry yellow jackets in order to protect her helpless pet. Now, more than ever, she was determined to help Darlene find the person who murdered her sister.

*****

Monday night, Mandy heard her cell phone ring in the privacy of her bedroom, quickly picking up to answer. She had asked Dave to call her after weeks of steady email, and now they would be hearing each others voices for the very first time.

"Red, this is Dave," he started. "I can't believe it's taken so long for us to actually talk to each other on the phone. What are you up to now? I'm here alone in my room, listening to some good Zac Brown music, looking at your picture, but definitely not that zombie one."

Mandy started to laugh, all of the tension quickly broken. "I wish you'd throw the zombie one in the trash. I must have been out of my mind to have given it to you. Guess what? Your voice sounds a little different than I thought it would. If someone were listening in, I'm pretty sure they'd know we're both from southwest Virginia."

Now it was Dave's turn to laugh. "Are you telling me I talk like a country boy? Me, a big-city boy living in the bright lights of Covington? You've got to be kidding! I thought I sounded like an ESPN announcer."

"Not exactly, but country's cool," Mandy reassured him. "It's really nice to finally talk with you." She hesitated, adding, "I had a secret motive in asking you to call me tonight. I finally got up the nerve to tell Dad that we've been emailing each other for the past six weeks, and he wants to meet you."

"I knew this day was coming," Dave replied. "Is your father PO'ed at me for going this long without meeting both of you?"

"He's probably more upset with me than you. But he didn't make a big deal out of it when I told him. He just agreed that I should have said something sooner. I told him everything about you, and then I showed him your picture."

"Oh, great! Now he not only knows who I am and where I live, but he can also pick me out of a line-up."

"Dad's a really good person, Dave. I believe that you're going to hit it off with him when you finally get to meet him. He played football in high school, too."

"I'm just joking with you, Mandy. I'm glad this thing between us is out in the open now. Pick a time that's good for you and your dad, and I'll drive over to New Court to finally get to see you face to face and meet him."

"What about next Saturday?"

"I work at Safeway on weekends, but I'll see if Mr. Painter will let me off early. I'll try to get to your house by 6:00."

"You realize this is could be considered our first date?"

"I guess so. Not many guys have to get checked out by the county sheriff before they get to take a girlfriend out, but I'm willing to pay the price."

"So now I'm your girlfriend?"

"You've been my girl since the night I first saw you. You just didn't know it until now."

"Since we're both being so open, I'll go ahead and tell you that you're my first serious boyfriend."

The two talked on and on about everything and nothing, growing more at ease with each other as they peeled away layers of adolescent reserve, openly sharing secrets. When Mandy put her cell phone back on the night stand, slipped into her PJ's, and turned out the light, she was still thinking about what Dave had said. She continued to mull over all of the possibilities that were miraculously taking shape until much later, when she finally dropped off into an easy sleep.

Chapter 25

"The autopsies confirm exactly what you thought," Coroner Scott Nelson informed Cole Wednesday morning, nursing a mug of the sheriff's infamous Courthouse Coffee. He took another sip, grimacing "Good Lord! This stuff is strong enough to eat a hole in your stomach. You ought to put a warning label on the cup."

"Quit your bitching and take it like a man," Cole replied, concealing a grin. "No one's making you drink it. Now tell me what you learned from the post mortem."

"The driver of the car, Norv Scaggs, and the front seat passenger, Janelle Farver, both tested positive for almost every drug in the book, but the predominant one was methamphetamine. I can see why you think the wreck was caused by drug-induced road-rage."

"It didn't take a rocket scientist to come up with that theory," Cole observed. "Scaggs and Farver were just hauled in here for domestic violence with a load of meth in their systems back in October. They've been our jailhouse guests for disturbing the peace so often that we've been giving them preferred customer rates.

"The other driver just happened to be in the wrong place at the wrong time. He passed Scaggs on Route 615, and all at once found he had an aggressive tailgater coming up and bumping him, trying to knock him off the road.

"Unfortunately for Scaggs and Farver, the other driver happens to race stockcars at the Radford Speedway on weekends, and our angry friends were the ones who ended up going off the road, hitting an oak tree head-on at fifty-five miles an hour. The tree held up a lot better than the Toyota. I know I'll have to do penance with Rev. McFarland for thinking this way, but I can't help but feel this accident was nature's way of cleansing the gene pool."

"I have to confess to having the same feelings," Scott replied. "We both have to deal with the same scum bags. The difference is that you haul them in while they're still warm, and I open them up after they've chilled down."

He set his half-full coffee mug back on the desk, slowly shaking his head. "I swear to the Almighty, I haven't drunk anything this bad since the night of my med school fraternity initiation. You ought to put a hazardous waste sign on your coffee pot."

"Like my daddy always told me, when it comes to quality, you get what you pay for," Cole replied. "Thanks for coming by with the autopsy reports. I'll tell my staff what you found, and you have my word, we'll keep on busting our chops to find out who's pushing ice around these parts."

*****

Carl Viello pulled off of US 460 around 9:00 and swung into Harlan's Truck Stop, spotting a dozen eighteen-wheelers, and about as many cars, pickups, and SUVs, clustered in the parking lot near the neon-lit restaurant. He swung by the nearest gas pump to top off his tank before cruising over to a remote part of the lot where he could see vehicles coming and going. The tantalizing smell of grilled hamburgers and french fries drifted his way when the breeze kicked up, reminding him that he had not taken time to eat dinner.

He looked over the collection of four-wheelers and studied the drivers carefully, seeing no one who jumped out at him as a county mountie hunkered down in an unmarked vehicle on a stakeout. He didn't need to be reminded that in the drug business you only got to screw-up one time, and after that you were off for a long vacation at a high security resort on the government's dime.

Viello looked around for the woman who was supposed to rendezvous with him, but saw no heavy-set, bleached-blonde anywhere on the premises. The only person he spotted moving about on foot was a young, slender, redhead in a very short skirt and high heels, the kind who get double-takes from men of all ages. He curiously watched as, with practiced ease, she scrambled up the steps and entered the cab of a Peterbilt tractor trailer parked at the end of the building, shutting the passenger's door behind her.

Twenty minutes came and went as he nervously sat in his parked van, trying to read the sports page of his newspaper under the dim light from a pole-mounted light, watching the redheaded business woman clamber down from the eighteen-wheeler and quickly walk away, this time heading for a nearby Volvo rig.

Still there was still no sign of the blonde, and Viello had become too antsy to wait for her in the van any longer. He stuffed the newspaper under the seat, locked the vehicle, and walked across the trash-strewn lot into the restaurant, ordering a cup of coffee and seating himself at the far end of the counter to continue waiting.

Two other men sat nearby, and one of them drew his attention. Something about the close-clipped hair, well-pressed slacks, and North Face windbreaker made him seem out of place, and Viello unobtrusively studied him to determine whether he might be a plain clothes officer. His apprehension evaporated when the man suddenly got up from his seat and disappeared, leaving only him and a young African-American man at the counter.

Viello felt a mix of relief and pent-up anger when he finally saw the blonde enter on the opposite side of the restaurant and glance in his direction. The woman casually moved across the room toward an alcove filled with NASCAR memorabilia, stopping as if to study the life-size cardboard figures of Dale Earnhardt, Jr. and Jimmy Johnson.

The two exchanged no words but made momentary eye contact again as Viello came past her and walked to the door. She waited until he had left the restaurant, then turned to follow him outside into the parking lot.

*****

It was serendipity that brought Maurice Jones into Harlan's Truck Stop on Wednesday evening. That, plus a growling stomach which reminded him he hadn't had a bite since wolfing down a Little Debbie cupcake at lunchtime. And maybe also the awareness that a Harlan Trucker Burger, with two quarter pound patties of Angus beef, topped with bacon and cheese, was as tasty as any fast food he'd ever eaten in his entire life.

He finished his HTB and the last gulp of draft beer from a frosted mug just as Carl Viello entered the restaurant, walking by him to the far end of the room, taking a seat at the counter. Jones had worked in the business long enough to recognize many of the drug dealers in the area, and he was almost certain that the Hispanic man was connected to the crystal meth trade.

He would have paid for his meal and walked out the door without so much as a glance in the man's direction only a couple of months earlier. But since Cole Grayson had spared him from a .40 cal slug at Slate Bank, Jones now saw the world through the eyes of a committed law enforcement activist, and a probable drug dealer was just what he had been looking for.

Jones watched a chunky blonde enter the restaurant, look toward the Mexican, and then trail him from the building. He followed them outside to stand behind a parked tractor-trailer, watching the man head toward a van across the parking lot.

The woman walked over to a dark Toyota nearer the building, unlocking the door to slide in behind the wheel. Jones slipped a pen from his pocket, jotting the license number on the palm of his left hand.

The woman started her car and drove toward the van without switching on her headlights, pulling up side-by-side so that she and the Hispanic man were only an arms length away through open windows. Something passed between them, and then the woman slowly pulled off.

Jones took his eyes off of her, concentrating on the van as it came past and continued out of the parking lot and onto 460. He stepped out from behind the tractor-trailer, struggling to get the pen to write on his sweaty skin, finally able to mark a second license plate number on his palm.

He was so focused on the balky ball-point that he lost track of the woman's whereabouts, and only a sixth sense made him turn his head as her car rapidly accelerated toward him from behind. An athlete's quick reflexes enabled him to step to the side just in time to avoid being run over.

There was no flash of brake lights to be seen when the fender of the green Toyota clipped his thigh, knocking him sprawling toward the ground, hands thrust forward to avoid going face-first onto the pavement. Maurice watched the woman drive off as he rolled over on his back, in a world of pain, trying to survey how badly he was hurt. Looking down at his hands, he saw that bloody road rash had erased both of the numbers he had worked so hard to record.

Two men in a SUV pulled into the parking lot, spotting Jones sprawled on the ground, where he was gingerly working his way back to his feet while still checking for injuries.

"What happened?" the first one out of the vehicle shouted. "Are you OK? Do you want us to call 911?"

"You should remain still and not be moving around until an EMT checks you out," the second one called out.

"I'm OK," Jones replied. "There's a twenty-four hour clinic down the road, and I'm heading in that direction right now."

"You want us to follow you in case you have any problems?"

"No need for that," Jones insisted, limping away. "All I need right now is something for pain."

He didn't mention one other thing he wished for even more than a heavy-hitter pain pill: clean, warm water to wash the blood and gravel from his hands. He could only hope that the remaining skin on his palm contained partial six-digit license numbers, and that might be enough information to finger two local drug dealers.

An hour later, Jones was back in his room at the Apple Blossom Motel with vicodin knocking the edge off of his pain, staring at his lacerated hands. The skin on both palms was gone, and with it, all traces of ink on the left one.

He knew that he'd blown a chance to strike a major blow against the drug trade in Courtland County, uncertain when he would have such an opportunity again. He mulled over things done wrong and lessons learned.

Jones gently eased his bruised body down on the bed, gingerly extending his arm to turn off the lamp, determined to put his earlier carelessness behind and look ahead to a second round. He directed a promise across the darkness toward the Mexican and blonde: "Tonight you beat me, but before long, I will take both of you down."

Chapter 26

Bayse Dillon held the door for Jane Barker to walk ahead and enter the Dairy Queen at noon, finding that they were the only two customers in the restaurant. "I feel guilty inviting you out to lunch and then taking you to a fast-food place," he commented with a smile as the two placed their orders at the counter. "I did better than that by my Nancy when we'd go out together."

"You shouldn't feel bad," Jane laughed. "I was the one who suggested coming here. To a country girl like me, having a cheeseburger and fries with a sundae for dessert, that's really living high on the hog."

Bayse paid for their lunches and picked up the tray, following Jane to a booth in the corner to sit directly across from her. Both having lost their spouses years before, they had become good friends who enjoyed warm companionship. Jane sensed from time to time that Bayse was looking for a more serious relationship with her, but she was not yet ready to take that step.

Their conversation started with friendly small-talk about family and neighbors, and then drifted into a topic that triggered strong feelings from both. "That Chicago outfit has started clearing the site for their wind farm," Bayse commented.

"I hear their chainsaws knocking down the trees when the weather's right. I imagine it won't be long before they'll start work on the new road coming up the other side of the mountain."

"Doesn't that make you heartsick?" Jane replied. "It certainly saddens me. I never dreamed that the County Board of Supervisors would grant a permit to build those monstrosities. Wesley will turn over in his grave when the first one goes up and our beautiful mountain top is changed forever."

She glanced toward Bayse with shared regret, adding, "Marvin Clark is the one who really disappointed me. I thought he was our friend all this time, and then he turned on us and cast the swing vote for approval."

Bayse unconsciously reached across the table to grasp Jane's fingers in his big, calloused hand, replying, "I never thought he would sell us out like that. There's something about him voting with Vince Johnson and Boyd Conner that stinks to high heaven. I can't help but wonder if there was some payoff in it for him. I wouldn't put it past Vernon to have made Marvin a deal he couldn't turn down."

"I don't like to think that either Vernon or Marvin would do anything dishonest," Jane countered. "As angry as I am about this whole ugly debacle, I can't believe that Vernon would offer a bribe, or that Marvin would accept it."

"We've both heard the proverb that everyone has his price, but I've never felt that way about Marvin in the past," Bayse commented. "I've always considered him to be a good businessman and an honest public servant. I suppose that's why we're both having so much trouble understanding what he did."

"It may surprise you to hear me say this, but despite all of the bad blood between Vernon and me, I've never thought of him as a dishonest man. He's on the board at the bank and he's a deacon in his church. But he's vindictive and mean as a rattlesnake, and as you are well aware, he will carry a feud to the grave.

"I'm convinced that he instigated that project as an act of pure meanness, to get back at me for something he thinks I did wrong a long time ago, something he considers to be an unforgivable sin against the Goode family.

"To him, the wind farm is a perfect act of retribution while remaining completely legal. Those enormous turbines will disfigure Indian Ridge and destroy the glorious view we Dillons have treasured for so many generations."

As Bayse continued to gently hold her hand, Jane got up the courage to ask the question she had never dared before. "Bayse, what in the world happened way back in the past between Vernon and you to cause this bitter feud?"

Bayse recoiled instantly, releasing her hand and angrily snapping, "Why'd you go and ask me that? I never dreamed you'd bring up such a hateful thing when I brought you to lunch today. I don't want to talk about what happened with anyone, not even you."

He watched the look of stunned surprise come across her face, and immediately tried to undo the damage he had caused. "I'm sorry, Janie. I didn't mean to jump on you like that. You know you're the dearest person in the world to me. It's just that when I recall what Vernon did, I lose control and spout off without even stopping to think about what I'm saying."

"I'll never bring that subject up again with you, Bayse," Jane replied, shocked and hurt by his outburst, pushing her lunch away. "I seem to have lost my appetite." She reached for her purse, getting up from the table, adding, "I'm going to go now."

"Please don't leave like that, Janie," Bayse pleaded. "I'd cut my tongue out before I'd ever say anything unkind to you."

Jane was still not willing to give him a pass for his conduct. "That was not a nice way to speak to me, Bayse. You really hurt my feelings."

"I know I did, Janie. I know I did. As God is my witness, it won't ever happen again."

He gently reached for her hand, and she reluctantly let him take it. "I have feelings for you, Janey. Please don't ever walk away from me mad."

Jane settled back into her seat, and the two finished their lunch in awkward silence, broken by snippets of mundane conversation as Bayse fumbled for words to restore the earlier pleasant atmosphere that had evaporated with his outburst.

After lunch, he insisted on buying her the chocolate sundae she had mentioned, sipping a cup of coffee while continuing to glance at her affectionately. When both had finished, Bayse walked with Jane to her car, opening the door for her to slip into the driver's seat. He inquired with concern, "Janey, you sure that you're not still angry at me for the ugly way I acted?"

She looked at him standing beside the car, seeing not big Bayse, the man that many found so intimidating, but rather little Bayse, the first grade kid who was trying his best to make amends for his misbehavior on the playground to the prettiest girl in the class.

Jane couldn't help but laugh. "Bayse, half of this county thinks you're made of pig-iron, but I believe that inside, you're nothing but a big marshmallow.

"No, I'm not still mad at you. If it will make you feel any better, I'll confess that I happen to be very fond of marshmallows."

She saw smile of relief break across on Bayse's face as she started her car and slowly drove away, glancing in the mirror to see him following her with anxious eyes until he disappeared from her view.

Chapter 27

Dave Barnett climbed into the worn front seat of his red Taurus on Friday afternoon, pulling out of the Safeway Grocery parking lot after a busy eight-hour shift stocking shelves and running a checkout counter. He would have rushed home, showered, and changed clothes, but he was cutting it close on time and needed to get on the road. A quick clean-up in the Safeway washroom and a fresh shirt would have to do.

The distance from Covington to New Court was only 35 miles. But he was aware that the winding two-lane state highway connecting the two towns would be shared with many overloaded logging trucks, requiring an hour of driving time. He would have to keep his foot down in order to be at the Grayson's by 6:00. He pushed his favorite CD into the player and turned up the volume, singing along to the familiar lyrics of Zac Brown's latest hit, *Keep Me In Mind.*

Dave had looked forward to the evening ahead since getting up that morning. He was aware that emails, phone calls, and photos could only go so far in building a relationship, and that the chemistry between two people would never really be known until they met face to face.

Dave had gone out with several girls in town, and knew from experience just how important early impressions are, how they stick in the mind long after the first date. He wanted his face-to-face get together with Mandy to be perfect. Everything up until now indicated remarkable compatibility between the two, and he knew they were strongly attracted to each other. She might to be that special girl.

He switched on his headlights against the deepening shadows quickly drifting from hills into hollows amid the leafless trees of December. In less that an hour he would enter Mandy's world to meet the other inhabitants, Dad, Buddy, and Grandmom. Undoubtedly the one giving him the most careful look would be her father. He had watched his own dad size up the adolescent boys who came by their house to hang out with his pretty, thirteen year-old sister, Karen. Fathers know everything that goes on in the minds of boys and young men. After all, they've been there, done that.

It was getting dark by the time Dave entered New Court, following Mandy's simple instructions to turn off Main Street onto Wagner Street and keep going for six blocks. The older two story brick homes along both sides of the pot-holed street, with their small front yards and large shade trees, reminded him of his own home town. The only thing missing was the unmistakable fragrance of the paper mill.

Finally, he spotted the brick bungalow that Mandy had described, pulling up in front and killing the engine to sit for a moment and take everything in. Then he jogged up the walk, pushing a battered skateboard out of the way, and bounded up the steps, two at a time.

Under a half-moon's pale light, the door lamp cast a welcoming glow on the broad front porch, a swing piled with cushions at one end, under which a math textbook lay cast aside unopened next to a far more interesting Iron Man Comic Book. A pair of girl's running shoes lay tangled with a New Courtland volleyball shirt in a worn but welcoming wicker rocker. He stood for a few seconds at the door, noticing the 625 house number plaque painted with a rather messy but altogether inviting humming bird. Then he whispered his football coach's rallying cry, Show Time, and rang the bell.

The door opened, and Dave saw a tall man standing before him with a friendly smile, comfortably dressed in blue jeans, faded denim shirt, and scuffed boots, arm extended to shake his hand. "I'm Cole Grayson, Mandy's father. You must be Dave Barnett. Come right in."

Dave returned the smile, shaking Cole's hand as he stepped through the door, relieved at his friendly greeting. "Yes, sir. I'm Dave. It's good to meet you." He glanced about the room to see an adolescent boy standing next to a slender, gray-haired lady with a warm, inviting expression.

"Dave, I'd like for you to meet my mother-in-law, Ms. Barker, and my son, Buddy."

Dave stepped across the room to accept the grandmother's hand and exchange a fist-bump with the boy. "Nice to meet you, Ms. Barker. Mandy's told me a lot of nice things about you. Buddy, you're taller than I expected." He noticed that his greetings seemed to go over well, particularly the one regarding the kid brother's size.

"Have a seat, Dave, before we get into the main event," Cole continued, smiling. "Buddy, run upstairs and tell your sister that Wideout24 is here."

Dave grinned, realizing that either Mandy or her brother had given their father his email handle, feeling his initial nervousness melting away.

Buddy commented, "She's been ready for an hour—she's just sitting around in her room waiting to come down and make her big appearance." He caught the frown that swept across his grandmother's face, and then was off like a shot, taking the steps three at a time.

A few minutes later, Dave watched a tall, slender redhead wearing a short powder blue dress come down the stairs. She looked older than sixteen, more like a young college student than a high school girl. Mandy was smiling, and Dave had to catch his breath.

Cole commented, "I don't suppose you two need any introduction, but I'll make one anyway, just for the record. Dave, I'd like for you to meet my daughter, Amanda. Mandy, your grandmother, brother, and I have just started interrogating Wideout24. You might like to know that so far he's doing fine."

"Daddy!" Mandy exclaimed, more in nervous relief than embarrassment. "Dave, my father's the county sheriff, but he tries to be a comedian. I told you that you'd like him after you get to know him, but right now you're probably beginning to wonder about all of us. Believe it or not, we're a pretty normal family."

Buddy turned toward Dave and whispered, "Don't believe anything she says."

Mandy retaliated, "I meant to add, except for my younger brother."

"Why don't you kids have a seat so we can all talk for just a few minutes," Cole suggested. "After that, I thought it would be nice to go over to Sal's Deli for a really good Italian meal. Then y'all can come back here and visit while I run Mama Jane back to her place."

*****

"Buddy, why don't you go upstairs and play with your new Nintendo game," Mandy suggested, as the three sat watching TV in the living room. "I'll make some ice cream sundaes when Dad gets back from taking Grandmom home."

"Not very subtle, Sis." Buddy wisecracked. "I know that you two just want to be left alone."

"Pretty much," she openly acknowledged. "But you'll get extra toppings if you play along."

Mandy and Dave sat side by side on the sofa, his arm casually draped around her shoulders, talking quietly about everything under the sun. "I can tell that Dad really like you," Mandy said. "He was on the all-district football team in high school, too."

"It gives us something in common," Dave answered. "He told me that he got de-cleated about as hard as I did when he was a senior, right on the same field during the district championship game."

"That was the night he won Mom over," Mandy confided. "He fractured a bone in his leg in the fourth quarter, and played the rest of the way without letting anyone know he was hurt. He went on to score the winning touchdown at the end, and had to be helped off the field when the game was over."

"So they started going together at that time?" Dave inquired.

"Not long afterward. Mom was on the girls' track team, but she thought Dad was a conceited jock. She wouldn't have anything to do with him until after he got hurt.

"The first time they went out together, he was still on crutches—I think she called it a pity date. But she discovered that night that he was a really likeable guy, and before long they were inseparable. You can see their picture across the room, on the far wall."

"What a great story! Your mother was really pretty. It's sad to look at her photograph and know that she died so young. I'm sure you hear it all the time, but I think that you look a lot like your mom."

Mandy's eyes began to tear, and Dave pulled her close, wrapping both arms around her, hoping to steer their conversation in a happier direction.

"So you and Dad really hit it off," she said, trying to regain control of her emotions. "Tell me what you think of my grandmother and brother?

"I like both of them, too. Grandmom's a very sweet lady who's obviously stepped in to pinch-hit for your mother, and that's a good thing for both of you.

"Your brother seems to be twelve going on twenty. I think Buddy sees himself as your older brother who likes to give you a hard time, but is really all about looking out for you. Some of the things he comes up with make me want to laugh, but I'd never take a chance on hurting his feelings."

"I can tell that they both feel the same way about you," Mandy observed. "A classmate I hang out with at school has a boyfriend who doesn't get along with her family, and it creates a lot of problems. She's always crying in the girl's room."

"We'll never have that kind of problem," Dave reassured her. "But now you need to come to Covington and meet my family. It's your turn to go into the Barnett family lineup. You'll get to meet my parents, Lowell and Pat, and my younger sister, Karen."

"I'm ready to come visit your family anytime you want me to," Mandy replied.

She paused to listen. "Wait a second—I think I hear a car pulling in. Dad must be back from taking Grandmom home."

With that, she leaned over to put both arms around Dave's neck, pull his face to hers, and kiss him lightly. "I wanted to do that before you leave, and I have the feeling that we may not be alone again for the rest of the evening."

Dave slipped his arms around her to draw her even closer, holding her for a long second kiss. "That's just in case you're right."

Mandy's prediction turned out to be on the money. Cole and Buddy joined them for ice cream sundaes running over the sides of the dishes from topping overload, and Buddy stuck like glue to watch reruns of Saturday Night Live long after his dad had said goodnight and gone upstairs.

At 11:00, Dave got up to leave for the drive home, Mandy noting that for once she was standing next to a boy taller than herself. "Will you call me when you get home?" she asked.

"You bet," Dave promised, noticing that Buddy was still watching them through the glass door. "It's been a great evening, hasn't it?" He turned as he got into his car to wave and call back to her, "You're beautiful, you know."

Dave turned his car around and slowly accelerated away from the Grayson's neighborhood, the Zac Brown Band sound again filling the car and spilling outside, as he headed back over dark country roads toward home, Mandy on his mind.

*****

Mandy propped herself on a pile of pillows, comfortably leaning back to turn on her laptop for a final check of her email. She discovered one unread message, from Beth Jackson, full of brief questions: "How'd it go? Hot as his picture? Get any time alone? Best part? No holding out—B."

Mandy quickly keyed in her short answers: "Incredible. Definitely. Better believe it. Great kisser.—M."

Chapter 28

Maurice Jones did not venture out of his room at the Apple Blossom Motel, a down at the heels dive which had been keeping secrets since the '40's, until late Monday evening. As both fugitive on the run and man on a mission, he kept the low profile of a wary coyote, hidden from view during daylight, holed up in a den inside the county line waiting for nightfall.

He knew that his adversaries, both the male drug manufacturer and female distributor, shared the same nocturnal world, trying to avoid attention while engaged in the lucrative business of supplying illegal drugs to panhandlers, prostitutes, and petty thieves as well as respectable folks with secret habits.

Jones could not afford to be stopped for even a minor traffic offense. His car had been purchased from a stranger for two-hundred dollars cash, complete with tags and registration card borrowed from another car left unattended under a farmer's shed. Neither he nor the vehicle would withstand scrutiny by a county mountie.

Jones knew from earlier days which of the truck stops, beer joints, and gas stations were frequented by users and their suppliers, and he planned his route accordingly. For over an hour, he cruised in and out of parking lots around the county and beyond, staying long enough at each location to observe the comings and goings of regular customers.

Nothing struck him as out of the ordinary until he drove into Pannell's Mini Mart, spotting a late model green Toyota with a crumpled left front fender parked out behind the building, backed up against a concrete curb stop.

Jones nervously scanned the premises for any sign of the woman he knew to have lethal tendencies, then pulled up beside her car, leaving the transmission in park and the engine running. His trunk served as a very large tool box, and he knew that, as usual, it contained exactly what he needed for the job at hand.

He lifted out a crowbar, a short length of metal chain, and two padlocks, prying up the six foot long, three-hundred pound curb stop to pass one end of the chain around it and lock it securely in place. Then he crawled under the Toyota, wrapped the other end of the chain tautly around the rear axle and secured it with the second lock. Job efficiently completed, he tossed the crowbar back into his car and drove away, leaving little evidence of his handiwork in sight.

Jones pulled in beside the closed dry cleaning business next door, taking out the TracFone he had purchased at Wal-Mart, knowing that it could not be traced to him. He dialed the number for the Courtland County Sheriff's Department, and when dispatcher Tammy Ewell picked up, he spoke quickly.

"I'm calling to help Sheriff Grayson shut down the drug dealers around here. Tell him right this minute there's a middle-aged, fat blonde at Pannell's Mini Mart dealing meth. She's driving a late model green Toyota with a banged-up left front fender, and she's got a three-hundred pound block of concrete chained to her rear axle." He could just make out the female dispatcher exclaiming, "What the . . ." as he turned off the phone.

*****

Tammy called Cole at his home. “Sheriff, you told me to call you 24-7 if there was a drug bust in progress. Tank and Jake are on the way to Pannell’s to check out a tip we just got claiming that some woman over there’s dealing meth.”

Minutes later, Cole was on the way, driving his own truck, still in civilian clothes, flashers on and pedal mashed down, running red lights with horn blaring. He arrived just in time to join in on the action.

Tank and Jake were pulling their patrol cars into opposite ends of the parking lot, while a stocky woman was hauling it across the pavement toward a dark colored Toyota out back, moving faster than Cole would have imagined possible. He watched her jump into the car, start the engine, and floor the accelerator, as he pulled his truck into line with Tank and Jake, their three vehicles fanned out in blocking positions.

Cole noticed black smoke pouring out beneath the spinning front wheels of the Toyota and sparks trailing from under the rear end, where a massive block of concrete was dragging. He recognized it as a six-foot concrete curb stop, twisting and gouging into the pavement as the driver desperately tried to make a tight turn and evade the blockade.

In quick succession, the left front tire on the Toyota blew out with an explosive bang, the car door opened, and the fugitive stumbled to the ground, hightailing across the lot toward the corner of the building.

He watched Tank run her down and grab her with both hands from behind, surprised when she broke free and sucker punched him with a round-house right to his face, causing blood to spurt from his nose. In a blur of twisting bodies, the blonde was suddenly sprawled on the pavement, flat on her back.

Cole would later be unable to recall seeing Tank strike her and knock her to the ground. It would be his opinion that his deputy used the minimum force necessary to restrain a violent offender, one who got tangled up over her own two feet while physically resisting arrest.

He could hear the blonde screaming at the top of her lungs, covering the spectrum of every obscenity he could recall, throwing in some commands which were anatomically impossible. Tank calmly replied, “Stick a sock in that mouth. Your mama teach you all that dirty talk?”

Jake walked over to Cole to observe, “That lady’s got quite a vocabulary. I hope the recorder in my car catches everything she’s spitting out, because there’s stuff I’ve never heard before. I’m going to have to Google a few of those words to find out what they mean.”

“Some of that stuff is new to me, too,” Cole replied. “When I was little, I recall my daddy saying that girls were made of sugar and spice and everything nice. I don’t believe he had this one in mind.”

Cole and Jake helped Tank complete the arrest, checking the woman for weapons and drugs, cuffing her hands behind her back, and reciting the Miranda rights. “What’s your name, and where’s your driver’s license and registration card?” Jake demanded to know.

The woman shrieked back in a high-pitched voice, “I’m not talking to you sons of bitches without my lawyer present. I’m filing a suit against you and the Courtland County Sheriff’s Department for police brutality, and I’m going to take all of you for everything you have.”

"You and your ambulance chaser scare us to death," Jake snapped back. "If you don't want to cooperate, we'll get the information we need another way." He spun around and spoke to Cole, "Ready for me to help you dig out the meth that Blondie's got tucked away in her car? It can't be hard to find. Anyone dumb enough to get a parking block wrapped around her axle is too stupid to hide Easter eggs."

Jake almost had to eat his words as the three men searched the Toyota for half an hour, with no luck. "It has to be stashed where she could get to it quickly," Cole insisted. "Keep searching behind the instrument panel. I'll keep checking back up under the front seat."

Jake resumed his blind probing, extending his arm deeper and deeper into the maze of wire harnesses connecting the electronic displays, until suddenly his fingers rested on a smooth plastic pouch bound with tape. "I think I just hit the jackpot!" he exclaimed, tugging until the package broke loose and he was able to pull it away in his hand. "Check this out."

He got off his knees, holding up a zip-lock plastic bag for all to see, then opening it to inspect the contents. "Yep, it's what we're looking for. Blondie has enough meth here to supply addicts all over the county."

"Good work," Cole replied. "I just found her wallet under the seat, and it's got her driver's license and other personal ID. Men, I'd like to introduce you to Jolene Burke. I imagine we'll find a lot out about her when we run a background check. I'd bet my last dime that she's been convicted of dealing drugs before. I'm guessing there will also be priors for assault and battery."

"Go to hell, Sheriff," Burke called out to him.

"Keep mouthing off, lady," Cole replied. "You're just digging yourself a deeper hole."

Cole pulled Tank and Jake to the side. "You two take her back and try to talk some sense into her. Tell her that if she'll give up her supplier, we may be able to cut a deal that will make things a lot better for her."

"That woman is as tough as nails," Tank commented. "I'll be surprised if she cooperates with us in any way, and I bet you a hundred dollars she won't give up the names of anybody working with her."

"Look for an Achilles' heel," Cole replied. "Does she have a family member that she doesn't want to leave behind by pulling a long sentence? Here's a chance for you two to help break another case and earn department commendations."

"I'd rather have a raise," Jake quickly replied. "I've got Courtland County Attaboys stuck all over my refrigerator door, right next to the kids' crayon pictures. None of them are worth a nickel at the flea market, or will get me a Happy Meal at McDonalds"

"I didn't realize you were such a mercenary," Cole laughed. "Maybe a raise is in the cards. And while you're figuring how to make our blonde friend open up, see if you can figure out how to get in touch with Maurice Jones, the new volunteer member of our department. I've got a commendation him, too."

Cole didn't know that the new volunteer was only a short distance away, watching everything going down and pleased that the woman who had tried to run over him was now in handcuffs and heading off to jail, much the worse for wear.

"One down," Maurice muttered under his breath, as he waited patiently for the sheriff and his deputies to clear the premises before heading back to his den at the Apple Blossom Motel.

Chapter 29

Cole drove up the rutted gravel road and turned into the Courtland County Gun Club on Thursday afternoon, feeling as guilty as a kid who had just sneaked out of school before the final bell.

He saw Connie standing next to the clubhouse door waiting for him, with her Browning twenty-gage over-under broken down under her arm. "Better hurry up," she called to him, smiling. "It'll be dark in an hour, and you have enough trouble hitting clay pigeons in full daylight."

He walked up and leaned in to give her a quick kiss, his Remington twelve-gage autoloader tilted toward the ground. "One of these days I'm going to outshoot you, and you're never going to hear the end of it. One of these days."

"Only in another lifetime or some parallel universe," Connie kidded. "It sure ain't going to happen here now. Maybe for Christmas I'll give you a ten-gage side-by-side with both barrels open choke. You could try shooting with your eyes closed and you might rack up your best score ever. The shot pattern would be wide enough to cover the side of a barn."

Competitive Connie was the nickname he had given her soon after returning to New Court, realizing that she was the antithesis of the proverbial southern magnolia blossom. The strangest part of it all was that her ability to beat him head-to-head in certain sports only made her more attractive to him.

They made their way around the course, shooting from each of the stations arranged in a semicircle between the high and low trap houses, exchanging good-natured gibes. At station six, Cole missed both targets, and Connie razzed him good-naturedly. "Are you deliberately releasing those things back into the wild?"

"That's exactly what I'm doing. Grandpa Grayson told me not to shoot all of the quail in the pasture, but always leave a few to mate, so you'd have some to hunt the following year. It's solid game management, whether you're dealing with bobwhites or clay pigeons."

"Sounds like a plan," Connie laughed. "I have a feeling that your grandfather was a better BS artist than wing shot, like someone else I know."

On station eight, Connie called "Pull" one last time, breaking both clay pigeons with two quick shots. Cole followed, hitting the first, missing the second, leaving him on the short end of the round with a final score of nineteen to Connie's twenty-three.

"Dropping a shooting match to a girl doesn't make a big man like you feel like a little boy, does it?" Connie asked innocently, walking ahead, but glancing back with wide-eyed faux-concern stamped on her face.

Cole's open hand delivered a swift swat and squeeze to her well-toned flank. "Only in another lifetime or some parallel universe, Ms. Balfour," he replied, mimicking her earlier words. Poker-faced, he added, "You'll find out for yourself before the evening's over."

The two made their way to Sal's Deli afterward, settling into a vinyl-upholstered booth to order pastrami sandwiches and draft beers. "A little excitement recently on the front page of the *Trib*," Cole remarked. "Nice article on Jolene Burke's arrest for pushing meth. I appreciate your giving Jake and Tank a pat on the back."

"What got the most attention was the photo of those two impounding her car, using bolt-cutters to remove the concrete block chained to the rear axle," Connie laughed. "I heard that the owners of the L & P Barbershop taped a copy of the front page up on their wall, and for once, fishing wasn't the main topic of conversation for all of the old-timers that hang out there."

Cole dropped his voice, continuing, "Ms. Burke has quite a criminal record, running the gamut from breaking and entering, grand larceny, and dealing drugs, to assault and even a count of attempted murder. She's a real piece of work—quite a handful for our jail staff.

"But she does have a vulnerable spot, and that's a twelve year-old daughter who's living with her sister in Bluefield. I think her attachment to the girl might help us to cut a deal. We reduce the charges and help her get a short sentence in return for giving up the names of others in the meth business. I don't think she'd be afraid to rat out her associates. I don't see Burke being intimidated by anyone."

"What have you learned about the man who set her up? Connie asked curiously. "Everyone wants to know who put the concrete boot on her car, and why he did it. Is there anything more you can share with me?"

"We know quite a bit about him, but treat what I'm about to tell you as off the record for now. His name is Maurice Jones, and he's a young former drug dealer and fugitive out of Henry County who still has time to serve on an earlier sentence. He's the same person that got away from me at Slate Bank. It turns out that he's also the one who ran off a man threatening Buddy and his friend on Halloween night, as a way of trying to earn points with me.

"He seems to have had a change of heart after I let him go instead of shooting him when he took off running from me that day. Now he's become an amateur crime fighter who's trying to win favor with the legal system by helping eliminate drug dealers in the county."

"You're not yanking my chain are you, Cole?" Connie inquired "You're really serious when you tell me that we have an amateur crime stopper here in Courtland County?

"I couldn't make up stuff this good, or I'd be putting out the next Superman comic book. If you don't believe me, I'll let you look at three sets of finger prints back at the office, the official ones on file for Maurice Jones taken when he was first convicted of dealing drugs, the ones found inside the wrecked Ford van, and now the ones we just lifted off of the locks and chain on the Toyota."

"Let me know when I can print this," Connie requested. "A good human interest story sells a lot of newspapers."

"I'll make a deal with you," Cole countered. "I'll let you break the Jones story if you continue to keep me informed about Megan's investigation of the serial murders. Has she turned up anything new?"

"She spent a day in Pearisburg last week trying to find someone who might remember the two carpenters that Darlene Barnes described, the ones who did some work for her sister Sally just before she was murdered. She had hoped that someone else besides Darlene might remember a local man who matched the description, but unfortunately she struck out.

"Megan now calls those serial killings the Mother's Day Murders. She has a calendar on the wall of her cubicle, with the second Sunday of May circled in red. She said it's a reminder that whoever committed those crimes is still running loose, and it builds a fire under her to keep at it."

"Maybe we should get off the subject of criminal investigations entirely," Cole suggested. "I never intended to get into a lot of heavy stuff when we came here to have dinner. So with that thought in mind, tell me, how's your pastrami on pumpernickel?"

"Absolutely delicious, as always at Sal's," Connie answered. "Tell me, would you like to come by my place for dessert and coffee? I have one of your favorite treats in the fridge, tiramisu."

"That sounds like a great invitation," Cole replied. "But do you think just offering me a fancy dessert is enough to compensate for humiliating me and destroying my male self-confidence on the skeet range? I would think your conscience would compel you to do more than that."

"You'll just have to wait until you get to my place to find out what else I have planned."

Cole glanced at her with wide eyes, waving his hand to get the waitress's attention. "Check, please."

Chapter 30

Irv Sutton eased his battered pick-up into a weed and trash strewn pull-off beside the deserted country road and turned off the engine. He was dressed in camo and looking, for all of the world, like any other hunter entering the woods in the early morning hours of turkey season. He lit up a cigarette, taking several deep drags, then settled back to wait.

He had just finished the smoke, rolling down his window and flipping the butt out on the ground, when an approaching Lexus sedan slowed to turn off the pavement and follow the same ruts until it reached the front of his truck. Both front doors swung open, and Irv found himself face to face with a major drug dealer from central Virginia, Floyd Greene, and a burly young driver he had never seen before.

Greene signaled for his companion to remain where he was, then came around to open the passenger side door and slip into the cab next to Sutton, reaching across the grimy seat to offer a firm handshake. "Have you thought over the deal I made you?" he asked, settling back carefully, as if to avoid grease spots on his eight-hundred dollar suit.

"Yeah," Sutton replied. "And I think you're trying to hustle me. According to your plan, you'd only have to push the product on the street. You'd dump all of the production headaches on me. I'd have to round up the chemicals, cook the meth, and then you'd come around in that big shiny new car and buy it just like you'd drive into KFC and pick up a bucket of chicken."

An angry look crossed Floyd's face, and he sat for a few seconds trying to control his temper before replying in a flat, tense voice, "You don't want to be giving me a ration of shit like you do the guys who work for you, or I'm out of here and my offer's off the table. Try getting the crap out your ears and listen to me, and I'll explain it all again in simple terms even you can understand.

"I told you I'd buy everything you make at the going price. You don't have to sweat getting busted by the sheriff or the state police while you're trying to sell it, since I'll be hauling it out of the area. If my employees get caught dealing, my tail's in the wringer, not yours.

"If for some reason I have to dump a batch to avoid getting caught with it, all that cost comes out of my pocket. Once you deliver the ice to me, my money's in your pocket, and you're home free. You don't have to worry about anything but laundering your income out of sight of the IRS."

Sutton realized he had gone too far, his tone becoming conciliatory as he continued. "You've got some serious risks selling it, but there's even more for me in making it. My people have to hire smurfs to buy the pseudoephedrine in stores without making the clerks suspicious.

"Cooking meth's a dangerous business where the chemicals can blow up in your face anytime, and things can go to hell in a hurry. People who've gotten careless have triggered fires and fried themselves. If you stay lucky and finish the run without anything exploding, there's six times as much toxic waste left behind to get rid of as there is product to sell."

"What if I get the ephedrine outside this area and sell it to you? That eliminates your biggest headache, except for controlling the production process."

Sutton ran his hand across his bearded chin, pausing to consider the revised proposal. "That'll work better for me, but I still think you're getting the best end of the deal. Anyway, go ahead and bring me a supply of cold medicine by next week, and I'll have a batch of meth ready for pick up on New Years Day."

Another quick handshake, and Greene was out of the truck, calling back, "I'll let you know when and where to meet me." He climbed into the Lexus beside his wide body driver, and minutes later they were on the highway, heading back toward Richmond.

Sutton reached into his pocket and pulled out a tin of Copenhagen long cut, dipping a pinch of tobacco and placing it against his lower gum, feeling the immediate hit of nicotine. He rolled down his window and sat back in the worn seat, watching the early morning sun light up the side ridges while leaving the nearby hollows in shadow, painting vertical stripes across the broad shoulder of the mountain before him.

His introspection ended when he heard a twig snap, as if someone were moving through the stand of rhododendron on the slope above. Sutton turned his head to scan the hillside behind him, listening for sounds of an intruder just out of sight. He breathed a sigh of relief and slouched back in a comfortable position after hearing the yelp of a turkey hen, reassured that only wildlife had witnessed the meeting with his new business partner.

*****

Maurice Jones flinched as a twig no bigger than a pencil snapped under his foot, making a noise that sounded like a cannon shot, causing him to silently mouth, "Oh shit!" He tried to cover his misstep by taking a turkey call from his pocket and placing it between his lips, emitting the yelp of a turkey hen looking for love. He crouched to anxiously watch the truck driver's reaction.

The driver turned his head, looking back toward Maurice's hideout, eyes scanning the hillside in an attempt to penetrate the green curtain of rhododendron. Seeing nothing out of the ordinary, the driver turned away, and Maurice let out a sigh of relief. Despite his carelessness, his quick thinking had prevented a major screw-up which could have cost him his life.

It was pure luck that he had spotted two well dressed men driving a luxury car along a remote country road during the early morning hours. The decision to tail them was a no-brainer. The pair stood out like high stakes players in a nickel-dime poker game. When he mentally questioned who they were and what they were up to, he had quickly concluded that there could be only one answer: out of town dealers here to buy or sell drugs. They were the targets he'd been seeking—and now they were marked.

He circled behind the battered truck on an old logging road and silently made his way into the rhododendron thicket above. He had arrived at his vantage point in time to see the entire meeting between the red neck and the suit, but the closed doors of the truck had kept him from making out what they were saying. All he knew was that they planned to soon meet again.

Jones recognized the truck as the one driven by the man he had rousted out of New Court on Halloween night to protect the Grayson boy. Now he could positively connect the truck to the driver, and this was a major break in squaring his account with the county sheriff.

He continued to watch as the man started his engine, pulling his pick-up out of the weeds onto the highway, then disappearing down the road. Acting on an impulse, Jones took out the turkey call and yelped again. High up above him, in the side of the ridge, a gobbler answered.

Jones stopped from time to time as he walked back to his car, hearing the gobbler call again and again as it worked its way down the mountain toward him, searching for the phantom hen. It comforted Jones to know that the natural world around him was still as stable and predictable as it had ever been. All he needed to get his life back on track was a little more time and a lot of luck.

Chapter 31

Mandy awoke to a silent house just before dawn on Christmas morning. Even the family cat, Snoopy, was still curled up on the chair across the room, taking catnapping to a whole new level. Reminiscing about how the unfortunate pet came to have that name brought a smile to her face.

Someone out in the country near Grandmom's house had dropped a tiny kitten soon after the Graysons had moved to New Court, and Mandy had insisted upon adopting it. Buddy demanded that the family also get a puppy, but their father had drawn the line at having two new pets without toilet training in a home with expensive new carpets.

Cole bragged that his solution would have impressed even King Solomon, pronouncing that the family would adopt the kitten, but would balance the scales between the two siblings by giving it a dog's name. He had settled on Snoopy before realizing that the tiny feline was a female.

Buddy was not pleased with his dad's solution, but then Buddy was often less than completely satisfied with his father's decisions. He had learned to grudgingly live by the credo, que sera, sera.

Mandy reached over to the night stand to retrieve her laptop, hoping to find a message from a special friend in Covington, Virginia. She checked the inbox, but saw there was nothing from Wideout 24. Just to pass the time, she keyed in a new message for Dave, certain that he would not find it until later in the day.

"Merry Christmas! Wake up, sleepy head. It's time to check your stocking and look under the tree for presents. Santa came while you were sleeping. I know, 'cause I'm friends on Facebook with him."

She was surprised when her computer scanned a new message soon after she hit the send key. It was from Wideout 24. "Merry Christmas back at you, Red. What in the world are you doing up at this hour of the morning? You must be expecting something big under the tree yourself. Glad you friended the head man at the North Pole. Dave."

Mandy continued the email chat, settling back in a comfortable cross-legged position on the bed with the computer in her lap. "I have a Christmas present for you. When will I get to see you again?"

"I don't know, Red. Maybe I can see you New Years Day. I'll try to get out of a family dinner party and drive over to New Court. I have a gift for you, too, but don't get your hopes too high. It's nothing like the new Porsche 911 Carrera I'm getting from my parents."

"I think you're totally out of your mind about getting a sports car. Anyway, try to come early. My volleyball coach, Mrs. Patton, has invited all of us to drop by her house for lunch. She told us that we can bring dates. You'll get to meet some of my best friends. They've heard me talk about you, and all of them want to meet Wideout 24. Do you have any big plans today?"

"Nope. I'm going to stick around the house and hang out with the family. Mom is big on having everyone together on holidays, like we don't already see each other 24-7. How about you?"

"Dad, Buddy, and I are going to Grandmom's house to open presents in a little while. She's also invited a good friend of dad's, Connie Balfour. Ms. Balfour is an awesome lady, and I really like her, but it feels weird to think of her dating my dad. Mom's been gone three years now, but I sort of feel like we're betraying her or something. Am I horrible to feel that way?"

"I think it's normal for you to feel that way. But how do you think your dad must feel about having someone like me dating his daughter after all of the years that he's been the only man in her life? He's dealing with some big changes in your family, just like you and your brother."

"I never thought about it like that."

"I think you ought to try. It might help make you understand where he's coming from. Anyway, I'll try to get to your house around midmorning next Sunday, all cleaned up and ready to stand inspection by a room full of your girlfriends."

"I can't wait. Will I hear from you again tonight?"

"You better believe it. Got to treat Santa's Facebook friend right until I get that Christmas gift. Say hello to everybody for me. And be nice to Ms. Balfour. She could be your stepmother someday, and that just might turn out to be pretty great. Love you, Red. Bye now."

"Love you more, Dave. Merry Christmas."

*****

The sun was well along in its trip across the southern sky by the time Cole and the kids arrived at Connie's house, Mandy and Buddy seated side by side in the back seat. Connie soon appeared, dressed for the holiday in a red skirt and a white sweater set off by a sparkly Santa Claus pin, carrying a big shopping bag overflowing with gifts in bright wrapping paper.

"Merry Christmas!" she called out, as Cole got out of the car to greet her with a warm kiss.

"Good morning, Mandy and Buddy," Connie said cheerily, turning a smiling face toward the back seat. "Thanks for letting me share Christmas morning with you."

"I'm glad you're going to Grandmom's with us today," Buddy replied. He'd already accepted Connie's relationship with his father and thereby with him, finding that she helped to fill the void his mother's death had left in his life.

"Me, too," Mandy chimed in after only a moment's hesitation, remembering Dave's advice to her earlier that morning. "I like your pretty sweater, and the Santa pin. You look like you're really into Christmas."

"Thanks," Connie replied, grateful for Mandy's friendly overture, having sensed the girl's reserved demeanor earlier. "My mother gave me that pin when I was twelve years old, and I really treasure it. I've worn it during the Christmas holidays ever since. It seems strange that something as small as a costume jewelry Santa can evoke such happy memories and take you back to your childhood, doesn't it?"

"I understand how you feel," Mandy answered. "I feel the same way about some of the things Mom gave me."

Connie redirected the conversation with a quick wink at Cole, continuing her friendly chat with Mandy. "Have you heard from anyone in Covington this morning?"

This time, Mandy laughed, replying, "Dave and I were in touch early, starting at the crack of dawn. He promised to come over to New Court next Sunday."

"Can you find a way to introduce me while he's in town? He sounds like a nice young man, and I'd really like to meet him. If the sheriff thinks Dave's good enough to call on his daughter, he must be pretty special."

"Buddy and I have looked Dave over pretty carefully, and we think he's a fine young man," Cole interjected. "But we'd welcome a third opinion from the newspaper editor. We might be missing something."

"I don't think you need another opinion about that young man. If he's won Mandy's respect and affection, he'll have no trouble winning mine," Connie replied.

Mandy looked at her silently, feeling a growing bond with this woman who had become so important to her father. Like her brother, she was beginning to feel that there was a place in their family for Connie.

"I promise I'll bring Dave by to meet you while he's in town, Ms. Balfour. I've already told him about you. I think you'll like him."

"If you want to give me a Christmas present, Mandy, here's what would really please me. Start by calling me Connie right now. Someday, I hope that you and I will be close friends."

Mandy wanted to acknowledge how much those words meant to her, but her emotions only allowed her to say, “Thanks, Connie. That’s very kind of you.”

Cole glanced at the generous, loving woman beside him, reaching across the seat to clasp her hand.

Buddy finally broke the silence. “I’m really looking forward to seeing Grandmom. She promised to have a huge turkey dinner for us, and told me that she was going to bake her special coconut cake.”

Mandy rolled her eyes, recovering her voice. “Same brother as always. All he can think about is food.”

“Apples don’t fall far from the tree,” Connie laughed, giving Cole a gentle poke in the stomach. “I’m with you, Buddy. There’s nothing quite as tasty as homemade coconut cake. Cole, can’t you drive a little faster? I’m starving.”

Chapter 32

Barbara Stevens, part-time deputy with the Courtland County Sheriff's Department, came on duty at 7:00 on Wednesday evening, taking over responsibility for the women's wing in the jail. She was expecting a quiet, uneventful second shift, knowing that only four women were locked up in holding cells. During recent weeks, there had been little excitement in performing the job, only having to break up arguments and shouting matches between bored and frustrated prisoners.

Nighttime duty in a small town jail was tame after retiring from a twenty year career with the Richmond Police Department, where she dealt daily with the underbelly of society, including drug addicts, prostitutes, and violent offenders. Checking the list of inmates made her feel even more confident of an easy night shift. Only a middle-aged woman with an attitude named Jolene Burke seemed to need her close attention.

Deputy Stevens settled in behind the desk and scanned the overhead monitors connected to closed circuit cameras strategically placed throughout the building. She picked up a clipboard to update the shift start check list, then dug out a training manual to go over the comprehensive list of jailer duties.

She patrolled the cell block at midnight, noticing that three of the inmates were sleeping. Burke, however, was wide awake, lying on her back, rolling slowly from side to side and moaning in pain. "It's my appendix," she muttered between clenched teeth. "I'm afraid it's going to rupture. I need to get to a hospital right now."

Stevens warily responded. "Why didn't you say something earlier when I first came on duty?"

"It wasn't hurting me then," Burke snarled. "Are you so stupid you think I can control when I get an attack of appendicitis? If you don't get me to a doctor and my appendix ruptures, I'll die. Do you even give a shit?"

"I'm going to call 911 and get an EMT over to check you out. The life saving crew can take you to a hospital in Roanoke if necessary."

"There's no time to drive me down 301 and over the mountain," Burke protested. "Come in here and take a look at my belly. I need a helicopter from the hospital on the way here right now."

Stevens had a sixth sense warning her not to open the door to Burke's cell, but she was conflicted by seeing the inmate in great pain and a possibly life threatening situation. She unlocked the door, watching Burke shift her clothing to expose the lower right part of her abdomen, touching the area and flinching in pain.

Stevens had walked closer to get a better look when suddenly Burke's right arm snaked out to seize her neck in a crushing choke hold, leaving her gasping for air. Burke whipped the deputy in a circle like a crocodile spinning its prey in a death roll, driving her head against the wall. Stevens fell limp, as everything around her went black.

One of the other prisoners was awakened by the noise, opening her eyes to silently watch the action. All it took to make her to close her eyes again was Burke pointing one finger at her. She heard the rustle of fabric as Burke stripped the unconscious guard of her uniform and exchanged it for her orange jumpsuit.

Burke walked toward the locked outer door of the jail, her blonde hair tucked beneath Steven's wide-brimmed hat, calling to the deputy on duty in the men's cell block, "Open the door for me. I've got to get something out of my car." No sooner had he complied than Burke was out the door and gone.

The escapee was on the road when Stevens started regaining consciousness, softly moaning in pain. At the same time the deputy controlling the outer door realized that no one had come back inside, smelled an escaping rat, and sounded the alarm. But it was all too late. Jolene Burke was outside the walls and on the run, a fugitive with the street-smarts to make recapture difficult.

The dreaded ring of his cell phone on the nightstand, heralding the bad news of the jail break, shook Cole awake just after midnight. "Sheriff, this is Deputy Crawford. I'm sorry to have to tell you, but Jolene Burke assaulted Deputy Stevens and has broken out. Cumbo's put out an APB to be on the lookout for her. We don't think that she's had time to get far."

"Is Stevens hurt?" Cole asked.

"She took a pretty good blow to the head, but she seems to be OK now. I think she's more embarrassed than banged-up, knowing that Burke took her down and escaped on her watch."

"I'll be there in just a few minutes. Tell Stevens that I said not to worry—I'm just glad she'd not seriously injured."

Jake, Tank, and other members of his staff were already assembled when he arrived. Darlene called out as he entered the door, "I put out a be-on-the-lookout bulletin to all of the regional law enforcement agencies and the State Police with Burke's photo and description. Road blocks have been set up in a twenty mile perimeter around the town."

"I want everyone to treat Burke as armed and extremely dangerous," Cole cautioned. "She's got one of our own side arms, and I have no doubt she'd use it." He noticed Deputy Stevens staring dejectedly at the floor, her head bandaged and her embarrassment palpable.

"How are you feeling?" he asked. "It won't take but a minute for you to give me a report, and then we'll get you to a hospital."

Stevens broke down in tears behind Cole's office door as she described how she'd been conned. "Sheriff, I'm OK. Knowing that I screwed-up is the worst part. I'm so sorry I let that woman make a fool out me. I've been around jails long enough to know better than to let a prisoner fake a medical crisis and get the jump on me. I'm ready to hand in my badge right now if that's what you want."

"Deputy, you aren't the first law officer to let misguided sympathy for a prisoner lead to carelessness," he replied sympathetically. "I'm not about to lose a good employee like you over one lapse of judgment.

"We're going to find Burke and bring her back. I'm glad you weren't killed. I'll never forget that Blacksburg prison break a few years ago. We lost a fine security officer and policeman trying to help a scum bag prisoner."

"I've learned a good lesson the hard way, Sheriff. I won't let you down again," Barbara replied, tears rolling down her cheeks. "If

Burke ends up back here, she better hope she doesn't have a real health crisis."

Stevens was a seasoned professional, and she gave Cole a detailed report, none the less concise for her injury. Cole walked with her to the waiting ambulance.

"Let us know what the ER doctors tell you. If they give you a clean bill of health and you feel up to it, report here for jail duty on second shift tomorrow. I hope by then we'll have that bitch under lock and key."

"I hope so, too, Sheriff. But I've learned that Jolene Burke is as tough and cunning as a coyote. It may be hard to run her to ground and get her back behind bars that quickly."

*****

Carl Viello pulled his van into the dark alley a few blocks away from the Courtland County Jail and waited for Jolene Burke to scramble out of the dumpster where she was hiding. "Get that uniform off and put on the jeans, coat, and cap," he tersely commanded as she climbed in, handing her a stack of clothing. "Leave the uniform back in the dumpster under some trash."

Viello lit a cigarette and waited until Burke was wearing the clothes and lying under a blanket in the back of the van. "How'd you get to a phone, and where did you get my number?" he growled.

"I broke a window to get inside the building. There was a phone on the wall, and I had memorized your cell phone number. I called you, and then I came back outside and waited in the alley. Someone loaded the dumpster with garbage, and I had to sit right in the middle of it until you got here."

"You didn't have to tell me that," Viello replied, rolling down his window for fresh air.

"You realize that I'm sticking my neck out a mile for you," he berated her. "Sutton is going to be mad as hell when I drive up with a fugitive every cop in this end of the state is hunting. The only reason he may let you stay is because his drug manufacturing business has taken off and he needs more help to run it."

"I agreed to sell crystal meth, not cook it," Burke protested. "I had a half-brother who got burned to death a few years back when a batch exploded on top of his kitchen stove. Just smelling the fumes would make me high as a kite when he was cooking. It would be safer working with your bare hands mixing arsenic to make rat poison."

"You don't have a damn thing to say about what you'll be doing, unless you're ready for me to let you out on the road so you can hitch-hike out of here. We both know you'd be picked up by the law and back in jail before you could even get your thumb up."

"I'll do anything to hide out at Sutton's place until things cool off and I can get out of the state," Burke fired back. She gave her answer a little more thought before adding, "That is, anything except screw the boss and the workers."

"I can promise you that the way you smell right now won't tempt Sutton, Fuller, or me to take you onto the petate," Viello replied with a crooked-tooth grin. "That is, unless you are offering us the pesos. All of us have limits on what we'll do for free."

Chapter 33

Cole, Connie, Mandy, and Buddy had just gotten home from Sunday early service on New Years Day and were starting a second pot of coffee when Dave Barnett pulled into the driveway in his old Taurus.

Mandy ran out the front door and flew down the steps to greet him, while Connie glanced through the window to get a quick look at Wideout 24. "Good looking boy, Cole," she observed. "I don't see any tats, piercings, dreads, or a skin head. He looks like a keeper to me."

Dave gave Mandy a quick kiss, following her up the steps onto the porch and through the front door, shaking hands with Cole, high-fiving Buddy. He trailed her across the room to be introduced to the attractive woman smiling at him.

"Nice to meet you, Ms. Balfour," the young man said, somewhat taken back by the wide, green eyes that seemed to read everything about him in a nanosecond.

"I'm Connie to Mandy and her friends, Dave, so you don't need to be so formal with me. I've heard some very nice things about you, and I'm glad to finally have this chance to get acquainted with the Covington football star. The editor of your paper, Virginia Thompson, happens to be a close friend of mine."

Connie chatted for a few minutes with Dave, then turned to the Cole. "Honey, let's slip into the kitchen to see if the coffee's ready, and let the young folks get caught up on what they've been doing."

Dave watched the older couple clear the living room, turning to Mandy to comment, "There are some things you failed to tell me about Connie. She's pretty hot for an older woman, a lot younger and more athletic looking than I expected her to be. She's easy to talk to. It's not hard for me to see why your dad's dating her."

"Is this what I'm going to have to put up with every time you come around a pretty woman?" Mandy inquired, half joking, half annoyed.

"Nope," Dave replied. "But when we had the conversation about Connie, I never pictured the lady I just met. I really like her."

Dave reached into his pocket and pulled out a tiny box clumsily wrapped in silver paper. "Let's talk about something else. Here's the Christmas present that I told you I had for you."

Mandy took the gift and quickly tore off the shiny paper, revealing a tiny box. She snapped it open, finding a silver ring crested by a heart-shaped blue gemstone. "A birthstone ring!" she exclaimed, "With an opal for October, the month I turned sixteen and first met you."

"You really like it?" Dave's question went unanswered, as Mandy threw both arms around his neck, taking his breath away with a deep, sweet kiss that handed her heart to him.

"I have something for you, too," she said softly, reluctantly breaking away to retrieve a small ribbon-tied gift not much larger than the one he had just given her. "Now it's your turn."

Dave gently removed the paper, finding a Case pocket knife box. He opened one end and slipped out a stainless steel lock back knife with a single blade, holding it up to the light to reveal the engraving on one side. Two lines of ornate script read, *To Wideout 24—Love Always, Red.*

"Do you really like it?" Mandy asked.

"More than you'll ever know," he replied, wrapping her up in his arms.

*****

Mandy and Dave had left for Norma Patton's party, and Buddy was off and away in the neighborhood with his friends, as Cole and Connie kicked back on the sofa and turned on the TV, hoping to catch a football game, but finding nothing of interest.

"I feel sorry for Dave, being thrown in with all of Mandy's friends and not knowing a single one of them," Cole commented as he flipped through the channels and settled on an old movie.

"I think he'll do fine," Connie replied, taking a sip of tea. "Kids used to be shy, but it's a whole different world today. They're much surer of themselves than we were at their age."

Cole remembered something he wanted to show Connie, getting to his feet. "Hold on while I get some old pictures out of the hall closet." He returned carrying a crumpled brown cardboard box which looked as if it had been retrieved from the basement of a museum.

"Guess what Pastor Tom found when he was cleaning out a storage room in the back of our church? It's a box filled with photographs taken during the 20's, 30's, and 40's, right on up through World War II.

"A lot of the church members in them are hard to identify, but fortunately, someone had the foresight to write names and dates on the backs of many of the photos. Tom loaned the collection to me because it includes several pictures of Grayson family members, including my grandparents."

Cole gently set the box on the coffee table, rubbing his hands together to knock off the dust, then pulling out a brittle manila envelope containing two 8 x 10 glossy black and white photos. "I never cease to be amazed at how sharp some of these old pictures are."

He lifted the one on top, handing it to her carefully by the edges. "This is the picture that caught my attention, the one I want you to look over closely. I think you'll be surprised when you see who's in it."

Connie took the glossy sheet carefully, studying it for a minute before commenting, "Now don't tell me the names yet. Even though I'm not absolutely certain about the man and woman, I think I recognize one of the girls, though I must say that she looks quite different in this picture than she did the last time I saw her. I believe the other two girls are deceased."

"I'm not surprised to hear that she looks different," Cole laughed. "That photo was taken almost seventy years ago. I doubt that she still has pigtails and wears a ruffled pinafore. Ready to take a stab at whose family you're looking at, or do you need a few hints to get started?"

"What's the prize if I get it right with no help?"

"Dinner at Bucky's Burgers with one of Courtland County's favorite personalities."

"I should have known big-spender Grayson would come up with something like that. But despite the chintzy prize, I'll tell you who I think it is. It's Bryce and Francis Goode and their children, photographed sometime around the early '40's."

"How in the world did you pick out Bryce and Francis?"

"There's a Trib file copy of their obituary pictures. They died quite a few years back. The three girls are their children, Mary Alice, Margaret, and Nancy.

"Now, as far as the boys go, I believe that the oldest and tallest is Jack, who was killed in a logging accident back in the '70's. The middle one looks a lot like young Vernon. But I'm stumped by the little one who looks like he has Down Syndrome. Who do you think he is?"

"You tell me," Cole answered. "It looks like he's a year or so younger than the one we both think is Vernon. I was unaware of a Downs child in the Bryce and Francis Goode family until I saw this photo. That's why I wanted you to look at it. I always thought there were only five children: Mary Alice, Margaret, Nancy, Jack, and Vernon."

"The boys in the photo look like they're somewhere between five and seven years," Connie replied, continuing to study the photo. "The one we think is Vernon has his arm around the smallest one, like he's protecting him."

"I've never heard anything about this youngest boy," Cole commented, taking the picture back to look at it again. "I would go right to the authority and ask that question if I didn't know Vernon's temperamental personality. He would probably go off if I brought this up. The older two girls are dead, but what about asking the youngest, Mary Alice?"

"Too late for that, I'm afraid," Connie answered. "She developed Alzheimer's and has been in a nursing home for several years. What about your mother-in-law?"

"Jane didn't move to Courtland County until after World War II," Cole replied. "The one other person who would know is Bayse Dillon, but he's got a short fuse, too. I don't know whether I want to get him stirred up."

"Go ahead and ask him if you're up for it, Sheriff. If you can get a straight answer without getting your head handed back to you, I'll give you a prize, maybe a chocolate shake at the DQ."

"You're the one starting to sound like a cheapskate now."

"I learned from the best," Connie replied, moving in to snuggle closer.

*****

"How did the New Year's Day party turn out?" Emily asked Norma, as she walked into the living room and tossed her keys on the coffee table. "I stopped for dinner at Sal's to be sure all of your guests had cleared the premises before I came back."

"I think the party was a big success, based on the noise level, and the way those kids went after the food," Norma replied. "None of them seemed to be in any hurry to leave.

"A few of my JV volleyball players brought dates from out of town, and I was really impressed by one boy in particular, Mandy Grayson's friend, Dave Barnett, from Covington. It did my heart good to see how well those two hit it off. I worried about Mandy at the start of the school year, but now she's turned into a very cheerful, happy young lady."

Emily went to the refrigerator, took out a Coke, and popped the top. "Marlene was my waitress at Sal's tonight. She told me something that happened earlier in the week that I find curious and a little worrisome.

"Marlene said that two men she'd never seen before came in for dinner on Wednesday. They both seemed to be quite familiar with this area, and they talked about people living around here as if they knew them, but they never dropped any names. One of them made a remark that it was nice to see younger folks renting farm houses way out in the country, like the two lady school teachers on Carter Creek Road."

Norma dropped the magazine she'd been lazily thumbing through to give Emily her full attention. "Something's not right, Em! How could those two know so much about us, that we teach school and share a house out in the boondocks? We don't put any personal information on Facebook, or anywhere else, for that matter. And why in the world didn't Marlene ask who they were and why they were so nosy?"

"That's exactly what I asked her. She said she didn't try to pry anything out of them because they made her feel uncomfortable. She didn't stick around any longer than necessary to take their orders, bring their meals, and hand them their checks. She was surprised when they left her a big tip."

"I find the thought of strangers knowing our living situation and talking about us as unsettling as you. This old house has always seemed like a cozy nest, a wonderful place to get away from the pressures of our jobs. Now it's beginning to feel like a frontier cabin. Couldn't Marlene have gotten their names from either their checks or credit cards?"

"They both paid in cash. The only other thing she told me was that one of the two men vaguely resembled Jay Leno." Emily finished her drink, tossing the can into the recycling box by the door before going upstairs, leaving Norma to feel, for the first time, that their home might be less a secure sanctuary than an exposed outpost.

Chapter 34

"We're pushing our luck trying to make two batches in one day, particularly on Friday the thirteenth," Carl Viello groused to Lew Fuller, as the two emptied over-the-counter decongestants into a ceramic dish, crushing the pills with a pestle before transferring the powdered ephedrine mix into a glass beaker. "The boss will be back before long with another big supply of cold medicine."

"We need that woman in here to help right now," Fuller replied, wheeling around and walking toward the adjoining room of the old log house now converted into a meth lab. "She ducks out of here to sit around and watch television whenever she gets a chance, like she's a guest at a luxury spa." He returned minutes later, trailed by Jolene Burke, who was looking quite different with her formerly long blonde hair cut short and dyed a dark brunette color.

"What the hell do you want me to do now?" she snapped. "Don't think that because Sutton's letting me hang out here for a few weeks you can start shoving all of the dirty work off on me."

"Shut up, and get some cans of engine starter fluid off the shelf," Fuller commanded. "I want you to take it outside on the table and add the ether into this beaker with the powdered cold medicine. That dissolves it and strips the binder off the ephedrine. Then you need to pour that mixture through a coffee filter into this other beaker.

"Throw the filter full of white sludge into the trash can when you're through, and let the filtered liquid in the second beaker evaporate. What you'll have left is a lot of white powder which contains all of the good stuff. Bring that back inside to me as soon as it's ready. One other thing, don't go sniffing that starter fluid or light up a cigarette while you're working."

Burke grudgingly carried the supplies outside and cautiously began the ephedrine stripping and filtering process. Meanwhile, back in the house, Viello was tearing small lithium batteries apart with pliers, extracting and collecting small pieces of the metal.

Burke returned with the beaker of concentrated ephedrine powder within the hour, complaining of a splitting headache. Fuller brought in a canister of anhydrous ammonia, setting up an apparatus to let it drip slowly into the beaker containing the combined ephedrine powder and lithium, watching the mixture quickly turn to a blue-black color.

The lithium began to react with the ammonia, boiling powerfully and almost uncontrollably, until finally the metal was fully dissolved. Viello slowly added water to quench the reaction, and the three took a deep breath, relieved that nothing had gone wrong.

"I don't mind telling you, I get nervous as hell every time I start adding ammonia in with the lithium," Viello confided. "Get too much of a reaction going and you can spew hot, caustic shit all over the place."

He took a softer tone with Jolene to explain the rest of the process. "The next step is to let the mixture evaporate at room temperature. Then you take the white meth oil paste, add ether to dissolve the meth, and throw away the crap on the bottom.

"After that, you bubble hydrochloric gas into the beaker to produce the meth crystals and run the batch through another coffee filter to remove the excess liquid. When it's dry, you have crystal meth collected in the filter ready to package and sell to tweekers for a pile of money."

"Sounds like a walk in the park from here on," Burke commented in a conciliatory voice. "What else do you want me to do?"

"We'll let you go outside and add the ether from more of those cans of starter fluid with the meth oil to separate the good stuff from the residue," Fuller interjected. "After that you can call it a day, and go back to your resort vacation watching TV."

"Do I really have to do that again?" Burke asked. "My head's just quit hurting, and now I'm going to be inhaling that damn ether again."

"Take a break, and I'll cover for you," Viello offered in a patently self-serving offer, hoping for some companionship later in the day. Jolene might not be a Sports Illustrated cover girl, but he knew that she was the only game in town.

"Thanks," Burke replied, flashing a grateful smile that made him think Friday the thirteenth just might be the day he would finally get lucky.

*****

Viello had processed meth oil paste with a solvent such as ether at least a hundred times before, always using great care when handling volatile chemicals. Today, he performed the procedure without conscious thought, his mind far away, enjoyably previewing some uninhibited sex in the hours ahead. It was like the lyrics in an old song, the girls get prettier at closing time.

He was not well versed in the basic sciences of physics and chemistry involved in making crystal meth. After all, he had little schooling while growing up poverty-stricken in the bowels of a Mexican slum, and he had added nothing to his educational resume since illegally crossing the border into Arizona.

The only technical training he had received while living in the USA with forged identification papers was on-the-job training in illegal drug production.

Viello began the task at hand, standing on a remnant of wool carpet beneath the work table to cushion his aching feet, pushing aside the 115 volt trouble light and large can of varnish solvent he had used the day before while working on an automobile wheel bearing.

He emptied the first can of starter fluid into the beaker, then the second. Without thinking he stopped to scuff his feet, clad in cheap new shoes, on the carpet below. Then he reached across the table to push the trouble light further out of his way.

A spark of static electricity, created by friction between wool carpet and synthetic shoe soles, leapt from Viello's hand to the grounded trouble light, instantly igniting the ether fumes in an explosive ball of fire. Meth oil paste and shards of glass flew at Viello's face, blinding him as his clothes combusted, leaving him futilely screaming for help at the top of his lungs.

The overheated container of solvent ruptured and exploded, the impact mercifully knocking Viello unconscious, his entire body now engulfed in flames. By the time Lew Fuller, Jolene Burke, and the just-returning Irv Sutton heard the explosion and rushed to him, frantically unloading an arsenal of fire extinguishers into the toxic fireball that had once been Carl Viello, he was lying on the ground, dead and barely recognizable as human.

Fuller and Burke stood in stunned horror, incapable of comprehending what had just happened to the Mexican. Only Sutton could muster his composure, quickly and calmly taking charge.

"Burke, help me roll him up in a tarp. Fuller, bring your truck over here and we'll load the body in the bed. I'm going to get the tractor with the backhoe, and meet you out at the pit where we've been burying all of our toxic waste. As soon as I can dig a deep enough hole, we'll get him in the ground and covered up with dirt. No one will ever know what happened."

"What about saying a prayer for Carl before we do that?" Burke asked, still in a state of shock.

"You can do that on your own later," Sutton snapped. "A county mountie or a fire truck may be showing up out here before you know it, and we need to have everything squared away before they get here. Otherwise, we're all in one hell of a lot of trouble."

"What do we do if the law starts asking about Viello?" Fuller nervously asked. "We can't just say he's moved out of town."

"Who's Viello?" Sutton answered with a sardonic smile. "A wetback who sneaks into this country with no legal documents and then drops off the face of the earth will never be missed by anybody."

*****

Buddy pulled his bicycle up beside Mikey as the two rode along the shoulder of Route 615, following Carter Creek on its meandering journey downstream. "I wish I'd gotten a new twenty-four speed for Christmas. I'm having trouble keeping up with you on the hills."

Mikey was clearly pleased to hear that. "You can really cover the ground on this thing. I was just checking the computer, and we've come eight miles, doing fourteen miles an hour since we started. We're almost out to the Meyer farm."

"Let's ride another mile and stop at the bridge," Buddy suggested. "I don't want to go much further. We're getting out near Psycho's place, and the old man warned me not to go anywhere near it again."

The boys pedaled on before stopping at the bridge spanning Carter Creek, getting off their bikes to stand at the railing and stare over the side, watching several large carp swimming around in the shallows below. Buddy broke the silence to ask, "If you were on a hunting trip out in the middle of nowhere, and ran out of food, would you eat one of those things?"

He never got an answer. A loud boom in the distance echoed off of the mountain sides, reverberating more faintly each time, followed by a faint plume of smoke, curling upward before dissipating in a cross-wind high overhead.

"Did you hear that explosion?" Mikey asked excitedly.

"Hell, yes," Buddy answered. "You'd have to be deaf not to hear that. Do you know where that smoke is coming from?"

"Somewhere on Psycho's property?"

"I'm pretty sure it is. Maybe he finally got what he had coming. I wouldn't care if he got blown up."

"Shouldn't we haul it back to town as quick as we can and tell your dad what just happened?"

"Yeah, that's probably what we should do, but we're not going to. The old man let me know back in October that he had better not catch me out here again. He'll find out what happened when one of the neighbors dials 911, and that way I won't catch any grief. Now let's get the hell out of Dodge before he or one of his deputies shows up."

"Your dad, your call," Mikey replied, wheeling his bike around, quickly clicking through the gears to lead the way home at top speed.

*****

Tank got the call from Tammy while running patrol near the Montgomery County line, whipping his cruiser around toward Route 615, picking up the story as he drove.

"The Meyer family said that smoke is still coming from Irv Sutton's property, but not as heavy as it was right after they heard the explosion. Tom and Lily were both working outdoors when they heard a booming noise that sounded like something had just blown up, and then what sounded like a man screaming something that sounded like, Auxilio! Auxilio!"

"Did they try to get closer for a better look?"

"Tom said he would have driven over to see if he could help, but that Sutton had been the neighbor from hell since he first bought the place, and Lily didn't want him going anywhere near his property. Tom told us that when Sutton first moved in, he put up a sign on the edge of his land warning, 'Enter Here and You Will Be Shot.'"

"He's a sweetheart," Tank commented. "Cole and I had a run in with him not too long ago, and I thought I might have to waste a load of buckshot on him to protect the boss. I'll drive up to his house and try to find out what's going on, if I can get past the gate. You better believe I'm going to be damn cautious."

"Do you want back-up?"

"Let me see what the situation is, and I'll let you know pronto. Don't go running off for cup of coffee until you hear back from me."

Tank reached the private road leading up to the Sutton house, turning in on the gravel road and taking it slow, then checking back in with the home office. "Tammy, just so you know, I'm coming to the bend up ahead where Smiley has set up his toll booth. Glad we replaced the shocks on this car last month, 'cause this road ain't nothing but one big washboard."

He was not surprised when he rounded the turn to find the gate closed and padlocked, and Irv Sutton nonchalantly standing beside it like he was collecting tickets at an amusement park entrance.

Tank ran his window down, calling out, "Good afternoon. I'm out here to check out a reported explosion and fire. Neighbors thought they heard a man calling for help."

"Everything's under control, deputy," Sutton replied flatly. "A can of gasoline got knocked over and exploded when it hit a hot engine block. No property damage to speak of, and nobody hurt. I came down her to wait for you to show up, figuring one of my nosy neighbors would be calling the law."

"If you don't mind, I'll drive on in and look around, so I can write up a 911 follow up report," Tank replied pleasantly."

"Not today, deputy. I told you that everything's under control here. That's all you need to put in your report. No need to waste your time."

"Don't tell me what I need to report," Krupski shot back, doing his best to control his temper. "I want to look around."

Sutton knew it would not be wise to continue baiting the officer, even though he would have enjoyed doing so. He had just played the winning hand, and it was time to walk away from the table with the money. No judge would issue a search warrant permitting the deputy to come onto his property without due cause, and justification was no longer anywhere in sight.

No one would ever know of the fatal accident, with Viello's charred corpse now buried six feet under ground, the grave marked only by scrub pine and locust seedlings that Sutton had hurriedly shoved into the rocky soil. Sutton was certain that he had dodged the bullet again. All he needed now was a good replacement worker, one who was green card challenged, and who could quickly be trained to take over a dangerous job.

Chapter 35

"Honey, I'm home!" Marvin called out to his wife as he came through the front door, tossing his coat on a nearby chair. "I've got some great news, and we're going for dinner at the Outback in Roanoke to celebrate."

"Throw some steaks and shrimp on the barby, mate," Polly replied in her best impression of Aussie slang. "Who would have ever expected such a treat on Friday the thirteenth? What's the good news?"

"We've just been awarded the contract for that new stretch of Route 697 east of Marion. There's a year's worth of work for our company by the time we straighten out all of the curves and make the cuts and fills that VDOT specified. Best of all, we should make a nice profit on this contract, unlike some of the others we've had to take recently. I'm thinking of the Route 642 debacle last year where we ran into nothing but rock, and the company took a bath in red ink."

"I take it that VDOT has announced this contract award through their web site," Polly commented. "I suppose that all of the area newspapers will cover a story about a local company getting some much-needed work."

"I'm certain that they will," Marvin replied. "Publicity is good for any business, including ours."

"And you have no concern about someone digging into the background details of how our small company came to get the order against some aggressive competition during a recession, a time when everyone's battling for orders?"

"We shouldn't be having this conversation, Polly," Marvin worried, trying to keep any sign of annoyance or concern from his voice. "It serves no good purpose. I don't know what transpired behind the scenes politically to result in ME&P winning the contract, and I'd rather not delve into that. I just want to celebrate our good fortune."

"I understand, dear," Polly agreed. "We'll focus on the wonderful news, and I won't bring up the award process again."

As they left the house, Polly recalled something she had intended to remind her husband earlier. "Don't forget that you have a Board of Supervisors meeting coming up on Monday evening.

"You told me earlier that one of the items on the agenda was the WindEnerG project to build those wind turbines on the Goode property. I know that there's a big flap about the access roadway construction and preliminary site preparation going on."

Polly did not see Marvin wince at the way her conversation had segued into a very unsettling part of his life. As he picked up his coat, he realized that he had lost his appetite for a tasty mesquite grilled Outback steak.

*****

Millard Freeman dialed up Johnny Carper, a former member of the Virginia House of Delegates, and now one of the most influential lobbyists in Richmond, taking only a minute for pleasantries before launching into the purpose of his call.

"Johnny, what the hell happened on that VDOT contract for the Route 697 project near Marion? I thought that Freeman Roadway Construction had the inside track. That's what you told me the last time we talked, right after all the bids were submitted."

Carper had known that he was going to get a call from Freeman, a big contributor to Republican candidates running for office in Virginia, one who expected quid pro quo from state government officials he'd helped get elected. FRC had been a dominant player in highway work in southwest Virginia for many years, and there had been few lucrative contracts let in recent months. FRC was now as hungry for business as any of its many smaller competitors.

"Millard, I swear to God, I was just as surprised as you were when that contract was awarded to ME&P. I was in close touch early on with a few key people who were involved in evaluating the bids, and none of them gave me a heads-up that a small company had the inside track."

"Lobbyists don't get paid big bucks for allowing their clients to get blind-sided like this," Freeman snapped. "What do you plan to do about it now?"

Carper dug deep for his most apologetic and conciliatory tone before replying, "Millard, we can't do anything now to make VDOT reverse their decision. I can go to work and try to find out if anyone pulled any strings to help steer the award to Mountain Excavating and Paving."

"You do that," Freeman commanded brusquely. "I want to know."

"I'll get on it for you. It's going to take some time to uncover what happened, but I'll call in some chits I have with insiders at VDOT, and get back to you when I find something out."

"Don't put this on the back burner," Freeman ordered tersely. "I'll be waiting to hear from you."

*****

We've got company coming to town," Connie informed Cole as the two sat eating lunch in the corner booth of the DQ. "I think that you're going to be called on to help with the hospitality."

"I'm half afraid to ask who it is, and half afraid not to," Cole replied, reaching out to rest his hand on hers.

"Ever hear of COT? That's an acronym for an organization of hard-core conservationists called 'Conserve Old Trees,' and they take tree-hugging to a whole new level. I heard from a newspaper buddy in Roanoke that activists are planning a demonstration to prevent the removal of more old trees on the top of Indian Ridge as part of the wind farm construction project."

"What's the ETA for this bunch, and how many will be showing up, according to your source?"

"Apparently they're keeping all of that info to themselves. I'm sure COT is savvy enough to know that WindEnerG security guards are already patrolling the posted Goode property and that the sheriff's department will be called out to arrest them for trespassing if they're caught before they can sneak into position."

"My guess is that they'll show up some time within the next month, certainly before the end of February. That's when the tree cutting will go into high gear according to the project schedule.

I wouldn't be surprised if quite a few activists show up. Think you'll be ready to handle a demonstration with national media coverage?"

"I'll deal with it if and when it actually happens. If you look at my track record, you'll find that I don't waste much time planning for hypothetical future events."

Connie opened her eyes wide, commenting, "I'm rather surprised to hear you say that, Cole, but it's certainly your prerogative to ignore what I consider to be a credible heads-up that activists are heading this way. After all, keeping the peace in Courtland County is why they pay you the big bucks.

"As for really important future events, I hope you'll take a more thoughtful approach. Check my track record, and you'll see that I do make plans. The time is coming when I'm going to want to know your intentions."

Cole bit back a laugh, replying, "This is turning into the kind of conversation I would have expected between your father and your boyfriend when you were graduating from high school."

"Dad's been gone for quite a few years, but when it came to making plans for the future, he set the bar pretty high. And you know very well that apples don't fall far from the tree."

"I'm starting to realize that. I guess that there's no turning back now, is there?" Cole asked, slipping close to put his arm around her.

"You wouldn't want to even if you could."

"You got that right."

Chapter 36

Mandy walked into the bustling New Court High gym early on Saturday morning, happy to see that a number of school friends were gathered in noisy groups, ready to join her in signing up for the girls' varsity and JV cross country teams.

She was pleased to spot Ms. Patton standing across the room, proving the school grapevine was as reliable as ever, and that Coach Patton might soon be helping her master a new sport.

Assistant school principal and cross country head coach Joe McCallister got things started by calling out in a voice trained to shake distracted teenagers into full consciousness. "Ladies, may I have your attention? It's time to get things started."

Mr. McCallister had been raised a Southern gentleman, and he knew how to charm an audience, particularly one made up entirely of females. It certainly didn't hurt that he still had the dark-haired good looks and crooked smile of the hot quarterback who had taken New Court High to the state championship two years running, the most successful era in the school's football history.

"I'm glad to have such a good turnout this morning for cross country season kick-off. We've won the district championship the past two years as most of you know, and I'm glad to see many of you who have already lettered back today.

"One change we're making this season to strengthen our program is the addition of a dedicated coach for the JV squad. Ms. Patton, who coached a number of you on the JV volleyball team this past year, has volunteered to take on this assignment. So, in just a minute, I'm going to have the varsity follow me to the far end of the gym, and we'll leave Ms. Patton to get things started for the junior varsity.

"We have seven races scheduled this season, followed by the Pioneer District championship. Our schedule includes a couple of schools in the Roanoke Valley with good cross country programs that will show us how well we stack up outside the Alleghany Highlands.

"We have a great tradition to uphold again this year, ladies, and that means a lot of hard, gut-busting training ahead. So if you're ready to run your way into the record books, let's get started. Good luck to each of you. Varsity, follow me. JV's, stay here with Ms. Patton."

Beth Jackson turned to Mandy to comment quietly, "Darn! I like Ms. Patton, but I was hoping we'd have Smokin' Joe this season." Mandy smiled, knowing better than to risk a reply that might be hurtful to her favorite teacher and new coach if she should overhear.

Coach Patton was no slouch herself when it came to athletics. Like Joe, she'd left her name on a plaque or two in the school trophy case, as the strikeout artist on the girls fast pitch softball team. In her NCHS track shorts, with her ponytail sticking out of a "Life is Good" ball cap, she clearly walked—or ran—the talk.

"I plan to be out on the cross country course with you at every practice," she announced. "If I can hang with you guys during training runs, I'll develop a good feel for what you're capable of doing in competition. We're going to train hard and win our races because we're going to be in better shape. We will refuse to settle for second."

Beth put her hand over mouth and said softly, "Do you think she's really going to push us that hard at practice?"

"I think Coach Patton's going to run our butts in the ground, and that's what we need," Mandy whispered. "Dad preaches that the way you practice is the way you'll compete."

After the kick-off ended, the gym went dark, and the girls headed out the door and on their way home. Mandy and Beth lingered behind. They stopped in the girls' locker room, where Beth fell into in a long-winded cell phone conversation with her new boyfriend.

"Are you finally ready to go?" Mandy inquired impatiently, opening the locker room door and entering the hallway a step ahead of her friend. She froze in her tracks, causing Beth to bump into her from behind.

The lights were off throughout the building, but Mandy could see the New Court High varsity and JV coaches standing at the far end of the darkened hallway under the illuminated *Exit* sign, locked in an embrace. She quickly stepped backward, pushing Beth into the restroom, putting her finger to her lips.

"What's going on?" Beth whispered. "Is anything wrong?"

"Lower your voice," Mandy urged. "If I tell you something, you promise that you'll never breathe a word about it to a living soul? You have to swear to me that you'll keep it a secret."

"I promise."

"I just spotted Mr. McCallister and Ms. Patton making out at the end of the hallway. I ducked back out of sight before they saw me. They're totally clueless that anyone else is in the building."

"Mr. McCallister was kissing Ms. Patton?" Beth squealed, her eyes wide. "I thought I saw him staring at her one day when he didn't think anyone was looking. I know there's a school policy that forbids teachers getting involved with their students, but I'm not sure whether it applies to other members of the faculty."

"I don't know either," Mandy replied. "That's why we're going to stay here for a few minutes before we go back out there."

"Who would have thought that Ms. Patton and Mr. McCallister would have something going on?" Beth exclaimed. "I wish I could post something on Facebook, but I gave you my word."

"And don't you ever forget it," Mandy admonished. "It might get both of them in trouble."

After waiting another minute or two, she opened the door again and glanced down the hall to be sure the building was now deserted, then both girls quietly stole out of the locker room and left the building.

Chapter 37

Dave was up early on Sunday morning, burnishing the shiny red Honda Rebel 250, observing that the tires showed little wear despite the bike's age. Some deep scratches in the metal frame reminded him why his cousin had sold it to him.

Eric had laid the bike over in loose gravel while home from William and Mary on Christmas break several years earlier, suffering a painful, slow-healing case of road-rash on much of his right arm and leg. He parked the motorcycle in the family garage under a canvas cover, never to ride it again.

Dave had heard his mother voicing her concerns about his purchase the night before. "Lowell, if our son has an accident while riding that thing, I'm going to hold you responsible. I read about people getting hurt on motorcycles all the time."

His dad's response had been typical. "Patty, I'm completely confident our son can handle that little bike safely. I had one about the same size when I was his age, and I still have all of my parts. Everything works just as well as it ever did, wouldn't you say?" Dave knew he was in the clear when his mother fired a pillow at his dad, her concern turned to amused annoyance.

Dave saddled up and made his way through the neighborhood, out of Covington and onto the highway, a spare motorcycle helmet bungeed to the seat back. He had timed the trip so that he would arrive in New Court after the Graysons were back from church, although the frisky bike wanted to go faster than the fifty mile per hour speed he intended to maintain. The cool February air on his face made him glad that he had worn a balaclava and warm gloves.

The morning was bright and sunny, but a few dark clouds in the west reminded him of the weather forecast for possible late afternoon thundershowers moving in from Tennessee. Still, there would be plenty of time for a Sunday date with his pretty girlfriend, and a return home ahead of any rain. It couldn't get much better than that.

*****

Mandy had just finished breakfast when she checked her cell phone and discovered a missed call. Seconds later, she had Dave on the phone, inquiring, "What's up?"

"Are you stealing Bugs Bunny's line?" Dave laughed. "I called to tell you that I have a new toy, something I bought last week. You'll never guess what it is."

"You just said that I'll never be able to guess, so why don't you save us both some time and go ahead and tell me?"

"I'd like to ride over to New Court later today and show it to you. Will you be home around noon?"

"I'll be here right after church lets out. Do you want me to pack a lunch? It's going to be sunny most of the day, and we could go somewhere around here for the first picnic of the year."

"Fried chicken, potato salad, and watermelon?"

"Nope. PB& J's and Cokes."

"Close enough. I'll see you a little after twelve."

"And you still won't tell me about the new toy until you get here?"

"I'll give you one clue. It has two wheels."

"A Harley?"

"Close. That's all I'll say 'til I get there."

Later that morning, Mandy sat in the dimly lit sanctuary of New Court United Methodist Church, between her father and brother, simultaneously listening to Pastor McFarland's sermon and studying a beam of sunlight passing through a stained glass window to paint a rainbow on the floor below. She glanced frequently at her watch to check the time, certain that it must have stopped.

Tom paused several times as though wrapping up his talk, but each time launched off again to make another point. Just when she had given up all hope, he drove home his central message and closed his Bible.

The congregation rose to sing all five verses of *Nearer, My God, to Thee*, leaving Mandy with the perception that somewhere in the cosmos the master clock had ground to a halt, and she would never again see either the blue sky overhead or Dave Barnett's boyish smile. But then the cosmic clock lurched into motion following a brief benediction, and the congregation filed out of the sanctuary.

Mandy was back at home in her bedroom changing into faded jeans when she heard the sound of a vehicle pulling into the driveway. She made it to the window in time to see Dave climb off a shiny red motorcycle, then jog toward her front porch and up the steps, two at a time.

She pulled on a long sleeve jersey, slipped into her sneakers without taking time to tie the laces, and ran down the steps to open the front door, almost bowling Dave over as she threw herself against him.

He wrapped her in both arms, lifting her off the floor to kiss her before slowly lowering her to the floor, laughing, "That was worth freezing my face off for the last hour. I'm so glad to see you!"

Mandy could see from the corner of her eye that her dad was sitting on the far side of the living room, trying his best to bury his head in the Sunday paper and tune out everything going on in the open doorway.

"Daddy, Dave's here," she exclaimed awkwardly, as if her father had just entered the room.

"So I noticed," Cole replied. He got to his feet and crossed the room with a smile and an open hand to greet red-faced Wideout 24. "Dave, how are you doing?"

"Fine, thank you, sir," Dave replied, releasing the sheriff's daughter to shake Cole's hand. "I just rode over here on my motorcycle to see y'all," he added awkwardly.

"Let's all go out and have a look at it," Cole replied. "Then I'll get back to reading the Sunday paper, and let you two have some time to get reacquainted, if you haven't already."

Buddy joined them as they stood looking over the sporty Honda Rebel. "How fast will it go?"

"About 70 miles an hour. That's a lot faster than I plan to run it," Dave replied, well aware of the protective father standing beside him. He quickly changed the subject, asking Cole, "Is it OK with you if I give Mandy a ride around town? We'll stay off the main highway. I have a helmet for her."

Cole paused to give the request careful consideration. "I suppose so, but I only say that because I used to ride my Harley with her mother on the seat behind me. You two be careful, hold the speed down, and watch out for cars and trucks pulling out in front of you.

"And keep an eye on the weather. The forecast is for a band of heavy rain to move through this area late today, and it's no fun riding a motorcycle on wet roads. We'd all feel better if you were home before it starts coming down."

*****

"I hadn't noticed how many more of those clouds had started to move in," Dave observed, turning his head to make himself heard as the young couple rode toward home late in the afternoon. The sky was a dark gray by the time he pulled his motorcycle into the driveway, and Mandy climbed off.

"I've had a great time with you today, but you need to get on the road right now," Mandy insisted, attaching her helmet to the seat back. She put her arms around him, asking anxiously, "Would you pull over and call me somewhere along the way to let me know everything's OK? I'll be on pins and needles until I'm sure you're home safe."

"Don't worry about me, I'll be fine," Dave replied. He called back from the end of the driveway, "Love you," before pulling out onto the street and accelerating away, noticing the water droplets starting to pepper his helmet visor. Now he wished that he had listened to Mandy when she had urged him to get started for home an hour earlier.

He was barely outside the town limits when the sky opened up, and he found himself riding through a driving rain at low speed, water thrown up from under his wheels to spray out on either side. He steered close to the double yellow lines where there was less standing water, still plowing through puddles deep enough to make him worry about hydroplaning.

Dave tried to stay calm, rationalizing that the rain couldn't continue to come down so hard for long, telling himself that he had only thirty miles to go and that he'd soon be home. He glanced up at the sky, but got no reassurance that things would get better. The clouds seemed to be as dark ahead of him as back toward New Court.

He did not know that a wet-weather spring near the Courtland County line had suddenly come to life, gushing water out of the hillside and across the highway, completely hidden from the view of motorists descending the steep hill and entering the curve below. Nature could not have created a better trap for a man on a motorcycle.

Dave spotted the rivulets at almost the same instant he felt both wheels lose traction, desperately fighting to keep the motorcycle from laying over on its side, but completely helpless to prevent it. Bike and rider went down, sliding across the pavement and through the gravel, the front wheel of the Honda slamming into the brush strewn bank.

Everything seemed surreal. One moment he had been riding toward home, and the next, he was wrecked and lying on the wet ground with his left leg trapped under the bike. Instinctively he reached for the ignition switch, turning it off before moving.

He struggled to push the bike up far enough to free his leg, then remained sprawled on the dirt in the rain, trying to assess his injuries, cautiously moving one limb at a time. A small patch of bloody road-rash showed through his torn Levis, and pain shot through his hip from impact with the pavement, letting him know that he had not gotten off unscathed. But despite the severe bruise and the burning sensation from a severely skinned hip, the pain seemed not a great deal worse than some he had felt after taking hard hits in football games.

Dave could see that the bike had not fared as well, its damaged front wheel wedged into the dirt and shale that had brought it to a stop, clearly no longer rideable.

He fished his cell phone out of his pocket, relieved to find it still worked, holding it under his jacket out of the rain while running through his options. He knew that the first thing he should do was dial 911, but confident that his injuries were not serious, he didn't want an embarrassing accident to end in an ambulance ride to a hospital in Roanoke.

He knew that he could phone home, report what had happened, and ask his dad to come get him. But there was a down side to that. His mother would be certain to pick up the phone, and he would have to explain to her that he had wrecked the motorcycle. That would surely cause her to max-out on the anxiety scale.

He decided to take the third alternative and call Mandy, to see if her cool-headed father would be willing to drive across the county to pick him up. The sheriff would certainly know how to downplay a minor accident. Cole could provide the help he needed to get things back under control without any unnecessary drama.

Mandy picked up on the first note of her ring tone, exclaiming, "Dave, I've been waiting to hear from you. Where are you now?"

"I'm out at the county line, and I've got a problem with my bike. Please take a deep breath and chill out—I'm fine. I just laid the bike over on a slick patch, went off the road, and busted up the front end. Do you think your dad would be willing to come out here in his truck and help me with my bike, maybe haul it back to town?"

"I'm worried more about you. Are you sure you don't want to go to a hospital and get checked out? What if you've broken a bone?"

"Mandy, I'm not hurt. The rain seems to be letting up, and all I need now is a way to get my bike moved to a place where it will be safe until I can decide how to get it fixed. I'll try to find a ride back to Covington after that."

"Dad and I will be there as quickly as we can. See if you can find a dry place to wait until we get there. I'm glad you aren't hurt bad. I love you, Dave."

"Back at you times ten, Red, and thanks for everything you're doing for me. For what it's worth, I believe the storm is over, but I have to admit that I'm starting to feel pretty chilly."

Dave was still inspecting the wrecked motorcycle when he recognized Cole Grayson's pickup speeding toward him, Mandy sitting beside her dad, Buddy in the seat behind them. He gave them a friendly wave, trying to conceal the shivers of impending hypothermia, as the three jumped out of the truck and came toward him.

He saw that Cole was carrying an armful of dry clothes and a blanket. Mandy ran up and threw her arms around him, paying no attention to the water saturating every stitch he had on.

"Son, get over there behind that oak tree and change into these, then wrap the blanket around you" Cole instructed. "Mandy, pour him a cup of hot coffee out of my thermos. He's starting to shake."

"What do you want me to do, Dad?" Buddy asked, trying to pitch in.

"Help me stand his bike up, and then you hold it. I'll back the truck up close, and when Dave's ready, the four of us will try to horse it up the tailgate ramp into the bed. It may look like a small bike, but I bet it will take all four of us to handle it. I'm guessing it weighs close to five-hundred pounds."

Dave quickly returned to join them wearing Cole's Levis, shirt, and jacket, and the four managed to work the Honda up the ramp into the truck, securing it upright.

"Are you going to take me back to New Court," Dave asked.

"We'll do better than that by you, son," Cole replied. "It's not that far to Covington, and we'll drive you on home. By the way, have you called your folks?"

"No, sir."

"Call them right now, tell them what happened, and let them know we'll be there in forty-five minutes. Mandy, Buddy, and I don't like to drop in on people unannounced, particularly when we're delivering an injured son and his busted-up motorcycle."

Dave climbed into the back seat of the truck beside Mandy and made the phone call. “Mom, I’m on the way home right now. I’ve had a problem with my bike, and Sheriff Grayson is bringing me back to Covington in his truck. Mandy and her brother Buddy are with me.”

His parents’ reaction was all that he expected and more, and he knew that worse awaited him when he got home. Finally, he managed to reassure his parents and end the call. With his arm around Mandy, both wrapped snugly in the blanket, he started to feel warm again for the first time since his immersion in the winter rain.

*****

“We can’t thank you enough for bringing Dave and that darned motorcycle home,” Dave’s mother Pat exclaimed to Cole as she, her husband Lowell, and daughter Karen, greeted the Graysons.

She turned to her son, her tone changing, and continued, “I never wanted you to buy that motorcycle from your cousin, and I should have put my foot down, but I won’t get into that again. I’m just glad you’re home.”

“How bad are you hurt?” Lowell inquired, noticing his son wearing different clothes than those he had on when he left the house that morning.

“Mostly scrapes and bruises on my hip,” Dave answered calmly. “I’ll run upstairs, clean up, and be right back.”

“I guess there’s one thing good that’s come from this,” Lowell observed, as Dave left the room. “We’ve been looking forward to meeting you, Mandy, and now we have the pleasure of also getting to know the rest of your family. We hope you’ll stay for a while. Karen, maybe Buddy would like to see your new skateboard ramp out back."

Pat walked beside Mandy, commenting, "I must say, you're even prettier that the picture Dave showed us. No wonder he picked you out of the crowd at the football game."

*****

Mandy and Dave walked back into the kitchen carrying the leftovers from an enjoyable improvised family picnic in the living room. "Anyone want anything else?" Dave called back to his parents and Cole.

"How about some coffee?" Pat asked Cole.

"No thanks," he replied. "It's getting late, and I suppose we'd better get on the road for home. It's not the way any of us would have chosen to meet today, but it's certainly turned into a nice visit."

"We seem to have lost Buddy and Karen," Mandy observed. "Where in the world do you think they are?"

"Those two still have the lights on in the driveway, and I've heard them having a big time showing each other skateboard tricks on a couple of plywood ramps I built for her," Lowell answered. "I'll round Buddy up for you and tell him that if he doesn't get moving, he'll miss the bus back to New Court, and he'll have to hitchhike home."

A minute later, Buddy came inside, following closely behind Dave's pretty thirteen year-old sister. "Do we have to go right this minute?" he asked. "Karen's got some really sweet jumps out behind the house, and she was showing me some cool stunts."

Dave turned to Mandy, and winked. "I should have warned you about Karen. Boys are always coming by the house to hang out with her. She's a magnet for skateboarders."

"I hope all three of you will come back soon," Pat said, watching Cole, Mandy, and Buddy climb into the truck.

"Bring your skateboard the next time," Karen called out, watching the three Graysons pull away into the foggy night.

"I'm glad that I finally got to meet the rest of Dave's family," Mandy commented, as they turned onto the main highway. "I really like his parents and sister. What do you think of them, Dad?"

"I think that they're extremely nice folks," Cole replied. "They certainly appreciated what we did for him."

"How about you, Buddy, what did you think of the family?" he inquired, looking into the rear view mirror to carefully observe his son's face.

"I think that they're nice," Buddy replied.

Mandy turned her head to glance back at her brother, noticing for the first time the conspicuous black scribbling on the back of his left hand. "Who in the world marked on you with a Sharpie?" she inquired curiously.

"Karen wrote down her email address," Buddy mumbled, radiating sheepishness.

"Good grief!" Cole exclaimed. "Here we go again."

Chapter 38

Cole gathered his deputies in his office for the mandatory Monday staff meeting, waiting until all were seated with a mug of coffee in hand before starting the session with his customary opening. "Glad y'all could make it this morning."

"The group of COT activists that we've been looking for slipped into town during the night, according to Vernon Goode. Conserve Old Trees is a national organization with excellent publicity skills, as you know from watching their stunts on national television. I'm sure that by now that all three TV stations in our area have been tipped off and are ready to run with the story.

"Vernon told me that several demonstrators got past the WindEnerG guards posted on the mountain, and a couple of women have set up camp in the top of a big oak in a portable tree stand. He's really torqued off, knowing that undoubtedly they were aided and abetted by Bayse Dillon, since they had to cross his land in order to get up the mountain into the construction site.

"Jake and Tank, you two draw the assignment of evicting them. I'd say the odds are ten to one that you'll end up having to arrest them for refusing to leave, but be professional and use the minimum force possible to get them off the property. Accusations of excessive force and a lot of drama between you and the demonstrators are the last things this town wants to have aired on the evening news. I know I'm asking a lot, but see if there's anyway you can climb that tree and convince them to come down without a big ruckus." Cole waited for the collective groan from both deputies.

"You're asking me to climb a hundred feet up a tree and swing through the branches like Tarzan, risking my butt in order to come across on TV like a southern gentlemen?" Tank asked, rolling his eyes. "Jeez!"

"That's the general idea, but the most important thing is to avoid having anyone get hurt," Cole continued. "I wouldn't ask you to do it if I didn't have confidence that you can work things out safely.

"Moving right along, I've posted the daily patrol duty assignments on the bulletin board for all of you. Keep your eyes open for leads that may help us nab the big dogs running the illegal drug trade around here. Our investigation's dragged on way too long."

*****

Jake wheeled the patrol car along the gravel road running up the spine of Indian Ridge toward the site of the future wind farm, commenting to his partner, "This assignment of clearing out a couple of young ladies squatting up in the top of a tree should be right up your alley.

"I recall your telling me that after high school you worked as a climber with a tree service. You said that you liked the money, and being able to work out of doors. Swinging around in the tops of trees with a chain saw hanging around your belt must not have bothered you at all."

"Yeah, but that was then, and this is now. Climbing is something that requires good physical conditioning, and I haven't spent much time doing that kind of thing in recent years. Kristen tells me to turn down the jobs when people call our house wanting me to take out trees for them. She thinks a man with a wife and a young family shouldn't be doing such chancy work, straddling a limb ninety feet off the ground and running a chain saw with both hands."

"Way too risky for me," Jake agreed. He pulled the patrol car over onto the shoulder of the road, adding, "Let's do like the boss asked us and try to handle this brouhaha calmly. Whether you're dealing with flies or people, you get better results with honey than vinegar."

"That's a big 10-4 on keeping it friendly," Tank agreed. "When I pay a call on those two girls in their tree house, I plan to charm the pants off of them and talk them into coming down without giving us any problems."

"Not a good choice of words, ol' buddy. I know what you mean, but you probably wouldn't want to repeat that remark in front of Kristen."

A television crew for the local NBC affiliate was already on site when the two deputies arrived, their camera focused on the upper limbs of a tall white oak. A conspicuous portable tree-stand, constructed of an aluminum pipe frame and a slatted floor shrouded by a snap-on canvas cover, was precariously anchored near the top. Two attractive young women could be seen peering out through an open flap in the front, watching to see what was happening on the forest floor below.

Jack Sanders, project manager, and Junior Goode strode toward the two deputies, Junior speaking loudly as he approached. "I want these damn hippies arrested and hauled out of here right now. They're trespassing on private property and delaying WindEnerG crews from clearing out the trees. This project is on a tight schedule and time is money."

"Hold on a minute, and let's try to handle this without putting on a big production for the television crew," Jake replied calmly. "We don't want to turn this into a reality TV show. Give us a little time and we'll take care of the problem for you without stirring up a lot of excitement."

It didn't take Tank long to lace-up his boots, strap on his climbing spikes, grab a coiled climbing rope, and start working his way up the tree limb by limb with professional skill, approaching the portable tree-stand from the rear until he was standing directly behind it. He quietly moved around to the front, stuck his head through the flap, and said with a friendly smile, "Good morning ladies. We can't go on meeting like this."

Both emitted startled yelps of surprise, then the blonde let out a nervous laugh while the dark-haired one replied calmly, "You're late, and your dinner's cold, deputy."

"Nice comeback," Tank acknowledged. "Since we're starting off on such a good footing, let me offer you a deal you can't refuse. Come down out of this tree peacefully, bring your little tree house with you, and we'll all pose for the TV camera crew. Everybody will walk away safe and happy.

"My partner and I will get credit for evicting you, and you'll get an interview with the local TV stations and fifteen minutes of fame on national TV as COT activists protecting the old trees on this mountain. The developer will get to move on with his site preparation work, which happens to have been legally approved."

"And if we refuse to leave peacefully?" the blonde inquired.

“Then I have to arrest both of you and physically get you down out of this tree. None of us will come away looking good. I have a wife about your age, and two young kids. Undoubtedly, you have families back home. Let’s don’t go there.”

The woman turned to discuss the offer with her friend. “What do you think, Marlene?”

“The deputy makes a persuasive case for us leaving peacefully, Carla. He seems like a pretty cool guy to me. If he weren’t married, I’d probably go out with him for a beer after we get back on the ground.

“Call Tom and tell him we’ve decided to come down peacefully, and we’ll join up with him and the rest of the team after we have a chance to talk with the TV reporters.”

Tank stepped back from the door of the tree stand, commenting, “Thanks for being sensible about this whole deal, ladies. For what it’s worth, my partner and I are both on the same side as you and the COT organization. We think it’s a damn pity that the Courtland County Board of Supervisors approved a wind farm on top of this beautiful mountain, but that’s strictly off the record.”

He swung his leg around to dig a gaff into the trunk of the tree, ready to descend, adding a final comment as he turned away. “Pretty impressive, the way you climbed way up here and hoisted that tree stand in place without any climbing gear.

Tank smiled at the brunette, adding, “You seem pretty cool yourself, Marlene. If I were still single, I’d take you up on that beer.”

*****

Millard Freeman leaned back in the executive's chair in his corner office at Freeman Roadway Construction to take the call from Johnny Carper, listening carefully to the lobbyist on the other end of the line. "Millard, I've finally found out what happened to steer that Route 697 roadway contract to Mountain Excavating and Paving.

"It's a pretty complicated deal, but here's the Cliff Notes version. The owner of ME&P, Marvin Clark, sits on the Courtland County Board of Supervisors. A politically influential Chicago based company, WindEnerG, submitted a request to the board for permission to build a hotly contested wind farm on top of an undeveloped mountain within Courtland County, and Marvin cast the swing vote that got it approved.

"Apparently, some strings were pulled afterward, and the Virginia Department of Transportation awarded the Route 697 contract to ME&P under the guise of a small business incentive program.

"The bottom line is that the roadway contract award appears to have been a payoff to Clark for his vote. Any ethical person would agree that that the manner in which the contract was awarded has the stench of a backroom deal, but it would be very difficult to prove that the contract is quid pro quo."

"Are you trying to tell me that I have to roll over and take this?" Millard snapped. "Apparently you don't know me as well as I thought you do."

"I'm not trying to tell you what to do, Millard," Johnny replied defensively. "I'm just saying that it will be not be easy to prove that Clark didn't vote his conscience in approving the WindEnerG construction permit, and that VDOT did anything out of line in awarding a road contract to a struggling small business."

“I’m going to look into this further with my lawyers, and find out what action I can take,” Millard promised. “I assure you that I’m going to give Mr. Clark some serious trouble, whether I can turn this highway contract around or not.”

Chapter 39

Connie leaned across the table at Sal's to speak quietly to Cole. "I'm glad you could join me for lunch today on such short notice. I wanted to tell you about the phone call I got this morning, with a charge of malfeasance against a local businessman and public official.

"An anonymous male tipster told me that the *Trib* should investigate and print a story on how Marvin Clark used his position on the Courtland County Board of Supervisors for personal gain.

"This informant alleged that Marvin sold his vote approving the WindEnerG petition to build on Indian Ridge in a deal that resulted in his company getting the VDOT contract for a stretch of highway near Marion."

"Who do you think the informant is, and why in the world would he want to stir up something like this?" Cole inquired. "Marvin's well respected in the community, and he has no enemies around here that I'm aware of."

"I'm sure that the man has an axe to grind. He may or may not live around here. Be that as it may, I wonder if there could be something to his allegation. I know much of what he told me to be true.

"We already knew that Marvin voted to approve the WindEnerG petition. And when I checked the records, it turned out that Marvin's paving company, ME&P, did recently receive a VDOT contract for construction of a new stretch of Route 697 that a number of companies were vying for."

"So what do you plan to do with this information?" Cole asked, reaching across the table for her hand.

"I've already got Megan digging into it. She'll be driving to Richmond in the morning to talk with the VDOT people who awarded the contract. When she gets back, she'll try to arrange a private discussion with Marvin Clark, and see what information she can pry from him."

"I hope for Marvin's sake that he's done nothing wrong," Cole replied. "But if he did land that contract as a payoff for his vote, his tail is definitely in the wringer, and county approval of the wind farm petition may have been illegal. The Lord only knows how this might get sorted out in the courtroom. I think Marvin stands to lose some sleep over the matter whether he's innocent or not.

"Speaking of Megan, has she been able to turn up anything new on the Mother's Day murders?"

"Megan's been hard at work sorting out whether a religious faction even stranger than the Branch Dravidians may have some connection to the murders. She's discovered that a secret cult has been practicing around the Appalachian region for at least the last decade. It's called the Fellowship of the Righteous, and it's made up of a group of radical men who have their own take on how to deal with women's sinful behavior.

"She's sure there are people who know all about the FOR cult, but she hasn't been able to find a single one who will talk to her. Everyone she's approached is completely intimated, like a lot of people were during the heyday of the Ku Klux Klan. It's all a little too close to home for their comfort."

"Hard to believe that same kind of terrorism is still going on today," Cole commented. "You'd never dream it could exist in this day and time."

"It does in some places, and we're out to roll back the rock and expose the people hiding under it," Connie replied with a wry smile. "I guess it's time for me to be getting back to the office, honey. Thanks for lunch."

*****

"Good morning, Mr. Clark," Megan began, setting her coffee cup on the desk. "Thanks for taking my call. I wonder if it would it be possible for me to make an appointment with you this afternoon to discuss a feature story I'm working on for the *Courtland Tribune* focusing on successful small businesses in southwest Virginia?"

"I think I can work a short interview into my schedule, Miss Porterfield. What about 3:00? Could you be a bit more specific about what you'd like to discuss with me?"

"Certainly. I know that that Mountain Excavating and Paving was recently awarded the contract to build a new section of Route 697, and I'd like to learn how small businesses can win their matches against bigger companies."

There was a brief moment of silence before Clark spoke again, and when he did, he sounded a bit less enthusiastic about the free advertising for his company. "I see. I thought the thrust of your article might be how a small company such as mine provides good jobs for people in our region."

"I certainly want to cover that," Megan continued, "but I also wanted to provide insight into how an entrepreneur succeeds against bigger competitors by cutting costs and increasing efficiency. I know that you personally must be very good at multitasking to be able to run a complex business while juggling duties as an elected official. I thought this would make a very compelling story."

Clark was ready with a quick response this time. "I would prefer to limit our discussion to the ME&P road building business, and defer the part about my duties as a Courtland County Supervisor to a later date."

"That works for me, Mr. Clark. Another story I'll be delving into in the near future targets the construction of the wind farm on Indian Ridge. I hope to talk with each member of the Board of Supervisors, including you, at that time. Thanks for working me in this afternoon. I'll look forward to meeting with you at 3:00."

Clark hung up the phone but remained motionless at his desk, contemplating why Megan Porterfield had just worked the subject of a controversial wind farm into her request for an interview concerning his road construction business. It was probably just a coincidence, but to him, a very unsettling one, particularly when an aggressive young reporter was involved.

*****

Jake Johnson led Boyd Dillon and Junior Goode, both in handcuffs, into the Courtland County Sheriff's Department and straight down the hall to Cole's office. Dried blood trailed from Boyd's battered nose. Junior also showed signs of a recent dust-up, his knuckles skinned, and a puffy black mouse half closing one eye.

"Here's Rocky Balboa and Apollo Creed, boss. Like I told you on the radio, they were duking it out in the parking lot behind Sal's. I had to physically restrain them and put them in cuffs to break it up.

"They talk a lot of trash, but after watching them through the first round, I'd have to say that neither's ready for a main event. I charged both of them with fighting and disturbing the peace."

"What the hell is this all about?" Cole coolly asked the two men. "Neither of you has ever been in trouble with the law before."

"You already know the answer to that, Sheriff," Boyd fired back. "Go look at the top of the mountain up above my place. The Goodes have has let that damn outfit from Chicago come in here and cut all those two-hundred year-old trees, and now the ridge looks like a plucked chicken, as ugly as a mountain top strip mine."

"We're helping to build a source of clean energy," Junior retorted. "The land has been in my family almost as long as those trees have been growing, and we can use it for any lawful purpose we want. No Dillon is going to tell us what we can or can't do with it."

"You two disgust me," Cole interjected, his mood darkening, as he looked from one to the other. "I suppose it doesn't mean a damn thing that you two played on the same championship football team back in 1975 and were good friends, despite all of the Goode-Dillon feud bullshit that was going on even back then.

"I used to go to all the high school home games on Friday nights. Boyd, I still remember you laying the key block that sprang Junior for a last minute touchdown to beat Clifton Forge for the district title. I looked up to both of you then, but I sure as hell don't feel that way about either of you right now."

"Do you want me to go ahead and book them for assault?" Jake asked.

"I ought to let you do that," Cole answered, glaring at the two handcuffed men who had become a lot less belligerent under the heat of his anger. "But I'll tell you what I'm going to do.

"Take the cuffs off them. We're going to let them go this time without pressing charges, based on their clean records up 'til now. They're both free to walk out of here with no pending felony this time."

"But I want both of you to hear me out. If you're ever hauled back in here again, you'll seriously regret it. There won't be another pass. You'll go before Judge Janette, and I promise that he will drop the hammer on you."

"I want each of you to go back home tonight and talk to your old man. Tell Vernon and Bayse that I'll be coming around to see each of them, and we're going have a come to Jesus session and get to the bottom of what started the Goode-Dillon feud. Let them know that the sheriff says their goddamn fighting has come to an end."

Chapter 40

Cole and Connie sat in a booth at the Outback in Roanoke, studying the menu over glasses of cabernet sauvignon and shrimp appetizers. The waiter returned to take their order, and as soon as he was gone, Connie inquired, "Would it spoil the romantic mood if I were to tell you something I found out earlier today about the Mountain Excavating and Paving road contract?"

"Just asking that question brought me back to the real world," Cole replied with a laugh. "Now you might as well go ahead and fill me in."

"I've already told you that Megan said Marvin Clark was very nervous when she interviewed him about his company winning the Route 697 highway contract. Since then she's met with the contracting officer at VDOT, and she told me that he's equally uncomfortable in discussing the matter.

"Megan thinks that a disgruntled competitor may have someone digging around in Richmond, trying to uncover possible collusion.

"She thinks the same person who made an anonymous phone call to me may be starting to spook both the contracting officer and the contractor. Innocent folks shouldn't get tensed up when reporters start asking questions."

"People get rewarded for filing whistle blower claims that lead to convictions in cases of fraud in federal and state government business," Cole observed. "If anyone discovers collusion between the two parties involved in this contract, they could blow the top off of a can of worms and make some big bucks."

"And then what would happen with the highway construction contract and the wind farm construction permit?" Connie asked.

"You'd need someone with more legal expertise than me to answer that one. My guess is that both projects would come to a screeching halt while the district attorney sorted things out," Cole replied.

"Now that we've kicked that can around, can we get back to small talk between a man and his favorite woman?"

Connie held her fingers to her lips and then reached across the table to touch his. "That works for me."

*****

Maurice Jones took a second look at the driver to be sure his eyes had not deceived him, then traveled a short distance down the road and wheeled around to begin trailing the green Chevy SUV up the highway.

Jolene Burke looked quite different now with her short, dark hair style, but he had instantly recognized her. There was something distinctive about her facial features that made her stand out, as though Mother Nature had puzzled over whether to make her male or female before finally deciding to withhold a Y chromosome.

Maurice dropped back even further to avoid detection, still keeping her in clear sight. Jolene was like a bird dog now, leading him to the covey of meth dealers in the area. Outing them to the sheriff would give him bonus points with the law, a short prison sentence which might even be suspended, and his ticket to a new life. No more living in the shadows and cringing each time a car with flashing blue lights sped by.

Maurice watched her turn from the highway into a gravel pull-off circling a grove of trees beside a stream. He knew that was an angling hot spot, where fisherman lined up each time the Virginia Department of Game and Inland Fisheries dumped another load of hungry trout straight from the hatchery. He slowed to pull off the pavement behind a tangled patch of green briars and wild grape vines, almost out of sight from the highway, yet with a clear view of the SUV up ahead.

He had not been parked long when a dark panel truck cruised slowly down the road, pulling in beside the Chevy, braking to a stop. Maurice took the binoculars from the seat beside him and stepped out of his car to determine the make and model of the truck and the identity of the passengers. He deciphered the license tags on both vehicles, writing the numbers on a scrap of paper, bending at the waist to quickly push the slip securely down into his shoe.

Maurice straightened, preparing to turn back toward his car, but before he could take a step, a gloved hand clenching a short piece of iron pipe delivered a crushing blow to the back of his head. He collapsed to the ground like a sledged steer, lying motionless, sprawled face-down in the dirt. His assailant dropped the club, rifling Maurice's pockets to take his car keys and wallet, leaving him for dead in a widening pool of blood.

The assailant broke off a tree branch and used it to sweep away his foot prints as he retreated toward Jones car, climbed inside, and pulled out onto the road. A short distance away, he swerved the vehicle off the road and down into a deep ravine, leaving it concealed under a thick stand of rhododendron. The man pushed the door open and got out of the car, threw Jone's keys and wallet as far as he could into the brush, then disappeared quickly into the deepening twilight.

*****

Cole and Connie were sharing a slice of cheesecake when his phone rang and he heard his second shift dispatcher, Darlene Cumbo, on the line. He knew that his dinner date was over even before she briefed him.

"Sheriff, we received a call reporting an unconscious man lying on the ground on Route 658 in the north part of the county. There's no one else around, and no motor vehicles are in the area. The rescue squad's been dispatched and Jake's on his way."

"You think the man may have been walking beside the highway and got hit by a car?"

"No, sir, this was clearly no accident. The victim is a young African-American male with a deep wound to the back of his skull. The caller saw a short piece of iron pipe covered with blood and hair lying on the ground beside the victim."

"Anything else?"

"That's all we know so far."

"Let me know as soon as Jake and the rescue squad get there."

"10-4. We should be getting a report from Jake very soon."

"Darlene, I'm going to hang out here in Roanoke until I hear from him. I expect the EMT's will be transporting the man to the Lewis Gale Hospital in Salem, and if so, I want to talk with the ER staff.

"Call Tank at home and tell him to get out there and give Jake a hand in securing the crime scene and collecting evidence. Call the state police and report everything that's going down. We need for them to dispatch someone to the crime site to assist in the investigation and expedite the lab analysis of the weapon."

"Will do, Boss. Sorry to break up your romantic rendezvous."

"Not your fault, Cumbo. Keep me informed of any new developments with the victim."

"Why? Do you think you know who he is?"

"I believe we've finally located the elusive Maurice Jones, but it may be too late to do any good for either of us."

*****

Jake knelt under the headlights of his patrol car beside the man sprawled on the ground, placing his finger tips over the carotid artery to check for a pulse. Feeling a weak but steady heartbeat, he said a silent prayer of thanks.

Jake reached into his pocket and took out his clean handkerchief, gently applying direct pressure to slow the bleeding from the gaping wound, noticing that he could not only see the fractured bone but also tissue inside the skull, his stomach lurching queasily. Seconds felt like hours as he looked up the road anxiously, watching for the rescue squad to appear in sight. He gently shifted the victim's head to clear his airway, and waited.

Finally, he heard the sound of a siren in the distance and saw the flashing lights of the approaching ambulance. Jake waved his arm to flag the driver, never moving from the victim's side as the truck rolled up beside him and two EMTs stepped out to take over.

"God, I'm glad you're here, Danny," Jake exclaimed. "This man's dying."

Dan O'Brien, and his partner, Caitlin Watson, went to work with the precision skill of a crack medical team, with sparse communications and no wasted motions.

"Hold that sterile pad in place, Cait, while I bandage his head."

"Looks like the bleeding's under control now, Danny. I'll get the collar on him to protect his spine before we set him onto the stretcher."

"Jake, give Cait and me a hand lifting him and turning him."

"OK, guys, we've got him immobilized, receiving blood and oxygen. Cait, keep a close eye on the monitor on the way. He's got critically low blood pressure and an irregular heart rhythm. We need to get him to the ER, stat, before he shuts down. Let's roll!"

Jake dropped his head in silent prayer as the ambulance pulled out, lights flashing, siren wailing, in a life or death race to the hospital in Salem.

Tank Krupski watched them fly past as he rounded a turn and saw the lights from Jake's patrol car ahead, pulling his vehicle off the road and into position so that his headlights also illuminated the crime scene, now circled with yellow tape.

"Grab your camera and start taking pictures," Jake instructed his younger partner. "I've already secured the weapon for the state police crime lab, and I've been searching for footprints and tire tracks, without much success."

"One thing you need to do first—call Darlene and tell her to get word to the boss that the rescue squad should be arriving at the Lewis Gale ER within thirty minutes."

"This was supposed to be Cole's big night on the town in Roanoke with Connie, wasn't?" Tank inquired.

"Yeah, but that's shot to hell now. I'm afraid that all of us are in for a long night."

*****

Cole sat with Connie in the ER waiting room, quietly talking and watching the news on a wall-mounted TV for an interminable length of time before a doctor in scrubs approached them.

"I'm Dr. Eugene Ballard, the ER resident on duty here tonight. Dr. Bowman, a neurosurgeon, and other members of our medical staff, are still working with the patient. Sorry to keep you waiting for so long."

Cole and Connie shook the doctor's hand, and then the two men stepped aside to confer. "I don't know whether he's going to make it or not," Ballard advised. "The prognosis at this time isn't good."

"We're dealing with major cranial trauma, trying to control the swelling and relieve the pressure on his brain. He's breathing with the aid of a ventilator, and his cardiac function is still unstable. The biggest factors in his favor are his youth and excellent physical condition."

"It's likely that he's sustained some degree of permanent brain damage, and if he survives, it might be in a comatose state. The assailant who struck him intended to kill him, in my opinion, and he almost succeeded. Can you tell me the victim's name?"

"My deputy sent me a crime scene photo, and I'm almost certain the victim is a fugitive we've been looking for named Maurice Jones. We won't be absolutely positive until we check his fingerprints against the ones we have on file."

"The EMTs who brought him here reported they could find no personal ID anywhere in his clothing," Dr Ballard observed. "But our staff did find something when they prepped him for surgery. Tucked down in his shoe was a slip of paper with two license tag numbers scrawled on it. I'll turn that over to you now, if you wish."

"Most definitely," Cole replied. "We'll run a quick check on those numbers. This could give us the lead to nail the mean son of a bitch who did this."

"I'll get that for you right now. Do you and Ms. Balfour plan to wait here, knowing the condition Mr. Jones is in?"

"No, I think we'll be on our way home now. I'm sure she'd like to get back to her office and file a story for the paper, and I expect to be up all night working on the case. Could you let me know if there's any change in Mr. Jones' status?"

"We have some very strict rules regarding patient privacy, Sheriff, but I'll leave a note in his file to ensure that you get any information you need."

Cole returned to Connie, asking, "Not the ending to the evening we both were looking forward to, is it?"

"That's pretty small stuff in the grand scheme of things," she replied slipping her arm through his. "The thing we'll both be praying for is that Maurice Jones recovers without permanent brain damage. You told me earlier that he was raised by a single parent. That means that somewhere there's a mother who loves him."

"You're undoubtedly right. For the record, Mr. Jones also has other people in his corner who are pulling for him, including you and me."

*****

Cole made a call to the Virginia State Police headquarters in Salem as soon as he got back to his office, finding that Lt. Tom Bowman was still on duty. His friend had already been brought up to speed by the trooper working the crime scene with Jake.

"Looks like things are heating up around here," Tom commented. "Trooper Stanley told me that the assault victim was in critical condition when your deputy arrived on the scene. Have you been able to identify him?"

"After seeing a photo, I'm almost positive that the victim is the man we've been searching for, Maurice Jones," Cole replied.

"I believe Jones may have been spying on some bad actors engaged in a drug deal at the time he was struck from behind. But something very positive has come from his foolishness or courage. He's succeeded in giving us information that fingers two big dogs in the drug business.

"We've just finished running the plate numbers he wrote down before he was mugged. One set of tags was issued to Irving Sutton, a Courtland County resident with prior felony convictions including assault and drug dealing.

"The other plates were issued to Floyd Greene, a Richmond resident, who also happens to have prior convictions that include running an illegal drug distribution operation."

"Fast work, Cole. Think it's time now to bring both parties in for questioning, before either one disappears?"

"I'm ready to move just as soon as you give us a crime lab report on that piece of pipe. With Jones hanging to life by a thread, we may end up classifying it a murder weapon."

"The lab's already dusted the pipe for fingerprints, and they found it to be wiped clean. But we've detected traces of skin shaved off by a sharp edge on the end that was used as a handle. Now we're working on DNA testing. That's going to take a little time, and we probably can't afford to wait for the results before we make our move."

"We're thinking along the same lines, Tom. The Courtland County Sheriff's Department has jurisdiction for Sutton, and the Virginia State Police for Greene. Both men should be considered extremely dangerous."

"When will you make your move on Sutton?".

"Early Sunday morning," Cole replied. "I know he and his associates won't be up for a church sunrise service."

"Be careful out there," Tom cautioned.

"10-4," Cole replied. "Good advice for all of us wearing a badge."

Chapter 41

"Anyone have any last minute questions?" Cole inquired, addressing the nine deputies gathered before him in the briefing room, all wearing protective body armor and helmets. There was no mistaking the nervous apprehension on every face.

"Remember, the way we handle violent people in this kind of situation is with overwhelming force. Nothing mano a mano about how we're going to deal with thugs. I want two or three of you in position to control each person we confront. Recent surveillance leads us to believe we're only dealing with Irv Sutton and three others, but we could run into more.

"We know that he keeps guard dogs on the property, and each of you has pepper spray to deal with them. Don't hesitate to shoot the dogs if you feel you are in danger of being bitten.

"Watch out for booby traps controlled by trip wires. People in the drug business will use every means in the book to intimidate intruders and keep them away from their operations. I want us to come away today with no injuries. I'm not as concerned with the welfare of the people we're going after.

"The warrant for entering Sutton's property is based on just one thin shred of evidence, a license tag number linking him to the assault on Maurice Jones. I was finally able to convince Judge Janette to sign it despite his misgivings.

"That's why it's so important to keep your eyes peeled for any signs of drug activity or other violations of the law. I have a strong suspicion that we'll discover a meth manufacturing operation on the premises, and if so, it will permit us to conduct a full investigation of the property, even if the license tag number turns out to be a dead end."

"Most importantly, I want every one of you back here safe and sound when we're through. Now let's load up and go. Rock and roll!"

Cole and his deputies drove away from the courthouse parking lot in a four vehicle convoy, quietly passing through the sleepy town and out into the countryside, turning off the highway onto the private road leading to Sutton's property.

The lead patrol car pulled up to the locked gate blocking the road, and Cole stepped down, calling out, "Irving Sutton, this is Sheriff Cole Grayson. I have a warrant permitting me to enter your property and investigate your possible involvement in a recent assault. Come out and unlock your gate."

He waited briefly, anticipating no response, then spoke again for the record. "Note that Irving Sutton has hereby refused to obey my order to open the gate and permit us to enter his property. Jerry, go ahead and remove the lock."

The young deputy already had the necessary tool in hand, and it took little time for him to step out of the vehicle, insert the shackle of the security padlock into the jaws of the bolt-cutter, operate the long handles, and snap the lock. He tossed the broken device onto the ground and swung the gate open, calling out, "Clear."

The four patrol cars traveled a short distance up the road, fanning out to circle a compound consisting of a log house and four sheds. Cole and his deputies, holding their weapons at ready, moved from the vehicles into perimeter positions.

Cole took a bullhorn from one of his men, walked up to face the cabin, and repeated the same message delivered at the locked gate, but this time with the clear intent of being heard. "Irving Sutton, this is Sheriff Grayson with the Courtland County Sheriff's Department. I have a warrant to come onto your property and speak to you. I want you and anyone inside the house with you to step outside right now."

There was no answer, so Cole repeated the command in a louder, more imperative tone, but the result was the same. A curtain momentarily fluttered at a window, suggesting a person peering out, but then again, possibly just a phantom hand created by a puff of wind.

"If you don't come out now, we're coming in."

The words were hardly out of Cole's mouth when three pit bulls silently streaked out from one of the sheds, coming straight toward him with open jaws and bared teeth. Two deputies moved forward holding canisters in hand to intercept them, hitting the dogs with streams of pepper spray when they were only feet away. All three were stopped cold in their tracks, dropping to the ground, rolling in the dirt, pawing at burning eyes, gagging and gasping for breath.

"Sutton, you son of a bitch, now you're under arrest," Cole shouted angrily.

All hell broke loose when the log house suddenly blew apart in a massive explosion, followed by a giant fireball soaring upward, fragments of the shingle roof and log walls flying out in all directions to fill the air and rain down on Cole and his men.

"Everyone take cover!" Cole yelled. "Watch out for gunmen under the sheds or behind the trees."

"Jake, Tank, move your squads into position and start sweeping the compound, one building at a time. If anyone points a gun at you, take them out."

"Sheriff, I've spotted a man a hundred yards back of the cabin, moving through the woods on the run, trying to get away," Tom Atwell called out. "Do you want Bill and me to leave our positions and head him off?"

"Yes," Cole yelled back. "Go get him! Don't let that man give us the slip."

Deputy Bill Nelson, carrying a pump shotgun, and Deputy Tom Atwell, armed with a military style carbine, took off running, taking a line to intersect the fugitive swiftly moving ahead of them through the woods. They had closed to within two hundred feet when the runner, clad in camo pants, jacket, and cap, stepped from behind a tree, leveled his assault rifle in their direction, and opened fire.

Both deputies dropped to the ground as slugs whizzed past them, Bill feeling fragments of tree bark strike his face from a near-miss. By the time they looked up again, the man was gone.

"He's probably still heading in the same direction," Tom called out. "We can pick him up again where the creek hooks back to the south if we cut through the ravine up ahead and work our way down through the rocks."

"Be careful that we don't walk into an ambush," Bill cautioned. "One of his slugs just missed me a few minutes ago. According to my count, he only let off five shots. That means he still has twenty-five rounds left in the magazine."

Tom's plan paid off, as the deputies emerged from the ravine and suddenly caught sight of their target wading across the creek directly below them, much closer than either had expected.

"Freeze!" Tom called out.

The gunman wheeled around and got off three quick shots, bullets whizzing like lethal hornets on either side of Tom's head.

Bill answered with a load of 00 buckshot, knocking the man backward, and Tom followed with a single .223 round. The gunman dropped his carbine and slumped into the creek on his back, eyes open, staring sightlessly at the sky.

"Shooter's down, Billy. Hold your fire, but keep covering me. I'm going to check him out."

Tom advanced on the man lying in the creek, not dropping the muzzle of his carbine until certain that the gunman was no longer a threat. "You can come on in, Billy," he called out to his partner. "I can't pick up a pulse. He's been hit several times and I think he's dead. I need you to help me pull him out of the creek."

The two deputies dragged the body up on the bank, leaving it lying in the same sprawled position in which they had found it, weapon still at hand.

Tom studied the face closely. "I'm almost positive this is Irv Sutton, the one Cole wanted to arrest. He looks just like the file photo. Let's get some pictures of him before he's moved again. We're going to need photos to prove that we acted in self-defense."

*****

Cole heard the sounds of gunfire erupting from the woods, an ominous silence, and then more shooting further off in the distance. His stomach was tied up in knots with concern for the safety of Nelson and Atwell as he turned to Deputy Kincer. "Head down that way and find out if Bill and Tom are OK. Be careful."

He shifted his focus to the unfinished job in the compound, striding over to catch up with Tank Krupski's team as they got ready to search the last structure on the premises. "Find anything yet?" he asked.

"A ton of stuff," Tank replied. "We came across a 2010 Chevy SUV with license plates matching the numbers on Maurice Jones's note. We've also uncovered drug supplies, lab equipment, and a lot of haz mat trash, indicating that meth production's been going on here for a long time. We haven't found any workers yet, but we're still looking, and sooner or later we'll pull them out from wherever they're hiding."

Suddenly a shout erupted inside the shed, and a deputy stepped out. "Come in here quick and take a look at what I've found. There's a trap door hidden in the back under a work bench. It's made of plywood grouted with concrete to look like the rest of the slab. I almost walked past without seeing it."

Cole and Tank followed the officer back into the building and studied the scene. "You want me to pull the bench out of the way so we can get to that trap door?" Tank asked. "I don't see anything that looks like a trigger for explosives."

"I don't either," Cole replied. "Go ahead and move the bench, but we need to be very careful when we raise the cover. No telling what's on the other side. We could be looking down a gun barrel, or worse yet, standing in front of a homemade bomb waiting go off. This place could go up in a ball of fire just like the log cabin did."

Tank dragged the bench out of the way, and asked, "Ready for me to pop the lid?"

"First let's clear everyone out of the shed but you and me," Cole answered, looking Krupski in the eye with a wry smile. "This is why they pay us the big bucks."

"You heard the boss," Tank instructed his team. "Everybody out of here on the double and away from the building. We'll call you back in when everything is clear."

Cole waited until he and Tank were alone, continuing. "Say a prayer. Then cover me with your shotgun while I see if I can do that open sesame thing and get us into the treasure cave."

He discovered a recessed finger-hold concealed along the edge of the plywood cover, inserted his hand, and tried to lift it. It budged ever so slightly, enough to show that it was latched on that side, hinged on the opposite end.

"Aim where my hand was and try to blow the latch off," Cole instructed, stepping back.

Krupski fired with devastating and deafening results. The load of buckshot blew a hole through the cover, causing powered concrete and plywood sawdust to spray across the floor, leaving both men's ears ringing. Cole let the dust settle before putting his hand into the shattered opening and lifting again.

This time the trap door swung up and over, dropping with a bang to lie flat against the floor, exposing an entryway with a set of wooden steps leading downward. A wisp of light and the sound of muffled footsteps were the only indications of life coming from the dark corridor below.

Cole and Tank froze, pistol and shotgun pointed down the staircase. Cole called out, "This is the Sheriff of Courtland County. Come out now, slowly, with your hands behind your head, and you won't get hurt."

Tank added a bluff, "If you don't, we're going to send down the dogs."

Movement could be heard below, followed by a woman's shaken voice. "Don't turn the dogs on us. We're unarmed, and we're coming out now."

Cole and Tank watched as Jolene Burke, Lew Fuller, and two other men climbed the stairs and passed through the opening into the faint light and dusty air above, stepping out onto the concrete floor. "How many more are hiding down in your spider hole?" Cole asked tersely.

"We're the only ones," Lew replied. That goddamn Fuller ran off when he saw you coming and left us here on our own."

"Deputy Krupski, have your men read the prisoners their rights and put them into separate patrol cars. Then you and I are going downstairs to find out what kind of five-star hotel they're running here."

Cole was still waiting for Tank when Deputy Kincer rushed into the shed to deliver welcome news. "Nelson and Atwell are both safe. The guy trying to run away looks like Irv Sutton. They shot him when he fired at them. His body's still lying down there on the creek bank."

"Find Jake and tell him to go down and help them. He's been through this kind of situation before, and he knows exactly what has to be done when there's a fatal shooting involving our people. I wish they could have taken him alive, but the important thing is that Bill and Tom are OK. Sutton was determined to live his life as a badass on the wrong side of the law, and, in my opinion, he got what he had coming.

"He may not be around for us to interrogate, but I believe Jolene Burke knows where all the bodies are buried, and she looked like a wreck marching up out of that hole in the ground. She was one tough bitch to deal with the last time we had her as a guest, but this time I think she'll talk."

"Jerry, I want you to stay here and help Tank check out the lower level of this boarding house. I need to break away long enough to call the State Police and ask Lt. Bowman for help in handling all of the contaminated crap. Sutton's methamphetamine operation has left us holding more toxic waste than there is at Chernobyl."

Chapter 42

Connie and Megan sat across from Cole on Tuesday, preparing for the interview with a recorder and laptop computer on the table in front of them. "We appreciate your releasing the full story to the *Trib* before it gets out to other members of the media," Connie remarked.

"Let's make that almost the full story," Cole countered with a smile. "I can't discuss any information that might compromise the prosecution of the case, but otherwise, it's full disclosure this morning. I'll signal you when to turn off the recorder if we get into anything I construe as sensitive.

"I'm glad to break the story through you for a couple of reasons. First, I wouldn't be holding office if it hadn't been for the help of the *Trib* during the election a few years back. Second, it's pretty widely known that I have a major crush on the editor."

Connie laughed and looked at Megan. "You can see that the sheriff is a smooth operator, but I cut him a lot of slack, 'cause he's my main squeeze." Turning to Cole she suggested, "Let's go ahead and get started. Lead us through what's happened up 'til now."

"OK, but be sure to put 'alleged,' 'accused of,' and 'charged with' in all the right spots, because no one has yet been convicted of any crimes. That said, here we go. Interrupt me with questions at any time."

Cole related how a slip of paper with two license tag numbers had been discovered inside Maurice Jones' shoe, and how that information had been the catalyst in breaking up Irving Sutton's crystal meth operation.

"He was clever to put that slip of paper where no one would think to look," Cole observed. "If he had put it in his pocket, it would have disappeared the same as his wallet, which has yet to be found."

"You say that Jolene Burke cracked, and she's now disclosing everything she knows about Sutton's operation, including information about what he did after he discovered a man secretly watching one of his drug deals?"

"Correct. She's agreed to testify that Sutton assaulted Maurice Jones while he was spying on a drug delivery. Burke testified Sutton thought Jones was as good as dead after he clubbed him, rifled his pockets, and walked away.

"She also informed us that an illegal immigrant named Carl Viello, who worked with Sutton, was accidentally burned to death while he was working, and that Sutton buried him near the bottom of a waste dump on the property. The State Police recovered a badly charred body yesterday.

"What broke Burke's feisty attitude was being trapped for months. She was hiding out at Sutton's place, being treated like slave labor in his operation, too intimidated by him to run away even when she had the chance."

"Has she given up the names of Sutton's suppliers and distributors?"

Cole raised his hand to signal the discussion was now off the record before replying. "Yes, she provided key information that triggered a big drug bust that's still going on right now. The State Police and the police departments in a number of localities are picking people up, charging them with running an illegal drug distribution ring. Nothing can be disclosed until the sweep is complete."

"What will happen to the Sutton property?" Megan inquired.

"I think that it'll cost the state seriously big bucks to clean up the contaminated meth production site, and that the property will be seized and sold to recover the cost. That's pure speculation, and also off the record."

"Do you think this drug bust will put an end to the meth problem around here?" Connie inquired.

"I think we've cut the head off of the biggest snake, and meth will be a much smaller problem going forward. But as long as there are addicts willing to fork out big money to buy that poison, someone will try to supply it. We'll just keep running the dealers down and locking them up when they do. I suspect that I'll have job security as sheriff for a long time."

"What's the latest on Maurice Jones' condition?" Connie inquired.

"He's still in a coma, and the prognosis isn't good," Cole replied. "I'm praying that he'll pull through. Anything else?"

"Think that takes care of me for now," Megan replied. "Thanks, Sheriff."

"See you at lunch, honey," Connie added

*****

Megan walked through her editor's office door on Monday, dropping into the chair across from her, inquiring, "Remember that discussion we had about a religious fringe group called the Fellowship of the Righteous?"

"Sure," Connie replied. "Are you starting to think of joining?"

"Not likely," Megan replied, laughing. "That outfit is a cult flying under the radar. But I just received something from Darlene Barnes in the mail. It's an old flier she found in her late sister's belongings. Darlene believes the two carpenters working on the Mountain Blossoms greenhouse shortly before Sally's death may have given it to her."

Megan passed a wrinkled black and white photocopy of a flier announcing the time and place for a Fellowship of the Righteous meeting in Pearisburg across the desk to Connie. "Last week I Googled Fellowship of the Righteous."

"And you found?"

"Zilch. Nothing came up when I searched that name. So then I started trying different variations, and when I entered Righteous Brethren, bingo! It took me to a website for a religious cult with a mission statement calling for the elimination of sinful conduct by women. That sounds like a great cause for a bunch of men to take up, doesn't it?"

"Yeah," Connie replied. "We ladies have gotten a lot of that over the last ten thousand years. What did you do then?"

"I read the rest of their message, which sounded like the rants of wing-nut bigots. The site struck me as a little scary, although it advocated nothing illegal. I let the matter drop for a few days, and then when I tried to go back to that website, I found it had been taken down."

"You think that someone may have started to worry about drawing unwelcome attention from a police investigator?"

"I can't answer your question about why it disappeared. But I have a strong suspicion that there's some sort of connection between the murders of Sally Barnes and Betty Crowell, and the Fellowship of the Righteous. Maybe murder is one way for a male cult to eliminate sinful conduct by women. What do you think?"

"I think you should report this to Sheriff Grayson," Connie replied.

"Thanks, Boss. That's exactly what I thought you'd say."

Chapter 43

"Good morning, Sheriff," Connie said, in a faux businesslike voice. "The following conversation is just between you and me, strictly off the record, until the story is officially released."

"OK, I know that drill by heart, and I accept your terms and conditions," Cole replied, laughing. "Please continue."

"The *Trib* has been tipped off by a Richmond source that the proverbial crap has hit the fan regarding the 697 road construction contract that VDOT awarded to Mountain Excavating and Paving.

"You and I spoke earlier about whistleblowers discovering illegal conduct in the awarding of state and federal contracts. It would seem that's exactly what's happened.

"A former VDOT employee has alleged collusion between VDOT, Mountain Excavating and Paving, and WindEnerG in Chicago. He alleges that the road contract is a payoff to a Courtland County Supervisor for voting his approval of the WindEnerG request to build a wind farm on Indian Ridge.

"You told me earlier that Marvin Clark might end up with his tail in a wringer. It looks like it's time for him to place a call to a rear-end rescue service and a good law firm. I'm just standing by waiting until official charges are made, before I run the story."

"There may be nothing for you to do right now, Connie, but there's some business I need to take care of. I told you earlier about my plans for a come to Jesus sessions with Bayse Dillon and Vernon Goode, and now looks like the right time for me to invite both gentlemen to come and see me. This whole ugly mess that Marvin's stepped in didn't have to happen."

*****

Cole opened his office door for Bayse Dillon, inviting him in to take a seat, then inquiring, "Would you like a cup of coffee?"

Bayse studied the expression on Cole's face before answering, seeing a smile but sensing the dead serious attitude behind it. "I think I'll wait until after you tell me what you want to discuss with me this morning."

Cole took a seat across from Bayse, looking him squarely in the eye, and casting aside all pretense of a social visit. "I want to talk about that fight between Boyd and Junior, and all of the conflict that's gone on between the Dillons and Goodes for the last sixty years."

"The Dillons helped elect you, Sheriff. Why are you starting up something with me this morning?"

"Because I want you to know that as of right now, the feud is over. I may not get elected to another term, but while I'm still the sheriff, I'm putting a stop to it."

Bayse made a move to stand, but Cole cut him off. "Hold up a minute. I didn't arrest your son or Junior when they got into a fight last month, but I could still bring charges against both of them for assault with intent to do bodily harm, and leave them with felony convictions on their records for the rest of their lives. Is that what you want me to do?"

The glowering bear of a man sat back in his chair, seething with anger at this treatment. He glared at Cole but held his tongue.

"I'm still hoping that you and I can have a friendly talk this morning, but that's all up to you. What I want to know is this: what triggered all of the animosity and bad blood between you and Vernon?"

"That's none of your damn business!"

"I'm making it my business!"

Bayse sat impassively staring back at him without speaking until Cole goaded him into opening up. "Are both of you afraid to talk about it because it might make you look like a couple of irrational, foolish old men?"

Bayse's façade of calm shattered. "You want to know what happened, Sheriff?" he snapped back, eyes blazing. "You demand that I tell you what happened, and sit there smugly threatening to hang a felony conviction on my boy if I don't? Then, damn you, I'll tell you everything that went on."

Bayse's words boiled over in an angry torrent, while Cole leaned forward, trying to conceal his consternation at Bayse's apoplectic outburst.

"Bryce and Francis Goode had six children. Most people can recall only five, Mary Alice, Margaret, Nancy, Jack, and Vernon, but actually there were three boys, a year apart in age. The youngest one was Larry, born with Down Syndrome. Back then he was referred to as a Mongoloid, a retard.

"Vernon and I were best friends growing up, from the time we started first grade, and we'd get together and play ball or ride bikes in the afternoons after school. I looked up to his big brother Jack, who was the leader when we got together. I was big for my age even then, about the same size as Jack, but he was stronger and faster.

"I liked Larry, but I didn't see much of him, since he never went to school, and his mother kept him in the house most of the time where she could keep an eye on him. Vernon tried to protect Larry when he did come outside to play, keeping other children from making fun of him and picking on him.

"Everything was fine between Vernon and me until we got to the fourth grade. It was on a Saturday afternoon in late September back in 1944, a day I'll not forget 'til they put me in the ground.

"We were passing a football in a vacant lot near the Goode's house when Jack came up with the idea that it would be fun to ride our bicycles over to Carter Creek. There had been a heavy rain the night before, and he wanted to see how high the water had gotten.

"Mr. and Mrs. Goode were away, so Vernon took Larry along, doubling him on the seat of his bike, standing up to pedal the whole way. We got there and saw that the creek was out of its banks, muddy water rushing downstream in torrents, and we should have had the sense to turn around right then and there and go back home. But we didn't, to my everlasting regret."

Bayse hesitated, lifting a shaking hand to his face, brushing something from his eyes.

"Jack wanted to go out on some rocks and throw sticks into the creek, like we were racing boats downstream. Vernon and I went out with him onto a wet, moss-covered rock half covered by water, never paying attention to the fact that it was slippery or that Larry was following right behind us.

"Little Larry picked up a stick and tried to throw it into the current just like us, but when he did, he lost his balance and tumbled into the water. I'll never forget the terrified look on his face when he fell in, or the way he called out, 'Mama', reaching out his hand toward us." Bayse's voice broke, his eyes filling with tears and his body racked with suppressed sobs, as he fought to compose himself before he could speak again.

"Jack and I were the closest to him, and we got down on our hands and knees and crawled out trying to reach out and catch hold of him. I got my hand on the collar of his jacket, but I wasn't strong enough to pull him out of the water. Vernon screamed that he was going for help, and he ran toward a farm house a long way off.

"Jack moved over beside me, leaning out to grab the front of Larry's coat. That's when he slipped on the wet moss, slid off the rock, and went down into the muddy water over his head. He came up gasping for breath, struggling to stay close to the bank and not get swept away.

"He managed to grab hold of a low-hanging tree limb and pull himself out, but he was not the same boy he'd been. Jack was paralyzed with fear, huddled up on the bank like he was shell-shocked, and shaking all over.

"I yelled to him to come help me, telling him I couldn't hold on to Larry any longer by myself, warning him that the current was about to pull me into the water. Jack looked at me, but it was like he was in a trance, paralyzed.

Bayse paused again, as if dreading the ending of his own story, wiping at the tears streaming down his cheeks.

"Tree limbs were washing down the creek, caught up in all of that fast moving water. A big log swept by, spinning around close to the bank, and it struck Larry and knocked him away from me. I lost my grip on his collar, and he was carried off downstream. I caught a glimpse of his face, and I still remember today exactly how he looked. I ought to. I've seen that sweet boy's terrified face in a hundred nightmares since."

"I just sat there in a stupor like Jack, knowing Larry was gone, and nothing I could do would bring him back.

"Vernon finally got back with help, a farmer and his son in their pick-up truck, but it was way too late. Larry's body wasn't found until a couple of days later, after the water had gone down. It was snagged-up in tree roots near a bend in the creek a half of a mile downstream.

"Things changed completely after that. Jack was scared to tell his father how he froze up instead of coming back to help me hold on to his brother. Instead, he lied to his family, claiming that he was bringing a pole over and would have pulled Larry out of the water to save him if I hadn't let him go.

"Everyone believed Jack, including Vernon, and his parents. Bryce came to our house and told my father that he never wanted me anywhere around his family or near his home again. My father told him to get off our land.

"Jack died in a logging accident years later, taking his lie with him to the grave. There's no way I could ever prove to Vernon that I didn't let go of his brother and allow him to drown. The two of us haven't talked since.

"All I've done is to keep everything private between the two families, and see to it that when the Goodes push us, the Dillons shove back. That's the whole account, so help me God. Is that what you wanted from me this morning, Sheriff?"

Cole felt emotionally drained from listening to the old man's intense account of the tragedy. "Yes, Bayse, you've told me everything I need to know. For what it's worth, after hearing your story, I think you've been wronged by Vernon and his family. It's time to set things right, and I intend to try and do so. I hope you'll have no trouble with my doing that."

Bayse stood and turned to leave, weary but relieved. "Everything I've told you here this morning is the gospel truth, and you can tell who you will. You're a good man, Sheriff."

*****

"Do you want me to give Bayse a lie detector test?" Cole angrily shouted at Vernon Goode, the two sitting tensely across from each other in the Goode living room. "If that's what you need to believe his story, tell me now, and quit beating around the bush.

"I'm convinced that Bayse is telling the truth, and I've interrogated a hell of a lot of people. Your brother Jack is gone. We've reached a point where it's time for you to trust your instincts about what really happened."

"Blood's thicker than water, Sheriff. It's hard for me to go against what my brother told my father and now start believing that Bayse did everything he could to save Larry."

"You seemed very determined to think the worst of Bayse and hang all of the blame for your brother's death on him," Cole commented. "I'm beginning to wonder why.

"Could it be because you've second-guessed yourself a thousand times for what you did on that day? Asked yourself why you ran off toward a house a quarter of a mile away to get help when your brother was up to his neck in cold, fast moving water and every second counted? Why you didn't stay to help, and look around for something that you could have used to pull him out of that flooded creek to safety?"

Vernon's startled expression told Cole that his shots had struck home. He couldn't have imagined the sudden change in the old man's demeanor, or the way he softly, slowly replied, "Ten times a thousand and more."

"I couldn't bear seeing little Larry struggling in that muddy water, knowing in my heart he was going to drown. I started running, not even knowing where I was going, trying find help. Then I saw a farmhouse off in the distance, and headed toward it. But I knew it was too far away and that even if I found a man at home, it would take too long for me to get back to the creek with him.

"I finally made it to the house, knocked on the door with all my might, and a man came outside to see what was wrong. He called for his son, and the three of us drove over in his truck as quick as we could. By the time we got back, Jack and Bayse were sitting on the ground with their heads down, Jack wet and covered with mud like he had been in the creek himself, unable to speak to me.

"The man sent his son to round up more neighbors, then started walking the creek bank looking for Larry. Before long, there were a dozen men out there, searching along both banks of the stream. My father and mother and my three sisters got there while the search was still going on. People were carrying kerosene lanterns, continuing to look throughout the night. But Larry's body wasn't found for a couple of days, after the water finally went down.

"It wasn't until then that Jack finally told us his account of what had happened, and how Bayse Dillon had let go of Larry. You know the rest of the story.

"It made it easier for me to live with what I'd done, knowing Bayse had done something so much worse. You can imagine the hatred we felt toward him. My father went to the Dillon's house to talk with Bayse's father, and was ordered off of the property. That was the start of the Goode-Dillon feud, and we're still fighting it today."

"Are you ready now to accept the truth, that Bayse did everything he could, that he was not responsible for Larry's death?" Cole asked quietly.

"I'm beginning to come around to that," Vernon confessed. "It may take me a little more time, but what you tell me he said happened on that day is starting to ring true."

"Vernon, I told Bayse the feud is over, and I'm giving you the same message. Whatever people did or failed to do at the time, Larry drowned, and that cannot be changed. Your brother's life was far too short, but you know that life isn't fair.

"Blaming Bayse Dillon for his death is misguided and wrong. It serves only to promote endless hostility and bitterness. No amount of finger-pointing or feuding with the Dillons will bring your brother back. Get your family together and tell them that now is the time to let it go."

Vernon rose without replying, opening the door for Cole to leave. To Cole's surprise, Vernon followed him onto the porch. As they stood together in the bright sun light, the older man spoke. "Let me study on what Bayse told you, Sheriff. I promise that I'll give serious consideration to this. It may be the time for the Goodes and Dillons to lay it to rest."

*****

Cole drove out to his mother-in-law's home on Friday afternoon, finding that Bayse had arrived shortly before, the two sitting side by side on the sofa in her living room.

Jane rose to set her cup of tea on the glass-topped table, greeting him with a warm hug. She whispered, "No one in this county will ever be able to repay you for what you've done."

Cole walked across the room to greet Bayse with a friendly smile. "I appreciate your coming here today," Cole stated. "I tried to pick the most pleasant place we could get together and decided that it could only be Mama Jane's home. Then, too, I was sure that you could find your way over here."

Bayse grinned sheepishly, knowing that his affection for Jane Barker was no secret in the community, enjoying the acknowledging smile spreading across her face. "My pleasure, Sheriff. I don't yet know why you want to meet with me again, but I'm here to listen."

"I'd like to give you some news about the wind farm project that hasn't yet been reported," Cole stated. "I'm certain you'll be pleased to hear that site preparation has been stopped, as well as work on the new access road. The trees are already cut, and the site has been graded, but nothing more will be done.

"The Commonwealth Attorney has ruled that the Board of Supervisors' approval of the project is invalid due to the alleged collusion by Marvin Clark in a quid pro quo VDOT road construction contract.

"Marvin still alleges he's completely innocent and has hired a defense attorney to represent him."

"I'm terribly sorry about Marvin's predicament," Jane interjected, "But as far as the stop-work order, I say hooray!"

Bayse reached out to take her hand, agreeing, "I'm with you, Janey." He turned to Cole to inquire, "What does this mean for Vernon? He leased his land to WindEnerG as part of a lucrative long term contract."

"Only a lawyer who was directly involved in drafting that contract could answer your question," Cole replied. "I would imagine that there's a clause voiding the lease if the land can't be used for the intended purpose, possibly with an agreement for a financial settlement with the land owner if the deal falls through."

"That sounds like the best thing that could happen," Bayse stated. "Those monster turbines never get built, and the Goodes get enough settlement money to reforest the cleared part of the mountain top."

"I'll go along with that thought," Cole said. "And then the Dillons and the Goodes can shake hands and live together happily ever after."

Bayse glanced toward Jane with a smile. "Sheriff Grayson never seems to know when to quit and leave well enough alone, does he?"

Jane gently reprimanded him. "Sheriff Grayson has turned out to be the best friend the Dillons and Goodes ever had. Don't you forget that."

"I'm aware of that, Janey. You may not believe it, but Junior Goode called Boyd last night to apologize for his part in the fight. He told me that the sheriff yanked a knot in both of them, making him ashamed of the way two old teammates had turned on each other."

"Maybe some day, Bayse, you and Vernon can talk things out and make peace," Jane suggested.

"Not yet, Janey, not yet. But down the road Sheriff Grayson may be able to get two hard-headed old men in the same room and convince them that childhood best friends should patch things up, too. He's a mighty persuasive man."

Chapter 44

"I really like your choice of restaurants," Norma Patton commented to Joe McCallister, as the two sat at a table by the window in Gregorio's. "What a beautiful view of the town," she observed, gazing out into the twilight. "I've never had dinner here before, believe it or not."

"It's a favorite of mine, and I was sure that you'd like it, too," Joe replied. "It's been two weeks since we've been out together, and I want this to be an evening you'll never forget."

"You're setting the bar pretty high, aren't you, sweetheart?" Norma inquired with a laugh. "Don't forget that you're living on an assistant principal's salary. You may have to take out a loan on your Honda to make this an evening I'll remember forever."

"You're probably right, but what the heck. If I lose my car to a loan shark, I can still ride my bicycle to work. Go ahead and order the steak and lobster, and the best wine on the list."

"The best wine would be wasted on me," Norma laughed. "I'm good with the house chardonnay."

The two lingered at the restaurant long after dinner and desert, talking about things they'd never discussed before, dancing to favorite songs, having the times of their lives.

"Do you suppose we should go before they throw us out?" Joe inquired.

"I've been thrown out of better places," Norma replied.

"In your dreams, Patton," he laughed. "You were never a wild child. But let's go, anyway. I want to take you off on the next part of our adventure."

"Where?"

"Mill Mountain."

"I think your Honda is safe from the repo man," Norma laughed. "The Mill Mountain Zoo is closed tonight, so you won't have to buy tickets."

The two had the world to themselves, driving from the Blue Ridge Parkway along the winding road toward the top of the mountain. They walked up past the neon-lit star and out on an overlook cantilevered from the hillside.

Joe slipped his arm around her as they stood looking out on the lights in the valley below. "Beautiful sight, isn't it? Biggest little village in the world."

"Are you sure you aren't confusing Roanoke with Reno?" Norma asked.

"Whatever. I still think the view is incredible, and I never get tired of coming here."

"I feel the same," she agreed. "Standing here with you, a million stars overhead and one very large one right behind us, how could it get any better?"

"That sets the stage for what I'm about to ask," Joe commented. He dropped to one knee, holding a diamond engagement ring in his hand. "Norma, will you marry me?"

Norma held her left hand toward him, allowing him the slip the ring onto her finger, answering softly, "The last thing I expected when we came here was a proposal. Yes, sweetheart, I'll marry you."

Joe rose to his feet, pulling Norma to him, hearing her whisper in his ear, "Joe, you mean everything to me."

"I'm going to spend the rest of my life making sure that you never change your mind. You've just made me the happiest guy in the world."

*****

"Emily, are you still up?" Norma called out to her housemate as walked through their door shortly after midnight.

"Yes, and I'm so glad you're back," Emily replied, walking from her bedroom into the living room, wearing her college vintage sleep pants, a Redskins jersey, and slippers that had seen better days.

"Being alone late at night out in the country gives me the creeps. I would have never have been able to go to sleep until you got home. I don't hear the porch floor boards creaking and the wind moaning around the chimney when you're here. Obviously, I wasn't cut out to be a pioneer woman living alone."

"I've got something wonderful to tell you, Emily!" Norma exclaimed, holding her hand under the lamp to show the new diamond engagement ring. "Joe and I are engaged. He proposed to me on the Mill Mountain overlook just a little while ago."

"Norma!" Emily exclaimed, rushing over to hug her. "I think that's wonderful. Congratulations!"

"Thanks, Em."

"Were you surprised?"

"Sort of, although maybe I should have seen something big coming when he talked about making this an evening I'd never forget. He certainly did that."

"What about Joe's situation? You've told me his divorce won't be final for a few more weeks, and that he still has a lawyer working out the details for shared custody of his son? Does that make his proposal a bit premature?"

"We'll have to keep the engagement a secret until the divorce is final. I won't be wearing my ring outside the house until then. But we know that we're committed to each other, and that's something incredibly important to both of us."

"Well, it looks like it'll be time for me to throw a big party soon. I hope that it won't be long after the end of the school year. Hard to believe that's coming up next Friday."

"Oh, I almost forgot something. I got a phone call from that strange Mr. Platt. You remember Calvin, Joe's and Jerry's uncle?"

"How could I ever forget that weird man. What in the world did he want?"

"He was surprisingly nice on the phone, Norm. He told me that he has some beautiful azaleas he'd like to give us, if we can drive out to their farm to pick them up."

"Who'd have thought that old guy would do something so nice. When does he want us to get them?"

"He was very specific about the time. He wants us to come on Sunday right at noon. I'm glad it's early, because I wouldn't want to drive that winding mountain road to Larkspur late in the day. Does that suit you?"

"It means I won't be able to go to church, but that's not a big deal," Norma replied. "I was going to sit with some of the cross-country girls. I'll send Mandy a text message and let her know that I won't be able to make it.

"Looking on the bright side, now I won't be rushed when I call the folks. You should call your mom, too. Don't forget that tomorrow's Mother's Day."

Chapter 45

"Ready to go, honey?" Cole inquired, as Connie joined him on the front porch, slipping on a tailored brown jacket to match her knee-length beige skirt. "As always, you look drop-dead gorgeous."

"What a sweet way for you to start my day. I'm surprised that no one has come along with you this morning. I though Mandy and Buddy might be joining us."

"Buddy had a sleepover with his friend Mikey, and I suspect he'll take a cut from church service this morning. Mandy is coming over with some of her cross country teammates, and they plan to sit with their coach.

"In a way, I'm glad it's just the two of us, since we haven't talked for a few days," Cole continued, leaning in for a quick kiss. "How have you been?"

"I'm doing great, sweetie. By the way, I need to ask a special favor from you this morning. Can you take me by Bailey's Shell on the way, so I can pick up my car? I dropped it off yesterday afternoon for an overdue state inspection, and the mechanic promised to leave it locked up next to their building for me. I have a spare set of keys, so I can get inside and follow you over to church."

"No problem, love. Then you can park next to me, and we'll walk in together."

"Sounds like a plan. Just don't forget to turn right at the next light."

"I'm not having a senior moment," Cole responded, laughing. "Sheesshh! Backseat drivers—everybody's an expert."

"Remember, it takes one to call one," Connie laughed, as Cole let her out at the service station and watched her walk to her car. He patiently waited until she pulled in behind him before continuing on to the church.

Inside the sanctuary, Cole and Connie found seats behind Mandy and her teammates. Cole leaned forward toward Mandy to inquire, "Where's Ms. Patton? I thought she was going to be here this morning to sit with you guys."

Mandy whispered a reply, "She texted me and said she wouldn't be able to make it. She and her friend, Ms. Latham, are going to meet a man who lives near Larkspur. He promised them some free azaleas."

"Ms. Latham shares that old white farmhouse house on Upper Carter Creek Road with Ms. Patton, doesn't she?" Cole asked.

"That's right, Daddy," Mandy replied. "The two of them have lived there together for several years."

A few minutes later the organist began to play, and the choir processed into the sanctuary. Cole and Connie settled back peacefully, holding hands, as Pastor Tom began the service.

Cole watched in amusement as two of Mandy's teammates unobtrusively texted each other continuously. He was still in a time-share attention mode, and Tom was wrapping up his sermon, when the minister delivered a reminder that caught Cole's flagging concentration and brought him to full alert. "Don't forget that today is a very special holiday, Mother's Day. Remember to visit or call your mother and thank her for all that she's done for you."

Cole sat thinking for a few minutes, then spoke to Connie in a concerned whisper, "I've got to go right now. It completely slipped my mind that today is Mother's Day. I have some misgivings about Norma Patton and her housemate meeting some man they hardly know. It's isolated out in Larkspur, and the road there is bad."

"Do you want me to ride along?" Connie asked.

"No need," Cole replied. "I'm probably overreacting because of Megan's theory, but I'll be uneasy until I know that Norma and her friend are OK. Tell Mandy where I've gone.

"I'll try to call you as just as soon as I get to Larkspur, but don't get upset if you don't hear from me right away. There may not be cell phone coverage that far out in the boondocks. Hold the good thought." Cole quietly slipped out of the church, climbed behind the wheel, and was soon on the way out of town, pushing the 35 MPH speed limit as he headed for Route 688.

Connie remained in her seat until the end of the service, filled with an unexplainable tension. She was not usually a worrier, but this time she could not get Cole out of her mind.

Her instincts shifted her route home in a new direction, her foot mashing the gas pedal toward the floor as she turned off on the lightly traveled road toward Larkspur.

*****

"Do you really think that three or four azaleas are going to fit in the trunk?" Norma asked Emily, as the two drove along the winding two-lane road toward the Platt farm.

"It's going to be a really tight fit, Norm." Emily replied. "We might have to put one or two in the back seat. It was nice of Mr. Platt to dig them up and pot them for us. His generosity makes me feel guilty about all of the bad things I've told you about him."

"I suppose we both need to remember not to judge a book by the cover," Norma commented. "I'm certainly glad he wanted to meet us at noon. This road is almost deserted now, and I imagine the traffic will be nil later in the day."

"I'm glad we don't live way out in the boondocks like the Platts," Emily replied. "Larkspur makes our Upper Carter Creek community seem like a metropolitan downtown area."

"And I'm glad to say that we're almost there," Norma rejoined. "The last steep stretch is a real piece of work. I'll never understand why VDOT doesn't straighten out that bad curve or at least put in a guard rail."

Norma steered the car toward the center of the pavement as she reached the top of the hill and eased through the hairpin curve. Halfway through the tight turn, less than a car length ahead, she noticed the pavement change to a dark and shiny appearance, as if covered by black ice.

The front wheels suddenly lost traction, then the rear ones, and the vehicle skidded sideways out of control toward the narrow shoulder. Norma screamed at the top of her lungs, "Emily, hang on! We're going off the road!"

Norma pumped the brakes to no avail as both the right front and rear wheels momentarily caught loose gravel and then nothing at all. The car tilted over on its side and then its top, slowly rolling once and then more quickly again and again as it fell away down the mountainside, the women flung back and forth in their seats like rag dolls.

Norma and Emily never felt the car's last drunken flip, as it came to rest on its wheels at the bottom of the ravine, with only a column of steam escaping from the punctured radiator and two startled crows taking off in flight to mark the wreckage now lying in a patch of green briars.

*****

High above them on the mountainside, two men wearing denim jackets over Kevlar vests stood watching, the tall, slim one passing his binoculars to his stocky friend. "No way they can still be alive after that ride down the mountain, particularly seeing how the top of the car is mashed in. Time for us to clear out of here before someone comes along."

"No need to hurry," the heavy set one with the prominent jaw replied. "There hasn't been a car come by in the last hour. I want to take a minute and enjoy the sight of two more sinners lying down there. It's taken us a while to punish them, but the job's done now.

"It may be a couple of days before Brother Calvin's two nephews happen to spot that car, the way it's settled in under that briar patch. If they don't, the buzzards will point it out to them by the end of the week."

He handed the binoculars back to his friend, shifting the military-style carbine slung across his shoulder. "I guess I'm ready to go now. In another couple of hours that coat of manure on the road will be dried out, and no one will ever know how slick it was when it was wet."

"Those two dykes sure found out," the skinny one replied, grinning at his friend. "I guess both of them are way beyond worrying about slippery roads now."

"Hold on a second!' the stocky one called out. "I think I hear a car coming up the hill." Both men crouched down, listening intently, seeing a car approaching the dead-man curve.

"Damn!" his skinny friend exclaimed. "Why's that son of a bitch way out here on Sunday morning?"

"I have no idea, but whoever he is, he's about to get himself into a heap of trouble. That patch of road is still slick as glass, and he'll never make it through the turn. I don't think we're going to have to worry about him."

The two watched as the car came around the hairpin curve, hitting the slippery patch, following the trajectory of the first vehicle as it skidded sideways off the pavement. The difference was in the quick reaction of the driver, who released his seat belt, pushed the door open, and rolled to the ground on his shoulder just as the vehicle flipped over and tumbled down the mountainside.

"I guess I was wrong," the big man said, unslinging his carbine from his shoulder. "I don't know how in the hell he got out, but I'm afraid we're going to have to go down there now and take care of unfinished business."

*****

Norma regained consciousness first, while Emily lay immobile beside her. She felt intense relief when Emily stirred in her seat, moaning in pain. "Em, wake up! Can you hear me?"

Her housemate's familiar voice helped clear the cobwebs from Emily's mind, and she responded weakly. "Yes. What happened? Where are we?"

"We skidded off the road at the top and rolled down the mountain. The Lord was looking after us, or we'd both be dead. We're trapped in what's left of the car. Your ankle's twisted, and I suspect it's broken. I must have fractured a bone in my foot, since it hurts like hell when I move it. I tried get out through a window, but the broken glass and sharp metal edges cut my hands. I'm afraid we're trapped here until someone finds us."

"We have no food or water," Emily whispered fearfully. "How long can we hold out?"

"Probably we can make it a few days if we have to, but surely it won't be that long until someone comes by and sees us. Maybe Joe or Jerry Platt is within earshot, and they can get help. Let's try shouting out loud enough to wake the dead, and see if we can catch someone's attention."

The two took turns calling for help until neither could speak above a whisper. Nothing stirred outside except a lone crow on sentry duty from its perch upon the topmost branch of a towering bull pine.

Then they heard the sound of metal pounding against rocky ground, growing louder and louder as a large object came rolling down the mountainside toward them. When it came to rest on its top no more than two-hundred feet away, they could see that it was another automobile, and that no one was inside.

*****

Cole gingerly fought to get to his feet, shoulder and hip badly bruised, hands skinned and bleeding, only to slip back to the ground on the slippery surface surrounding him. He managed to stand on the second try, wiping his hands on his pants, trying to sort out what had just happened.

Cole spotted movement on the hillside above, then saw that two men were working their way toward him. He called out, "I need help down here!" He started to identify himself as Sheriff Grayson, but an instinct told him not to until he knew their intentions. Adrenaline surged as the larger man stopped and aimed a military style carbine at him, firing three quick shots, the slugs narrowly missing his head.

The puzzle pieces locked as he dove off of the shoulder and huddled on the steep hillside just below, bloody right hand reaching behind his back for his holstered .40 Glock. It was Mothers' Day, and two women had been lured out into the countryside. A treacherous curve was rigged as a murderous trap, and two hostile armed men were now coming to kill him.

He tried a ruse, calling out to them, "Quit shooting. I'm a member of the Fellowship."

"What's your name?"

"It doesn't matter. I belong to the Fellowship of the Righteous, just like you."

"You're lying. Stand up so we can see you."

Cole gauged the sound of the voice, estimating that the two were now within a hundred feet of him, waiting for them to come nearer.

Finally, he sensed the two were close enough to offer parity between his pistol and their carbines. The odds of survival were as good as he was going to get. He jumped to his feet, taking a shooter's stance and holding his weapon in a two-hand grip. Cole got off two shots point blank into the chest of the nearest man, watching the impact of the slugs knock him reeling backward, but fail to take him off his feet.

The big man swung his carbine up to shoot, and Cole spotted body armor under his jacket. His third shot was directed at the forehead. The man dropped his weapon and collapsed to the ground on his back, his feet futilely digging into the dirt.

The second gunman leveled his carbine at Cole, firing several rounds, the third one striking home, entering and exiting Cole's arm just below the shoulder. The sheriff was spun sideways by the impact, and his pistol landed on the ground. He waited for the impact of another slug, hearing the man's muttered threat, "You've killed my brother, and now you're a dead man."

Instead, he heard the bang of a shotgun and the sound of shot whistling past. The thin man wheeled around to level his carbine at another adversary, blood running down his neck where lead pellets had peppered the back of his skull.

Cole saw Connie, standing in a shooter's position thirty feet away from him, pointing her over-under skeet gun above his body armor, directly at his head.

Her second shot leveled the man, causing him to drop his rifle as he fell. Blood running into both eyes, his threatening tone gone, he pawed at his face in panic. "I can't see! Don't shoot me again!"

Connie kicked the carbine away from him, then apprehensively turned to Cole. "How bad are you hurt?"

"He put a hole through my shoulder, and it feels like a hot poker, but I'll make it. You just saved my life. How did you know the trouble I was in?"

"Hold the questions for later. The first priority is to stop your bleeding. Then I need to call for help. Is there a cell phone tower close enough for me to get a call through to 911?"

"No, you'll have to drive back toward town until you're able to make a connection. Don't waste time trying to help me. I can slow the bleeding. You need to go.

"There are two wrecked cars at the foot of the hill, mine and a red one that I'm certain belongs to Norma Patton. She and Emily are probably inside, and may still be alive. Get all the help heading this way that you can."

"You've lost a lot of blood, Cole. Are you sure you can hold out until I get back?"

"Yes. Go now."

Connie ran to her car, made a tight turn with gravel kicking up beneath the wheels, and started back toward town with the pedal down, as Cole stood trying to staunch the flow of blood from his shoulder, watching her drive away and disappear from sight.

*****

Norma and Emily talked about mundane things, trying to take each other's minds off of their situation and the relentless pain, until several sharp reports in the distance broke the silence. Someone was not far away.

"That sounded like gunshots on the mountain above us!" Emily exclaimed. "Maybe someone's spotted us and is signaling for help." More shots rang out, a fusillade echoing from the surrounding hills.

"I don't think so," Norma replied. "It sounds more like a battle going on." Then the shooting stopped as abruptly as it had started, and silence enveloped them again.

*****

It took first responders only thirty minutes to reach the scene after receiving the 911 call from Connie, and within another half hour, the mountain top was overrun with law enforcement officers and medical personnel.

A team of EMTs quickly tended to Cole's gunshot wound, while others began working their way down the hillside, listening intently for any faint calls for help as they approached the two wrecked cars below.

At first Norma and Emily thought it was just their imaginations—a little trick played by minds wracked with pain and fear. But certainty grew as they both heard voices calling out to them, growing louder by the minute.

"Norma! Emily! Can either of you hear us? We're coming to get you out of there."

Norma turned to Emily, observing with a wan smile. "I don't know who's heading our way, but those are the most beautiful voices I've ever heard."

Emily reached over to squeeze her hand, replying, "I think it's a band of angels coming after us, coming for to carry us home."

*****

The rescue team found Norma and Emily alive, but battered and bloody. Red handprints on a broken window told of their struggle to get out of the crushed metal box, despite injuries which made escape all but impossible.

One member of the crew began cutting away the side of the car, using the Jaws of Life to shear the steel frame and skin of the cabin.

"You're both safe, now," he called out as the last metal part fell away, and one of his buddies carefully crawled inside to begin treating the two women's injuries. "That must have been one hell of a ride down the mountain," he commented.

"The first part was terrifying," Norma replied. "But after a couple of flips, we were both unconscious."

Their voices were drowned out by the sound of a medevac helicopter descending to land nearby. Soon both women were securely on board, and the helicopter was under full throttle, powering upward out of the deep valley and headed for the hospital in Salem, the chop of its blades reverberating across the rugged mountains of Courtland County.

Chapter 46

Cole eased into a chair in the living room, carefully protecting his bandaged shoulder, his left arm resting in a sling. "How much does it hurt, Daddy?" Mandy asked.

"Not too bad. That is, until the pain pills start to wear off. I don't need an alarm clock to tell me when it's time to take the next one."

"You said the surgeon thinks you'll be able to use your arm again, didn't you?" Buddy asked anxiously, hoping desperately that his dad would make a full recovery and be able to throw a football and baseball with him once again.

"That's what he said, but he also told me that I'll need a lot of rehab before I regain full use of the arm. I'll have to catch and throw with one hand until then, but we'll make it work."

"Then things will be back to just the way they were, won't they?" Buddy pleaded.

"Maybe even better that they were before," Cole replied. "Life improves sometimes. Having Dave Barnett as a boyfriend has made your life better, hasn't it, Mandy?"

She put down her magazine and came across the room to very gently hug him, softly answering, "Yes."

Cole reached over with his right arm to pull her closer, asking, "Wouldn't you say that your brother's life is better since he and Karen exchanged email addresses and started going back and forth with other a half dozen times a day?"

Buddy looked at his father with a sheepish grin, commenting, "You think you know everything."

"At least six times a day, maybe even more," Mandy agreed with her father. "But why are you bringing all of that up now?"

"It's because I need to ask you two a very important question. You're well aware that Connie and I have been going together for quite some time, and that we've come to love each other. Would you two approve if I were to ask her to marry me?"

"You told us how she risked her life to save yours," Mandy replied. "You also know that we both like her." She turned to her brother for confirmation, inquiring, "Right?"

"Right."

"Go ahead and ask her to marry you, Dad. We'll be a happy family."

"When will you two get married?" Buddy asked.

"That will be up to Connie, if she'll have me. Don't ever let her know this, but she could do a lot better."

"We disagree on that," Mandy said, kissing her dad's cheek. "Everybody thinks you're awesome, including your kids."

*****

"You're a good man, honey," Connie observed, gently slipping even closer to Cole on the wooden bench where the two sat on the Blue Ridge Parkway overlook at sunrise. "Stop and consider how many things have taken a turn for the better because of you."

She paused to refill her cup from the thermos of coffee. "The crystal meth epidemic in this area has almost disappeared since you busted Irv Sutton's drug manufacturing operation."

"You're giving me more credit than I deserve, Connie," Cole replied. "The person who provided the information to break the case is still lying on a hospital bed in a coma. We need to keep praying that Maurice Jones recovers without permanent brain damage."

"Sutton's gone, and the drug dealers who worked with him are heading to jail," Connie added. "I believe that the Courtland County Sheriff deserves a lot of the credit, despite what you say.

"Then there's the Dillon-Goode feud that would have gone on forever if you hadn't strong armed Bayse into telling you how it all started, and leaned on Bayse and Vernon to end it. You were the one who got Junior Goode and Boyd Dillon together as friends again."

"Things really started to get better between the two families after the wind farm project was terminated," Cole observed. "It will be a long time before the courts finish sorting out all of the backroom intrigue between Marvin Clark, WindEnerG, and VDOT, but it's certain that the lease of the Goode property is permanently vacated and the mountain top will be reforested. "But before you go any further, you should be aware that I'm starting to get a swelled head."

"You've always had a generous head, sweetheart, but I wouldn't change a single thing about you. Furthermore, I intend to keep building your ego. You deserve it, acting like a cowboy in a western movie, riding out to rescue Norma and Emily from the Fellowship of the Righteous cult, and almost getting yourself killed by the Karcher brothers."

"Megan Porterfield deserves the credit for exposing the FOR cult, Connie, and you know it. She was the one who first realized all of the killings happened on Mother's Day, and theorized that boys' hatred for their mother was behind it all. We later learned that Megan was dead right. It turned out that the Karcher brothers' father had been an abusive husband, and their mother had abandoned them when they were still children, running away with a female lover.

"Jake and Tank rate a pat on the back, too. They put on a good cop-bad cop interrogation of Neil Karcher on the way back to town, causing him to spill a lot of information. Somehow he got the idea that Tank was going to pull the lead pellets out of his head with a pair of rusty pliers.

"But you're the real hero, Connie, the way I'll see it forever. You saved my life. I continue to ask myself, what kind of person would close in on a psycho who's wearing body armor and armed with a military style carbine, while carrying a 20 gage skeet gun loaded with #9 shot. A woman would have to be out of her mind to do something like that."

Connie gently disagreed. "Or so much in love with a man that she would risk everything to save him, knowing that she wouldn't want to go on living without him."

Cole reached for her with his good arm, pulling her tightly to him for a long, sweet kiss. With her face just a breath from his, he asked, "Will you marry me?"

He had to listen closely for her whispered reply, "Yes," before her lips found his again.

Cole fumbled in his pocket, pulling out a diamond ring and finding it a perfect fit on her finger, just as he'd hoped.

"When did you buy it?" Connie asked. "When did you decide that you wanted me to be your wife?"

"I knew that I had to have you the day you put me through the Balfour baptism out in front of your house."

"What in the world are you talking about?"

"I'm talking about that chilly day I came to your house to make-up with you, and you turned the water hose on me. I figured that it was some sort of Balfour commitment ritual. The next day I went to the jewelry store and put a down payment on the ring. When did you decide that you'd settle for me?"

"Same day, only a little later, in a much more intimate setting. We both sealed the deal in our own special way."

"Sealing deals can be really good, if you go about it properly," Cole observed, loving the light in her brown eyes. "We're definitely committed now—all the way."

Chapter 47

"Time to saddle up and ride out," Cole called out to Mandy, Buddy, and Mama Jane. "I don't want to leave my bride-to-be waiting at the altar. She might find a better man before I get there."

"I know Connie pretty well, and I don't think she's still shopping around," Jane replied, laughing.

"Daddy, I appreciate you and Connie inviting Dave." She turned to look at her brother, adding, "I'm not sure you needed to ask Karen, but I suspect that Buddy had something to do with that."

"Ya think?" Buddy inquired, poker-faced.

"The Barnett kids seem to have joined the family," Cole replied. "We limited the wedding invitations to family members and friends. Connie and I plan to make up for the small wedding by throwing a big beer and pizza bash later this summer, and inviting every Tom, Dick, and Harry in town. We seem to know everyone around these parts, between the two of us.

"I suppose it's time to finally get the show on the road," Cole added, starting the engine. Are you good to go?"

"We certainly are," Jane replied, speaking for everyone. "This is going to be a very exciting day for all of us."

Cole pulled the family car into the church drive, discovering that many had arrived earlier, surprised that the parking lot was beginning to fill. "I suppose it's time for us to split up," he commented. "I need to speak with Rev. Tom, and you three probably want to tie in with your friends. Let me give each of you a hug before the curtain goes up."

*****

Neither Cole nor Connie realized that the number of invited guests had grown like dandelions in summer during the weeks before the wedding, and what had started as a small, intimate affair had blossomed into a major social event.

Norma, Joe, and Emily caught up with Cole to give him a warm greeting as he walked toward the church. "You deserve a medal," Norma exclaimed, giving him a hug. "Em and I might still be in that wrecked car if it weren't for you."

"I owe you big time for what you did," Joe added. "Norma and I have announced our engagement, and we'll be following behind you and Connie before the summer is over."

As Cole continued across the lot, he encountered the ultimate odd couple, Bayse and Vernon, standing side by side. "Congratulations, Sheriff," Bayse called out. "We appreciate your including us today."

"Bayse won't be sitting with me," Vernon added, smiling. "He's already spotted Ms. Barker coming this way."

"That doesn't mean you can't join us," Bayse replied. "Jane has a very high opinion of you."

As Cole entered the church, he glanced back and saw that the Barnett family had arrived from Covington, and that Mandy and Buddy had already tied in with Dave and Karen. A wave of nostalgia swept over him as he realized the circle of life was continuing to turn for the Grayson family, his two children in new relationships and with lives of their own. He watched the four young people wave to him, and silently raised his hand in return.

*****

Connie stood talking with her brother Steve and Mandy, waiting for the moment to enter the sanctuary and start up the aisle on Steve's arm. She stepped to the mirror to check the match of her bouquet with her simple ivory silk sheath. "What do you think?" she asked.

"You look gorgeous, Sis," Steve replied.

"Totally awesome dress," Mandy added. "Connie, I have something for you, if you'd like to carry it." She held out a blue, heart-shaped charm hanging from a velvet ribbon. "It's borrowed and it's blue. I thought it might bring you good luck."

Connie slipped the token into her flowers, giving the girl a quick kiss as the sound of the wedding march reverberated throughout the church. Mandy led the way out the door and up the aisle, a beaming maid of honor.

Cole stood looking out over a sea of smiling faces, watching Connie walk toward him. He glanced to the side, seeing his best man, Buddy digging in his pocket to check that the ring was still there.

The couple exchanged their wedding vows as they stood facing each other with loving smiles, and then Tom brought the ceremony to a conclusion. "I now pronounce you husband and wife. You may kiss the bride."

Cole put his good arm around Connie, staring into her eyes before gently leaning toward her for a tender kiss. The nagging pain in his shoulder disappeared as they came together.

A reception in the church social hall followed the service. The pianist surprised everyone with her opening selection, *Have I Told You Lately That I Love You*. Cole turned to face his new bride and ask, "Ms. Grayson, may I have this dance?"

As they walked out onto the floor, he curiously inquired, "Did you know Evie was going to play this song?"

Connie smiled, replying, "Yep. She did it at my request. I call it our song."

"It brings back great memories," Cole laughed.

Later, as the couple said their goodbyes, preparing to run beneath a hail of bird seed toward a shaving cream covered escape vehicle and a Hawaiian honeymoon ahead, Tom caught up with Cole, holding out his cell phone. "There's someone who wants to speak to you before you get away."

"Who is it?"

"You'll see."

Cole took the phone and answered, "Sheriff Grayson."

He was surprised by a voice he had never heard before. "Sheriff, this is Maurice Jones. The doctor says I'm going to make it. I want to get a fresh start and turn my life around. Will you help me get things squared away with the law?"

Cole swallowed a lump in his throat, managing to answer, "I'm glad to know you're out of the woods, son. You and I'll work this out together as soon as I get back to town. I know what it means to be given one more chance."